The Spirit

By d. Nichole King

The Spirit

Limitless Publishing, LLC
Kailua, HI 96734
www.limitlesspublishing.com

Formatting: Limitless Publishing

ISBN-13: 978-1-68058-194-2
ISBN-10: 1-68058-194-5

Dedication

For my husband, David. Without you, this book
wouldn't exist.
Thank you for showing me what true love looks
like. You are my everything.

Chapter 1

Yep. I was doomed.

The rinky-dink town had shut itself down. Already at nine-thirty at night, the streets were deserted. And the creep factor didn't help. The buildings, the homes, everything had an eerie feel to it.

The perfect place to spend my summer vacation.

I parked in front of a line of stores on the town square, surprised—scratch that—downright astonished that I found The Coffee Shop still open.

Feeling the dried tears on my face, I checked my make-up in the rearview mirror. Sure enough, it was gone. Washed away like everything else in my life. After dabbing on a little lip-gloss, I stepped out and breathed in the warm Iowa air—hay and alfalfa, mixed with a touch of lilac.

A cold breeze rushed past me, and I shivered. It wasn't an ordinary gust that swept up on normal summer days. No, this was different. Like twenty-degrees-lower-than-the-temperature different. I swallowed and stood perfectly still.

1

Get a hold of yourself, Carrie Anne Reese!

Another gust sped past, chilling me to the core. I jerked my head to the side in the direction it went. The sidewalk was empty, as it had been five seconds ago.

With my heart pounding, I waited, expecting another gust to follow.

I held my breath. Nothing happened. Letting it out, the tension drained out of me.

"Stupid town," I muttered to myself.

After taking another glance around, I went inside The Coffee Shop and ordered. I rubbed my arms as I waited. Despite the warm May evening, the strange blast of cold air had left my skin cool.

All too quickly, the barista handed me my drink. I lingered for a few minutes, wondering how long I could avoid heading to my grandparents' house. My anticipated arrival created a swell in my chest.

I reached for the handle and hesitated. Something didn't feel right. I swiveled my head to the counter. The barista's back was to me, but I couldn't shake the feeling someone was watching. Swallowing, I scanned the empty sidewalk through the glass pane. Seeing no one, I pushed the door open and stepped back outside, sipping on the hot coffee.

I tucked a loose strand of hair behind my ear. The back of my neck tingled, sending shockwaves of ice under my skin. I slapped the back of my neck expecting to kill the mosquito I knew had to be there.

Fumbling for my keys, I started walking toward my silver Honda Civic. I stopped halfway there and glanced over my shoulder. Someone was watching me...*touching me.*

The barista gave a small wave from inside the shop and flipped off the lights. Now, only the moon and a dim streetlamp lit the square. I nodded back at her, forcing a smile.

A lump formed in my throat. My grandparents were expecting me, and I couldn't delay any longer. I didn't want them to worry.

I'm not sure what made me turn around again. The breeze hadn't returned, and I didn't feel eyes on the back of my neck. But something compelled me to look up.

A man stood under the shadow of the eve at The Coffee Shop. His hands were stuffed in his pockets, and he was leaning up against the door.

My breath caught at the sight of him. I couldn't make out his features. Slowly, his head turned toward me, and his eyelids opened. I sucked in a breath and clasped a hand over my mouth. I'd never seen a brighter green in my life. They glowed in the blackness—a perfect shade of emerald.

I hadn't seen him arrive, and he wasn't in The Coffee Shop. He didn't say anything; he just stood there, staring at me.

I opened my mouth to ask if he needed anything, but nothing came out. The hair on my arms stood on end, and I shivered again.

His head tilted sideways, and his eyes narrowed, the glow compressing, as if he was summing me up. I should have screamed. Or run. But I couldn't take my eyes off him. Something about him drew me in.

Then he looked away, leaving only his dark

outline in the doorway. Embarrassed, I dropped my head. Who was this guy? After taking a deep breath, I lifted my eyes.

He was gone.

My drink slipped from my hand and onto the ground. I ran up to the sidewalk. Turning in a circle, I checked in every direction. The whole square was deserted.

It was as if he hadn't been there at all!

As the thought crossed my mind, that frigid breeze brushed past me again. My teeth chattered in the wake of the cold. I hugged myself, trying to warm the goose bumps spreading across my arms. Taking one final glance behind me, I ran to my car, squashing the Styrofoam cup that used to hold my coffee. Hot liquid rolled over my toes.

I closed the door and locked it as fast as I could. My hands trembled, making me miss the ignition. I dropped my keys.

"Oh, come on!"

Snatching them off the floorboard, I jammed the key in and started the car. I threw the gearshift in reverse and stomped my foot on the gas, spinning out of the parking spot. I didn't look back.

People don't vanish into thin air! Or so I thought.

Chapter 2

I gripped the steering wheel until my knuckles turned white. I was still unsettled over the mysterious man and freaky bursts of cold wind. Trying to calm myself, I took a few deep breaths and drove through town.

The house loomed before me in the darkness. No porch light—no electricity. I only saw it by the reflection of the lights of neighboring homes. I hadn't forgotten; it just hadn't crossed my mind. The Moore House, on Lot 310.

Two pick-up trucks pulled out of another driveway. I stepped on my brakes. Coming to a stop in the middle of the road, I couldn't help the way the house drew my eyes to it.

The sign hanging on the porch read, "The Villisca Axe Murder House." There was something seriously wrong with the place. My lower lip began to tremble as the temperature inside the car suddenly plummeted.

Again? Really?

But this time it felt different somehow. On the

5

square, it had been just plain weird. This time, fear took hold, twisting my insides.

I pressed my lips together and forced my foot off the brake, my eyes glued to the upper three windows of the house. I blinked, and that's when I saw it. It was only a split second … in the middle window. I could have sworn I saw a flash of red light and the curtain move.

I shook my head and wiped my eyes. Squinting, I stared harder.

HONK!

I jumped. The car behind me flashed their bright lights. I took a deep breath. My senses returned, and I stepped on the gas.

"Sorry," I mouthed.

I laughed at myself. For a second there, I'd almost gotten caught up in the delusion of ghosts.

I drove out of the city limits of Villisca. The Reese farm was situated five miles outside of town. Though it had been ten years since the last visit to my grandparents', I still remembered how to get there. I slowed down as the familiar white picket fence came into view and beyond it, the farmhouse. The place looked the same as it did ten years ago.

I parked my car in the gravel driveway. After a moment's hesitation, I opened the door and stepped out. At the same time, Grandma Renae walked out of the house twisting her graying hair into a clip at the back of her head.

"Carrie!" she exclaimed, wrapping her arms around me. She smelled as if she'd just baked an apple pie—my favorite. "How was the drive?"

"Um, fine. Where's Grandpa?"

"On the phone. He'll be done soon, I hope."

After she released me, I started gathering my stuff from the backseat, avoiding further conversation.

Grandma helped me take my things to the guest bedroom upstairs. She and I unpacked the car, and I was grateful when she decided to go downstairs and check on Grandpa.

As soon as the door closed behind her, the tears began to form. I wiped them away in a hurry. Exhausted and creeped-out, I collapsed onto the mattress.

This sucks.

My favorite Coldplay song rang on my phone—the same ring I'd heard almost the entire drive from Sherman, Texas. It was Stacy, one of my best friends that I'd left behind.

I grabbed my useless smartphone, only good for making phone calls now that my mom had dropped data and unlimited texts due to our new financial strain.

Thanks, Dad.

Reading her text took me back to my own bedroom in Texas. We used to text until two a. m. on school nights.

The nostalgia didn't last long. In the middle of my reply, my phone rang. The number belonged to my father. If it were a voodoo doll and my dad had the capacity to feel, I'd chuck the phone across the room. He was the reason our family was sleeping under different roofs. I never wanted to speak with him again. Unfortunately, he didn't seem to get the picture.

"Where were you?" Mom had yelled two days ago. "Your father was here. He wanted to take you to dinner."

"Yeah, and what are you, Mom? His spokesperson?"

"We're trying for *you*."

"Well, stop! He left both of us, remember?"

"Carrie Anne Reese, you can't do that!"

"Can't do what?" I screamed back, furious.

"He's still your father."

This is ridiculous.

At that moment, I didn't care that I'd be living with my dad's parents in "Farmville" for the summer. I'd be far away and wouldn't be forced to talk with them about how they'd betrayed me.

"Carrie, he wants you to call him."

"Whatever. I'll do it later."

Later never came.

***

The memory enveloped me. Heat began to rise, flushing my face. The numbness had evaporated during the ten-hour drive. Now I felt it all, again: the pain, the anger, the sadness. And it sucked.

I grabbed the folded clothes from the suitcases on the four-poster bed and started hurling them around the room.

I hate them. I hate them.

When I'd emptied the suitcases, I picked them up and chucked them against the closed door. I didn't care if I broke something. No one seemed to care about destroying my life, so what were a couple broken suitcases and a cracked door?

The bedroom door opened, but I didn't look up. Instead, I turned my back to it. I wasn't in the mood for a lecture about controlling my temper. Besides, these were Dad's parents. My dad, who walked out of my life to bang his twenty-five-year-old secretary.

Bastard.

A hand rubbed my back and Grandpa Robert's voice, so soft and tender, reached me. "Hey, Care Bear," he said, calling me by the nickname he had given me when I was born.

"It's gonna be rough for a while. I'm sorry, hun." He said nothing more, just sat next to me as I cried into the heap of clothing clutched in my hands.

I wondered what they thought of their son walking out on my mother and me. But, then again, maybe I didn't want to know. Maybe it was better to just forget any of it happened.

Unfortunately, memories don't empty as easily as suitcases.

Grandpa cradled me in his arms like I was a toddler with a skinned-up knee. I buried my face into his shoulder, breathing in his Old Spice aftershave. Out of the corner of my eye, I saw Grandma Renae in the doorway, her lips pulled tight and a tear falling from one eye. Her expression reminded me of my mother's before I left.

I sat in Grandpa's arms longer than I needed to. Eventually, with three people in it, the room became claustrophobic.

"I...I just need to be alone for a while," I said. "I'm sorry."

He smiled, understanding. That's why I loved him so much. He got me—even though we didn't see each other often.

"We'll be downstairs if you need us," he said, kissing me on the forehead.

Grandma Renae nodded and set a slice of freshly baked apple pie on the bed.

"Thanks," I muttered.

After they left, I wiped the waterlogged mascara off my cheeks with a pair of jeans and stood up. I placed the warm pie on the dresser and started picking up the clothes from the floor. I folded the handmade floral quilt Grandma had won at the Montgomery County Fair and placed it on the top shelf in the closet. Then I remade the bed with my own comforter and pillows. On the wall above the bed, I hung my burnt orange Longhorn banner. Thankful that I hadn't broken the picture of Stacy, Jessica, and me, I set it on the dresser next to my laptop and iPod. The place was beginning to look like home—if there was such a place.

My stomach churned. These rooms, this house, weren't mine. I felt like I was living someone else's life. How could my whole world fall around me in just a few days?

One day I was hanging out with my best friends, Jessica Phillips and Stacy Stevens, at the mall in Dallas, celebrating our last day of junior year at Sherman High. The next my mother told me she'd arranged for me to spend the summer with my grandparents because *she* needed some space. She thought I did too.

I should have noticed my parents acting strange

and my father not coming home at night. But I didn't see what was happening around me. Between study groups, Bearcats football, Longhorn football, Jessica's basketball games, shopping with Stacy—I don't know, somehow, I'd just missed the signs. Now I didn't know my parents anymore.

Hell, I don't even know myself!

When I finished unpacking, I collapsed on the bed. Cheer Bear, the Care Bear Grandpa had gotten me when I was little, sat against the footboard though I didn't remember putting her there. I smiled and shook my head in bewilderment. She was a reminder of when life was simple. I toyed with her matted ears.

Grandpa.

Glancing over to the double windows overlooking the south fields, I stood up, gently placing the little pink bear on my pillow. I untied the curtains and let them fall closed. After changing my clothes, I decided my mom deserved to know I'd made it safely. Part of me did feel guilty for how I'd treated her that morning. I dialed her cell; she answered before the phone even rang on my end. As soon as I heard her voice, I clammed up. The conversation was short and one-sided, and I was relieved when she said goodbye.

When I hung up, the emptiness returned. I could do nothing to stop the pain except sleep.

Chapter 3

I awoke just after nine to absolute silence. Grandpa was in the fields by six, and Grandma's store opened at eight-thirty. I sighed, thankful to be alone.

I sat up, rubbed my eyes, and glanced around the room. Everything was as I had left it—not that I had expected anything different. Even the apple pie sat untouched on the dresser. After showering and dressing, I went downstairs to search the kitchen for breakfast.

The old house still had all of its original charm, including uneven floors and hideous kitchen cabinets with doors that refused to close.

I crunched down a half-burnt breakfast of eggs and bacon and grabbed my keys and headed to town for my first day working at my grandma's store. I was forced to pass the Moore House on my way to the town square. Even though I knew last night's vision was all in my head, I caught myself speeding past it.

I parked on the square in front of Renae's

Antiques. Grandma Renae had said a girl my age, Megan, would be training me today.

I got out of the car and blinked several times, astonished. The blanket of shadows that had covered the town the night before had lifted. In its place, morning sunlight brightened the quaint storefronts.

It was almost as if I'd stepped back in time. A mom and small child were holding hands walking down the sidewalk. Two older men were sitting at a small table in the courtyard playing checkers and sipping from their ceramic coffee mugs. A group of older ladies sat in The Coffee Shop, drinking coffee and playing bridge. I smiled thinking of a picture I once saw that depicted this very scene. The only thing missing was a glass bottle of Coca-Cola with a straw.

As I passed The Coffee Shop, the same cold breeze as the night before rushed past me. Again, I shivered. I looked around but saw no one. *Overactive imagination much?* I heaved a sigh.

Shrugging it off, I stepped inside The Coffee Shop and asked for a Pepsi.

As I went back out to the sidewalk with my drink—a glass bottle complete with straw—the cold breeze pushed against me. This time, it lingered for a few seconds before moving on.

What the hell?

My body stiffened and my eyes darted around, expecting to see a man with insane green eyes. Clearly, my eyesight had played an evil trick on me the night before. The hallucination had shaken me up.

Still, my pulse sped up. I knew that ghost stories were nothing more than scary fairytales, but I walked quickly to Renae's Antiques, refusing to look back.

The store was void of customers. Behind the small counter, a young girl shuffled through invoices. She glanced up as the door behind me closed, ringing the bell hanging above the frame.

She smiled. "Good morning! Can I help you?"

Her auburn hair fell to her shoulders. In the dim light of the store, her skin was the perfect shade of olive and her eyes a glistening hazel.

"Um, hi. I'm Carrie."

"Oh! I'm Megan Miller. Your grandma said you'd be coming."

"Is she here?"

Megan walked out from behind the counter and beckoned to me. "Yeah, she's in the back working on some new pieces. She'll be out in a bit."

She suddenly grimaced. "So, what do you think of Villisca? Or Iowa, for that matter? It's probably not as cool as Texas, huh?"

"It's great, actually," I said, thinking about the charm of small-town living I'd witnessed this morning instead of the eeriness I still felt all around me.

Megan started right in, showing me around and rattling off my duties.

The store overflowed with treasures. As she talked, I was impressed by Megan's knowledge of the rustic pieces. Behind the counter, she showed me how to use the antique bronze register.

"That's about it," she said. "Do you have any

questions? Renae's always here, usually in the back."

"No. I think I've got it. I'm not sure I'll remember all the information about the pieces, though."

"That's okay. Most people don't really ask. They just look around for something pretty."

"So, are the customers usually tourists or something?"

"Ah," Megan said with a hint of animosity in her voice. She rolled her eyes and shifted her weight, putting her hands on her hips. "You mean the Moore House?"

Surprised by her tone, my cheeks flushed a little. "Well, uh, no, not really. The town is just small, and I guess I was wondering if everyone here decorates with antiques."

Megan's expression softened immediately.

"Oh," she said, all traces of bitterness gone. "We get some tourists and people passing through. But Renae's store is known all around this county and the surrounding area. She even gets a lot of people from the larger cities."

At that moment, the small golden bell over the door chimed.

"Why don't you go?" Megan urged, nodding to the customer who'd just walked in.

"Sure." I swallowed and stepped out from behind the counter.

If I screw up, no one knows me in this town anyway.

"Good morning! What can I do for you today?" I asked, trying to sound as cheerful and confident as

15

Megan.

"Ah! You must be Carrie."

I didn't even try to hide the surprise on my face. How did she know my name? Had Megan thrown a nametag on me when I wasn't looking? I checked my pink button-up shirt. Nope, no nametag.

The middle-aged woman smiled. "Don't worry. I know Renae. She said you'd be helping here this summer."

"Good morning, Mrs. Taylor," Megan said from behind her work, smiling. "Mom said your tomatoes made the best salsa she's canned in years."

The woman winked at her. "Glad to hear it. I've got plenty more if she wants some. Just have her drop by."

"I'll tell her. I have your lantern under the counter."

"Perfect!" Mrs. Taylor said. "My husband will love it. Tell Renae thanks for me and to let me know if she comes across others."

Mrs. Taylor turned around, her light blue sundress flowing behind her. "It's good to have you here this summer, Carrie. I hope you enjoy it. I'm sure we'll see each other again."

"Yeah," I said. "Thanks."

Megan laughed as the bell rang. "Mrs. Taylor's my neighbor. Her husband collects antique lanterns."

"Does everyone already know who I am?"

"Small town," Megan said as if that was enough explanation.

I stared at her. She went on, a smirk on her face. "In this town, it's everyone's business to know everything about everyone else's business. It's hard keeping secrets. You get used to it."

Get used to keeping secrets?

I studied Megan, wondering what secrets she had tucked away that she didn't want the town to know. It didn't matter. It's not like I didn't have my own secrets to hide.

The rest of the day went smoothly. Grandma worked in the back while Megan and I ran the front. Megan had me handle the customers, most of whom were out-of-towners. The two from town also knew my name before I could introduce myself.

When I finally got off work and returned to the farm, an old, rusted Ford truck had taken my spot, so I parked in front of the barn.

I went inside and headed for my room. Sprawled across the bed, I opened up my laptop and checked my email. Just as they'd said in their texts earlier, Stacy and Jess both sent me an email.

OMG! I got on full-time at the pool this summer, and guess who the assistant manager is? Ben Rice! SO HOT! And he totally asked me out for Friday night! We're going to Dallas. I promise to tell you all about it. It really sucks that you're so far away. So, are you like out in the middle of nowhere? Anyway, I miss you. Talk to you soon!
Love ya, Stacy

I rolled my eyes and shook my head. If Stacy was excited to be dating Ben, I was happy for her.

In the back of my mind I knew it would end up like all of Stacy's relationships; she'd have a new guy by the end of the summer. I moved on to Jessica's email.

I miss you so much! After work today, I almost drove to your house to tell you how it went—not like there's a lot to tell—and halfway there, I remembered you weren't there. Today, I just had orientation stuff. But tomorrow I'm going with the sports reporter to the boys' baseball game.

How are you? Tell me about your first day at your grandma's store. And do be careful up there. I can't explain it, but something tells me ... well, just be careful, okay?

Did I tell you I miss you?

Jess

I missed Jessica most. We'd been neighbors forever and grew up playing in her sandbox. Unlike me, Jess was very superstitious. She'd love this town. Sometimes she tried to convince me supernatural beings really existed; she said she could "feel it." I usually rolled my eyes at her. She did have an uncanny ability to predict things, though, like the weather, sports scores, and school gossip. But, mostly I just teased her about broken mirrors, black cats, and walking under ladders.

After I began responding to the emails, I heard Grandma holler up the stairs. I closed my laptop and ran down to the kitchen to help.

"Mike Carson is staying for dinner tonight,"

Grandma said, handing me a bowl of potatoes to peel. "Every Tuesday and Thursday."

"Who's Mike?"

"Bill Carson's boy. Your grandfather hired him last summer to help on the farm after he had the pacemaker put in. He's about your age."

Great. Someone else to meet.

The small giggle that shot out of Grandma's throat when she said his name didn't escape me, either.

***

Taking their places at the table, Grandpa and Mike drank their entire glasses of milk in one swig. Grandma was right there pouring them another glass. They both thanked her and took another drink. It was automatic—almost robotic. I had a feeling I'd get to see the same scene again on Thursday.

"Now that we're all settled," Grandpa announced, "Carrie, this is Mike Carson. Mike, Carrie."

Mike shot a glance in my direction. "Could you pass the corn?"

"Yeah, sure," I said, passing him the bowl. "Good to meet you, too."

So much for pleasantries.

Mike went back to his food without saying anything else. Not very polite, but boy, he was handsome. His smooth skin and full lips gave the impression of sweetness; his strong jaw more accurately fit my perception of his demeanor. As he ate, I noticed his large hands and thick fingers, hands built for working. His chestnut hair dripped with sweat. I couldn't help but stare. He was probably a conceited jerk; guys who looked as good as him usually were. I ripped my eyes away from him and went back to my dinner, listening to Grandma's apparent conversation with herself since Mike and Grandpa clearly weren't interested.

"And I bought two beautiful wall mirrors. I couldn't believe it; I got them for only twenty-five dollars each! I need to replace the glass in one, but the other—aside from a little cleaning—is perfect. I hope to have them ready by the beginning of next week. Remember that stingy dresser? Well, I finally got that put out today. Someone considered it this morning, but nothing came of it. I think Carrie had a good day, though. Right, dear?"

"Yeah…it was a good day," I said, too distracted by Mike to say anything more.

Neither he nor Grandpa looked up from their dinner. They were both on their third glass of milk.

When I didn't elaborate, Grandma continued talking about her latest finds. A few minutes passed before Grandpa looked up and said, "Well, we'd better head back out. We'll probably put in a few more hours tonight."

"Thanks Renae," Mike said. "Dinner was amazing, as usual." He winked at me and turned to follow Grandpa outside.

I huffed at his back. How dare he wink at me after being a prick during dinner? What an…Yeah, he wasn't worth the time to stew over.

Grandma and I finished our dinner and cleaned

up. I went back to my room and finished my emails to Jessica and Stacy, telling them I was doing fine and that I'd just had dinner with the biggest jerk in Villisca. He was still on my mind even though I was trying not to think about him.

A few hours later, as the sun was beginning to set, I decided to visit Goldie in the horse barn. The last time we'd been up, she'd just been born and Grandpa let me name her. She was beautiful, with a light brown mane and a shiny golden coat. Dad's brother broke her, but no one was around to ride her anymore.

"Hey, girl," I said as I entered the barn. Standing in the far corner, she crunched on her hay. I walked over to the gate and watched. She stepped around and shook her mane before coming to me. I held out my hand and caressed her nose. I didn't have much experience with horses—or any animals, for that matter—so I stroked her the way I'd pet a small cat.

"This town weirds me out," I said to her. "I mean, it's nice and all, but something about it gives me the heebie-jeebies. The bipolar temperature thing, for one, is just creepy."

I paused and stroked her silky mane.

"And what's up with this Mike guy? It's like he has his head shoved so far up his—"

"I hope you were about to say 'butt,' because we make it a point not to swear in front of the livestock. Ticks 'em off, you know."

I jumped and swung around.

Directions: stick foot in mouth and walk away.

Mike sauntered toward me and hopped up on the gate. Suddenly, I gained an insatiable interest in the amount of dirt on the barn floor. I considered brushing him off, but when I lifted my eyes, the cute smirk on his face made my heart flutter.

"Uh, I didn't mean…"

He held his hands up in front of him in surrender. "You're new here. I'll give you a break. This time." He grinned.

"Thanks," I muttered, feeling like a dork.

"Sorry about dinner. Rob and I don't have much time to eat. We try to get as much done as we can before the sun goes down. But it sounds like Renae found some great stuff for the store. She's got an eye for that sort of thing."

My eyes narrowed. "You were listening?"

"It's called multi-tasking, you know, eating and listening—all at the same time. You should try it." And with that, he jumped off the gate and started to walk away.

I felt guilty…again.

"Hey, I'm sorry."

Mike stopped, and I saw his broad shoulders rise and fall. He turned, grinning from ear to ear. "Good. I didn't want to have to avoid you all summer. But that *is* your second strike of the night, new girl."

He walked back to me and leaned against the poles.

Okay, maybe I over-reacted at dinner. Give him a chance.

"Well, on your next pitch, I'll make sure to hit a home run."

His eyes lit up. "I think you just did."

My heart sped up at the tone of his voice. Standing beside him, I was distinctly aware of how close our hands were.

Goldie whinnied, and Mike reached over to pat her on the side. "You ride?"

I shook my head. "No, I don't."

"I can teach you, if you'd like. It's not difficult."

"I'd like that. Thanks."

"Hey, do you want to sit on the porch? It's nicer outside, and it doesn't have that faint smell of, you know, horse," he said, nodding toward Goldie.

I giggled. "Sure."

He wiped his hand on his dirty jeans and we started to head outside. Before we reached the double barn doors, Mike slipped my hand into his. My eyes swung in his direction. He kept his head facing forward. I bit my upper lip, suppressing a smile.

Yeah, he's not so bad.

The night air felt cool against my face. We walked in silence to the front porch and sat on the swing, the coolness finally evaporating off me. I hadn't noticed his eyes inside, but outside in the moonlight, they were a sparkling caramel.

"You like sports, huh?"

I blushed. "Mostly football. I'm from Texas. If you're not a fan, they kick you out of the state."

Mike raised his thick eyebrows, the sparkle in his eyes brightening.

"Go Longhorns?" he asked, a little cautious.

"Of course! What other team in Texas is worth rooting for?"

He laughed. "Nice."

In the moonlight, his blond highlights stood out.

"Do you play?" I asked, trying not to stare at

how well his t-shirt clung to his chest.

"Tight end."

"Really? Are you any good? I mean, you're not really that tall."

"Thanks," he replied, grimacing. "I guess I'm okay. Good enough to have some colleges scouting me."

A cold breeze blew through the porch. I tensed as it settled on my shoulders. Mike didn't seem to notice.

I cleared my throat, forcing myself to focus on the conversation. "Maybe a future Longhorn?"

"Ha! No BCS schools. I'm not *that* good."

"No plans of going pro?"

Mike contorted his face. "Uh, no. Just college."

"That's cool."

I giggled then, finally relaxing again and thinking about what Dad and his brother did for fun when they were younger.

"What's so funny?" Mike asked, a confused look on his face.

"I have to ask—do people really tip cows here?"

Mike cocked his head to the side. "Oh, yeah! All the time. Tip 'em. Paint ball 'em. It's about all they're good for."

I shook my head, chuckling. "Have you ever done it?"

"Why, you wanna tip a cow?" Mike's smirk accented his high cheekbones.

"No! My dad used to tell me about doing it when he was younger. He said Grandpa would get so mad."

Mike chuckled, his eyes full of amusement.

"Rob would. His sense of humor doesn't extend that far."

The front yard was lush and green with two large oak trees standing on either side of the walkway. From under the porch, a squirrel darted out, sped across the porch and up one of the trees. I jumped about a half mile off the swing.

"That is what we in Iowa call 'a squirrel.' Mean little buggers."

With my hand on my heart, I sucked in a breath and glanced at Mike. His rugged good looks gave me goose bumps.

He shot me a crooked smile. "I'd better go. I've got an early morning." He stood up. "I guess I'll see you around." He glanced over his shoulder at me before he left.

After watching the cloud of dust settle behind his truck, I went inside. Grandma and Grandpa were in the living room watching TV.

"So, what were you and Mike out there talking about?" Grandma had a soft grin on her face.

"Nothing. Just talking. He said he'd teach me to ride Goldie," I said, ignoring her expression. "I'm going to bed. See you in the morning."

"Wait a second, Carrie," Grandma said. "Griffin called earlier. Wanted to know if you'd arrived yet. He said you haven't spoken to him."

Resentment swelled at the mention of his name; it flushed my face. I folded my fingers inward, making a fist. I didn't want to get upset in front of my grandparents, but I didn't want to explain myself, either.

"Don't pester her 'bout it, Renae," Grandpa Rob

said. "She's here to process this, not to get the third degree from us. She needs space and time. I'm sure she'll call when she's ready." He looked at me and winked.

I nodded and flashed him a half-smile before I walked up to my room. On my way, I heard Grandma trying to defend herself.

"All I said was that he called," she said.

"You implied somethin' completely different," Grandpa replied.

It was hot upstairs, and I wondered how soon Grandpa would install an air conditioner. After getting ready for bed, I lay awake staring at the ceiling, trying not to think about Mike. I was only going to be here for the summer. Dating would be pointless, even if he liked me.

How did he not notice the temperature drop on the porch? And why hadn't it stayed at The Coffee Shop? Was it following me? How paranoid was *I*? The breeze had sent shivers down my spine.

"Stupid, stupid town."

Chapter 4

I was standing on the porch of the Moore House with Megan. The orange glow of the recent sunset disappeared, and a crescent moon shone in the blackness. She'd called earlier and wanted to meet me there—I couldn't figure out why. Wearing a long black dress and matching stilettos, she paced slowly.

"Megan?" I asked, my voice steady.

Her heels clicked on the wood.

"Megan? Why are we here?"

She stopped and gradually turned to face me. "We're waiting."

Suddenly, a howl of wind erupted. A cold breeze rushed onto the porch and engulfed me, swirling around me in a vortex of wind. The frigid air trapped me inside.

"Megan! What? Help me! Help me!" I hugged myself, trying to keep from freezing.

Megan's eyes narrowed. With a sly grin on her face, she reached her hand into the icy air.

I grabbed for it, relieved that she wasn't going to

leave me. But when I touched her, my hand went through her. "What?" My voice shook.

"Be careful, Carrie," she said. Then she vanished.

The cold air suddenly turned into flames of fire, rising in a circle around me. My scream echoed in my ears.

I awoke in a cold sweat, bolting upright. Sucking in air, I stared at myself in the dresser mirror; my brown hair stuck to my face and neck. I felt like I was still suffocating in the ring of fire.

My mind was racing. What were we doing at the Moore House? Why was Megan there? And why couldn't I touch her? Goose bumps rose on my arms when I realized the resemblance between the frigid wind in my dream and cold breezes in town. Was there a connection?

It's just a dream. Just a stupid dream.

***

I followed Grandma into the store the next morning. It was a cool day for June. The sky was turning gray, and the sun struggled to be seen from behind the endless stream of clouds. Megan already waited outside, wearing a pink jacket. She smiled at me as we approached, and the dream flashed in my mind.

"Nice weather, today, huh?" she said.

I had awakened several times in the middle of the night after dreaming of Megan. I hoped to ask her more about the Moore House today. Maybe I was overreacting to local superstitions, but I couldn't shake the feeling that there was something strange going on.

Was I looking for something peculiar here because this was a tiny town with a century-old murder mystery? I wasn't in Villisca to play Nancy Drew. I hoped she didn't think I was crazy.

Maybe I am.

Grandma unlocked the door, letting us in. After asking Megan to show me what needed done in the mornings, Grandma retreated to the back room.

We checked the messages, cleaned, and at eight-thirty, Megan flipped the sign to 'Open.' The cleaning continued, and by a quarter after nine, rain began to fall in heavy sheets.

I stood by the door and watched as the wind blew the rain toward the storefront windows. The sloshing was soothing compared to the noise the storm made on the metal roof. Small trees bent almost to the ground in the courtyard. Soon the rain fell so heavily I could barely make out the park just across the street. Megan appeared next to me, following my gaze.

She sighed. "It's going to be a slow day. Rain keeps the customers away."

I pursed my lips together. If I was going to ask Megan anything, now was the time. My paranoia needed to be tamed, and the only way I would get any sleep was to stop obsessing.

"Megan?" I mumbled, trying not to act nervous, even though the hairs on my arms were standing on end.

"Yeah?" She didn't look at me but continued to

stare at the downpour.

"Um, I was just wondering about what you said yesterday…about the Moore House?" I hoped she didn't notice my hands trembling.

"What do you mean? I don't remember saying anything about it." She still didn't look at me, her voice steady.

"You just sorta mentioned it, but you seemed…annoyed," I said, half under my breath.

Megan shrugged. "Crazy paranormal people and supposed psychics come here all the time, doing their experiments on the place, trying to stir up trouble. Why can't they just let the family rest in peace and leave the rest of us alone instead of trying to get interviews with people in town?"

"I'm sure they don't mean anything by it. They're just curious."

Her eyes narrowed at me. "Yeah, well, my grandma always used to tell me that curiosity killed the cat. Now the new owner went and fixed it up and released them to make the town even more of a tourist attraction. The place should have been destroyed a long time ago." She turned back to the counter, leaving me alone at the window. "Only it can't."

Putting us at risk? At risk of what?

I frowned. And what did she mean by "*released them*?" I hoped she was referring to the paranormal scientists, but I had a feeling she meant something else. Did Megan believe in ghosts?

She slumped down on a stool behind the counter.

With her back to me, she bowed her head. I debated on whether or not to say anything.

After a minute, Megan turned around, a small smile gracing her face. "I'm sorry. I didn't mean to snap like that. It's just that, in this town, that is all we're known for. It's all anyone asks about. Honestly, it's annoying. My family sees the house differently than some people. My great uncle was visiting my great grandparents in Villisca when it all happened. Because he was a stranger, they accused him of the murders. The townsfolk began to shun my family; all their friends bailed. Our family still isn't looked upon very highly. Old prejudices die hard."

I nodded. The conversation wasn't making me feel any saner. In fact, it made me even more suspicious. This must be what Jessica meant when she talked about the "feeling" that something just wasn't right.

"You said the owner released them? You think it's ghosts?" The words were out of my mouth before I could stop them, and as soon as I spoke, I regretted it.

Megan glared at me. "I didn't say he released anything. You must have misunderstood. There's no such thing as ghosts." And with that, Megan turned her attention to sorting the few items on the desk, making it perfectly clear the conversation was over.

The door dinged and Megan and I both looked up to see who walked in. I hoped, whoever it was, they'd be able to break up the tension. Instead, Megan went rigid.

A cold breeze rushed through the store. I hadn't realized the temperature outside had dropped so much with the storm.

"Oh, great," she mumbled under her breath. And then she smiled at me as if I hadn't heard. "Why don't you handle this one, I need to use the restroom."

Megan left, and I stared at the most gorgeous guy I'd ever seen, standing seven feet away. I fell into a sort of trance. I swallowed and took a deep breath, letting it out slowly.

Movie stars didn't compare to the six-foot, black-haired beauty standing in front of me. His wavy hair somehow wasn't wet from the rain, yet it still glistened under the lights of the store. He wore an old pair of faded jeans with scuffed brown shoes and a brown button-up suede jacket. Drops of rain should have been dripping from his perfectly shaped ears and nose, down to his broad shoulders, but he was completely dry.

He looked up at me and caught me staring. I blushed and averted my gaze, but not before noticing his bright green eyes, made greener in contrast to his tanned skin.

"Hi, there," he said with a crooked smile and perfect teeth.

I slid off the stool and tucked my hair behind my ears, hoping to look more presentable. "Hi," I managed. I wasn't sure if I could say anything else.

"Do you work here?" he asked, his voice gentle, making my pounding heart stop and melt.

I cleared my throat and in an embarrassingly squeaky voice answered, "Yes." Apparently, I could only manage one word at a time.

He looked at me sideways. "I'm looking for a mantel—for a fireplace."

"Okay."

Oh, goody! A two-syllable word this time. Progress!

My mind went fuzzy. I couldn't think straight with those emerald eyes on me. Nothing in this world could be so mesmerizing.

After a few long seconds, he asked, "So, what do you think?"

He caught me off guard. "Uh, about what?"

"The mantel?"

Was it me, or did he seem oblivious to my trance?

"Oh," I said, reality returning. "Uh...I don't know. There isn't one out here. I can check with Grandma...uh, Renae, though. There may be one in the back."

"Is she busy? 'Cause I don't want to bother her."

Ah. Sweet.

"I, uh, I don't know. I'm sure it would be fine."

"That's all right. I'll just come back another time." A slow smile spread across his face. "Besides, it'll give me another excuse to see you."

That did it. My whole body was now a puddle on the hardwood floor.

He pushed his fingers through his hair; the grin replaced by...regret? His hand covered his mouth as if he'd just said something he hadn't meant to say. "Um, yeah, I guess I'll see you later, then," he said and went back out into the rain.

I stared at him through the glass until I could no longer see him. The way he acted before he walked out left an odd taste in my mouth. I searched behind me for the stool I needed for support. I'd never acted like that in front of a guy before. I couldn't get his face out of my head. And his eyes. Those eyes.

"You okay?" Megan asked as she approached. "Did you handle everything all right?"

I nodded, not wanting her to think I was nuts. "Yeah, he was, uh, looking for a mantel for a fireplace. We don't have one. Did you know him?"

She shook her head. "Never seen him before. He's not from around here; probably passing through or something. Are you sure you're okay? You look…feverish."

"Oh, yeah. Yeah, I'm fine. I think I'll run down to The Coffee Shop and get a drink. You want anything?"

"No, I'm fine. Thanks, though."

I grabbed my purse and hurried out the door. The rain had slowed to a drizzle, but it was cool against the heat of my face. A quick scan of the block confirmed what I already knew—the guy was gone.

As I approached The Coffee Shop, a swift, cool breeze brushed past my cheek. I tried not to think about the strange shudder that immediately electrified my body.

I must be losing my mind.

The Coffee Shop looked the same as it had the day before, with the same bridge club sitting at the same table. It was the monotony of real small town living, and I was starting to get used to it. Even like it.

I studied the beverage menu written in bright colors on the black chalkboard wall and opted for a French vanilla latté with extra foam and an egg salad sandwich on a croissant.

As I waited for my order, I leaned up against the counter and watched the bridge club ladies. Eight older women sat, each with a cup of coffee and a pastry. Their topic of conversation: the weather. And, according to them, Villisca was expecting a "doozy" of a thunderstorm that evening.

"Your latté, ma'am," the barista said from behind the counter.

"Thanks," I murmured.

When I walked outside, I was disappointed that I didn't feel the cold breeze again. I knew it was strange, but I missed it. Almost longed for it. Hesitating for a few moments, I waited, hoping the breeze was running a little late. When it didn't come, I bowed my head and walked back to the store.

Renae's Antiques was just as I'd left it—no customers. Grandma, I assumed, was still in the back. I pulled up the stool to the counter and ate my egg salad in silence. Megan's attention rested in the book in her hand. She hadn't said a word to me since I returned, and I hoped she wasn't harboring any hurt feelings over our earlier conversation. "Conversation" to put it nicely.

I took a deep breath and tried to make small talk. "Did you hear about the storm, tonight?"

"Yep."

"It's supposed to be big."

"Yep."

This wasn't working. Megan was *not* in the talking mood. I entertained myself by thinking up different scenarios between me and the gorgeous guy who had come in. I was being stupid, acting like a dumb school girl crushing over a guy whose name I didn't even know. Something about him...*What's wrong with me?*

As Megan predicted, the rainy day didn't bring in many customers. She didn't say much to me, and I couldn't help but feel that her less than cheerful mood was my fault. It wasn't my intention, of course, but my curiosity and paranoia had gotten the best of me. And to top it off, it started pouring outside again, this time with small pieces of hail.

We closed the store at four-thirty sharp. Megan managed to smile at me and say goodbye. Grandma held the door open for me and instructed me to park in the barn. I didn't argue.

With keys in hand, I sprinted out to my car. I dove into the front seat and wiped my face of dripping rainwater. The engine started easily, and I flipped on the wipers, wondering if the high setting would be fast enough. Rain was falling so hard that I couldn't see two feet in front of me. It took me over thirty minutes to drive home—a drive that should have taken just over five.

The barn doors were open, and as I inched in, I noticed a familiar face waiting inside for me. I slammed the car into park, and Mike closed the doors behind me. He was drenched and covered up to the knees with mud.

"Nice day, huh?" he said as I opened the car door and got out into the musty barn.

"Absolutely beautiful. I considered a picnic dinner tonight, wanna join me?"

"Mmm...tempting."

I laughed and wrung out my hair as Mike watched with a grin on his face.

"You know, that really wasn't worth the effort. You're not going to get from here into the house without showering again."

"Yeah, I suppose you're right. Are you working out in this weather?" I asked, nodding toward the mud on his jeans and work boots.

"Rain or shine. Like the postal service, just more profitable. We're almost finished, though. Not much we can do in this mess."

"Then what? You go home?"

"Actually, Rob told me to stay here tonight. It's supposed to get real nasty, and I live twenty minutes away on a nice day."

Mike opened the barn door for me, and I ran across the gravel and into the dry house. I threw off my jacket and stepped out of my shoes and socks, both soaked. Barefoot, I ran upstairs and headed straight for the bathroom and a nice warm shower.

Warm showers were great for two things: getting clean and clearing your mind. I used this one for both. Needless to say, my mind was running images of Mike and Mantel Guy in steady spurts, and I had to get them both out of my head. I wasn't interested in a summer fling; it was, I kept reminding myself, very stupid.

I dried off and donned a pair of sweats and a Longhorn T-shirt—trying to impress Mike?—and dabbed on some make-up. *Stupid.* I decided to email Jess and Stacy to try to calm my pounding heart.

```
Hey guys,
I  think  I'm  going  crazy.  Really
```

**nuts. In my first few days here I have
turned into some psychotic person. I'm
paranoid, easily distracted, and I may
be more hormonal than usual.**

I stopped. Were they going to think I was as out
there as I felt? That wouldn't help. I wasn't looking
for a confirmation; in fact, I wanted the opposite.
This would be a long email.

I asked Jess about her "Sixth Sense" theory,
explained about the cold breezes, and talked about
Megan, her aversion to the Moore House, and her
odd reaction to the guy who came in. Then I wrote
five long paragraphs about Mantel Guy, describing
him to the tiniest detail, including his strange
behavior before he left, and giving a word-for-
word—mostly his—recap of the conversation.

I took a little break from writing, stared at the
ceiling, and pictured his green eyes and dark hair.
Ah.

Then I ended the email talking about Mike and
how I was wrong about him before.

I read through it again, decided I needed therapy,
and hit send. I lay back on my bed and closed my
eyes, allowing my thoughts to take over. It felt good
to write it all out. Thankfully, all this drama was
interfering with sorting through the real reason I
was in town.

"Hey." Mike's voice at the doorway startled me.
I sprang up, surprised. "Sorry. I didn't mean to
scare you, but Renae told me I could come up here
to shower. Is that okay, since she said it was your
bathroom now?"

It took me a few seconds to answer. I wondered

how long he'd been standing there.

"No problem," I sputtered.

He grinned that gorgeous smile of his. "Thanks."

Good Lord, what am I going to do?

He turned and went into the bathroom, and I collapsed back onto my pillow. I was more than surprised to see him standing there, covered in mud and wet. His disheveled chestnut hair dripping onto his shoulders made him look like a beach model, and, whether or not I wanted to admit it to myself, he took my breath away.

I went to the kitchen to help with dinner, but Grandma had it under control. Grandpa was still in the shower downstairs, so I took a seat on the sofa. The Channel 7 local news blared from the television, the newscasters chatting about the storms ravaging through the state. Three tornados had already touched down, causing minimal damage. The heavy rain outside continued to pound against the windows. The lights flickered, and the thunder roared, shaking the glass.

"Crazy out there."

I glanced up to see Mike leaning against a wall, arms crossed in front of his chest. He sauntered over and sat at the opposite end of the sofa. I pretended not to notice the smell of my shampoo radiating off his clean skin.

"Yeah...crazy," I said, trying to keep my eyes on the TV. "Clean clothes?"

"I hope you don't mind, I had to search all of your drawers before I found something that fit," he teased.

"You look good in women's clothing. Brings out

your masculine features."

I can't believe I'm flirting with him.

Mike laughed. "I keep an extra pair of clothes in the truck, for occasions such as these. Thanks for letting me use your shower."

Grandpa walked in, sat in his recliner, and put his feet up. The wind howled and the lightning created strips of silver across the sky. We sat in the living room, our eyes glued on the TV until Grandma announced dinner. Mike and I stood up at the same time.

Mike nodded at me. "Ladies first."

"Well, thank you, sir."

"Ouch! Sir?" He stuck his hand over his heart as if I'd just stabbed him.

I led the way into the kitchen. Everyone sat down in the same seats as the night before. The only difference was that Mike and Grandpa were involved in the conversation. Grandpa talked, not surprisingly, about the weather and hoped the storm wouldn't ruin too many young corn stalks. I sat back and enjoyed listening to their voices.

After everyone finished, I helped clean up the kitchen then joined Mike and Grandpa in the living room. Mike had taken my spot on the sofa, so I glared at him as I walked by to sit in his earlier seat.

"What?" he asked. "This is *my* spot!"

I peered out the window behind the sofa, and through the heavy rain, I noticed Goldie running around in strange patterns in the field. "Hey, what's wrong with Goldie?"

"Horses sense danger, and they react to it," Mike said without looking outside. "I left the barn door open; she'll go inside, I'm sure."

"They do *that*?" I said, pointing toward the window.

Mike turned and had to focus hard to see through the rain. "Huh. Hey, Rob, check out Goldie."

Grandpa stood up and peered outside. With a questioning look, both Mike and Grandpa went to the side door. I followed.

"I've never seen her act like that before," Mike said.

"Yeah, me neither. Guess we'd better check it out," Grandpa agreed.

They both put on their wet and dirty boots and grabbed two of the raincoats hanging on pegs.

Mike winked at me. "Be right back."

They headed into the pouring rain. From what I could make out, they stood at the gate, trying to get Goldie to come to them; when she wouldn't, they went to her. She swished her tail and stood on her back feet. Her head shook back and forth, whipping her long wet mane side to side. Grandpa and Mike backed away. Mike motioned to her from inside the barn, hoping that Goldie would go in. Grandpa stayed off to the side, reaching toward her, trying to calm her. When she finally went inside, Mike shut the door, and the two of them jogged back to the house.

"What's wrong with her?" I asked as I handed them towels.

"Got me," Mike replied, rubbing the towel over his hair. "Horses get spooked when they sense danger. Maybe there was a coyote or bobcat nearby."

"There's always coyotes. Never bothered her before," Grandpa pointed out, thinking. "I hope we're not having a mountain lion problem again."

"No one has seen one of them around here in over a year."

"Probably just the storm," Grandpa said, shrugging it off, and he went back to his warm recliner in the living room.

Grandma sat in her recliner, Grandpa in his, and Mike and I on opposite ends of the sofa—each of us with our eyes on the television. No one spoke except for the occasional weather comment.

Tired of staring at the TV, I meandered into the kitchen for a glass of water, and that's when all the lights went out. I froze. Small clicks tapped on the window; there were no trees outside the kitchen to make such a sound. I turned toward the noise and saw two bright green eyes staring in at me. The water glass fell from my hand and shattered on the floor as an ear-splitting scream echoed down the hallway. The scream was mine! Three pairs of feet came rushing to my rescue. I shook in fear; Mike got to me first.

"Carrie? Where are you? What happened?"

"There…at the window." My voice cracked. "Eyes." When I looked again, they were gone.

Grandma appeared, holding a candle, and looked at my face, then to the floor. "Don't move, Care. I'll get a broom."

Grandpa Rob stood at the doorway, and Mike went to check the window. He looked around and opened the door. "I don't see anything."

"Probably one of those damn cats," Grandpa

said. "They're always trying to sneak into the house."

Grandma returned with a broom and swept up the glass. "You okay, Care?"

"Yeah, I'm fine." I tried to mask the tremble in my voice.

She glanced at Mike and handed him a candle. "We're headed to bed. Goodnight, you two."

Mike pulled out a chair, and I sat down at the table, still shaken. I knew those were not cat eyes, but they weren't human either. Human eyes were not that color. Mike brought over a new glass of water and sat across the table.

He studied my face. "You okay?"

I took a deep breath and exhaled slowly, trying to steady my shaking hands. I took a drink of water and sighed. "Yeah, I think so. Those eyes were like...nuclear waste or something."

"Rob's probably right. It had to be a cat."

I looked up at him. "How about a mountain lion?"

"They wouldn't come up to the house."

I nodded, unable to shake the image from my mind. The eyes were haunting. I closed my own eyes and concentrated on breathing.

"Come on," Mike said, standing up. "Let's go back to the other room."

I stood up, and Mike wrapped his arm around my shoulder, leading me back to the sofa. A white sheet covered the cushions; a white pillow and a thick light blue comforter were folded nicely at the end. Mike set the candle on the end table.

"I never asked, but why are you spending the

summer here, anyway?" Mike asked.

I shook my head. "Things at home. I don't want to talk about it."

"Fair enough. You sure you're okay?'

I thought about it for a second. I was fine; I was sitting next to Mike alone in the living room. Somehow, that made me feel better. "Yeah. So, this is your bed, here?" I asked, patting the sofa cushions.

"No, but you took mine, so I have to settle for this one."

Mike smiled his half-crooked smile. "As nice as it is to have a girl in my bed, I think I'm going to have to tell you to scram so I can get some sleep. Unless..."

I stood up and shoved his thick shoulder lightly. "Good night." I felt his gaze on me as I walked away.

I wandered up to my room, holding the candle, and crawled in bed. There was something about those eyes that were both eerie and strangely familiar. My body tingled with confusion and fear, paranoia creeping in again. I wondered if Jess or Stacy had emailed me back yet, so I decided to check; I had one new email, from Stacy.

So, you're living in Spookville? You're not crazy, Carrie. Anyone would feel paranoid in a town like that. Remind me again why anyone lives there? How do they get anyone to move into that town, anyway? Hauntings can't be a great selling point.
   Congratulations on the two guys,

though! Wow! That is totally cool.
    Here's the thing: Megan probably knows the guy from the store; my guess is she's dated him and was embarrassed. Don't blame her for bailing or lying about it. Either that, or she started her period. The period thing would explain her moodiness, anyway. I really wouldn't worry about any of this if I were you. Just enjoy it.
    Oh, and try to get a date with him! If he makes you that speechless, it's a good sign you're totally into him. I'm still not sure about your Mike guy, seems a little schizo to me.
    Love ya, Stacy

I grinned, same old Stacy. Her email did make me feel better, though. It was exactly what I wanted to hear, especially after tonight—I wasn't crazy. Her Megan explanation made perfect sense; I was just reading too much into everything. And Mike was probably right about the cat, too.

After turning off my laptop, I glanced out the window. The rain had stopped; at least that would help me get to sleep. I closed my eyes and soon I entered the land of dreams.

A dark-haired man stood outside in the pouring rain, earbuds in, rock music blaring in attempt to drown out everything around him. He wore jeans and a white long-sleeved T-shirt, which was, despite the rain, dry. He leaned up against a brick wall in an alley, hands in his pockets. His green eyes darted around, obviously waiting for someone. The muscles in his jaw clenched, and he shifted his weight from one foot to the other. He stared straight forward to another brick wall, and then down at his feet, sighing.

Already, he'd screwed up too many times. He didn't exactly need the reminder.

Footsteps echoed between the two brick walls in the alley. They were hurried, and all of a sudden, she *stopped in front of him.*

"What do you want?" he said, refusing to look up. He hated her calling this little meeting. It was none of her damn business what he did.

The dark figure in front of him wore a long, black hooded cloak that flowed down to her ankles.

"You're messing with fire," a woman's low voice said from under the hood. "And you will get burned." It wasn't a statement—it was a warning.

"Why do you care?" he asked, finally lifted his eyes at her.

"If you are exposed, we all will be."

"Don't worry. I'll be careful."

He hadn't been so far, but things had to change. Fast. Something made it impossible for him to stay away from her like he should.

"You have no idea what you're doing. This cannot end well. You have to know that." The woman's voice pleaded with him. "What can you possibly gain from this?"

He dropped his gaze back down at his feet. "I don't know yet. I can just feel it. There's something there, and I have to find out."

"Find out another way."

"I don't know of any other way," he said through clenched teeth.

She sighed.

"I'll be careful. I promise."

"You'd better be. This is extremely dangerous."

He nodded. "I know."

The woman in the cloak glared at him. "I really don't think you do."

His jaw clenched again, and he stared back. Then he closed his eyes and faded into the night. The woman stood alone in the alley. She turned and walked away, her cloak trailing behind her.

I sat up, my heart pounding. It was still dark outside, and it had begun to rain again. The dream had been so vivid, so strange. I took a deep breath and glanced at the clock—three a.m. I groaned and lay back down.

It was just a dream.

Chapter 5

I woke up late the next morning feeling groggy and achy. I hadn't slept well after the weird dream and spent the rest of the night tossing and turning. A couple times, I even dreamed about an older woman—Megan's grandma?—surrounded by a bunch of cats who ended up killing her.

Weird.

When I finally got to the store—at exactly eight-thirty—I was quick to notice Megan's absence. Instead of Grandma tucked in the back room, she stood behind the counter talking on the phone. I flipped the sign on the door and scurried inside.

Hanging my purse on one of the pegs, I waited for Grandma. When the bell above the door dinged, I sighed.

"Good morning. Can I help you?" I asked, walking toward the customer.

"Yes, Renae's working on a bedroom set for me. She said it would be ready today," the woman said.

"Oh," I said. "Hang on a sec."

I went to the back of the counter and mouthed to

Grandma that someone was waiting to see her up front. She nodded and held up one finger.

The woman was admiring one of the wall mirrors that Grandma had just finished restoring and had put out on display the day before.

"She'll be with you in just a moment," I told her.

"Thank you."

The bell above the door rang again. Customers seemed to pour in all morning, including Mrs. Taylor with a bag of peppers from her garden for Grandma. Of all the days not to be here, why had Megan picked the busiest one? It was past eleven when I finally got the chance to ask Grandma where Megan was.

"Oh, she never comes in after a storm. Their basement floods, and she and her mother spend the whole next day pumping water. Poor thing."

Every time it rains? Wasn't that what a sump pump was for? I had a hard time imaging Megan with an empty gallon ice cream bucket, scooping water into a drain. Her words repeated in my ears: *Small town. It's hard to keep secrets.* Though I couldn't quite figure it out, something didn't add up. Then again, maybe I needed to tame my suspicions before I freaked out over every little detail I found strange. I didn't have more time to dwell on the matter as another customer rung the bell.

The flow of traffic into the store slowed down enough that by one o'clock, I was able to run to The Coffee Shop for a sandwich. It was a beautiful day. Warmth from the sun pounded on my shoulders. I wasn't looking for warmth, though. An ache stirred in my stomach, and I longed for the coolness to brush over my skin again. Sadly, I didn't feel the cool breeze, confirming that I was just being paranoid over nothing. I got my chicken salad and walked back to the store.

My constant paranoia had to stop. It was utterly ridiculous, and my mind was in a flurry of motion, making me dizzy. For my own mental health, I had to get a better grip on myself.

As I entered the store, Grandma flicked her wrist in what she called "the farmer wave." "I'll be in the back if you need me."

I pulled up the stool and began to eat my lunch when the bell rang. Shivers raced up my spine at the cold breeze suddenly circling the room.

Did Grandma leave the A/C on too high?

I swiveled around on the stool, and the sandwich nearly fell from my fingers.

He puffed out a laugh. "I didn't mean to scare you."

The butterflies in my stomach began fluttering wildly. This time, however, bravery did the speaking for me.

"Oh." I glanced down at the croissant. "It's fine. Uh, we still don't have a mantel, though. Sorry."

He shrugged. "I didn't figure you did. But I didn't introduce myself yesterday; you probably thought I was rude." He held out his hand. "I'm Lucas."

I took it. It was cool, reminding me of the breeze I'd just felt, but his touch pulsed warmth through my hand and up my arm, spreading throughout my whole body. Out of nowhere, a jolt went through me, and suddenly I felt like...like I'd known him forever!

Lucas jerked his hand back, staring at it. Then he lifted his green irises to me.

Impossible. Before yesterday, I'd never seen this guy before in my life!

"Carrie," I managed, scrutinizing him.

He dropped his hand, a blank expression clouding his face. Coming to, a smile slowly played on his lips, revealing the hint of a dimple on his cheek. "It's nice to meet you, Carrie."

"Yeah. You too."

He seemed to relax, leaning against the counter.

"So, are you from around here?" My attempt at small talk made me sound childish. *Obviously,* he didn't reside in Villisca. If he did, he'd have already know my name, where I lived, my cell number, and possibly my shoe size.

Hmm. I wondered what his lips would feel like against mine.

Oh, God! Did I just think that?

His eyes searched mine. "I guess that depends on what you mean by 'around here.'"

I pushed hair out of my face. "From Villisca?"

"I've been all over, really."

Maybe he was an army brat? I shouldn't probe. He was a stranger, and I couldn't figure out why he was here talking to me in the first place. Did he come by just to introduce himself?

"*You're* not from around here, right?" he asked grinning, and I had to remember to breathe.

I scrunched up my nose. "Is it that obvious?" Did I wear it on my face?

He laughed, making my insides flip-flop at the sound. "It's just that you don't see too many Texas Longhorns T-shirts in this area."

I looked down, completely forgetting what I had put on that morning. "Yeah. I guess not, huh? I'm up here visiting my grandparents for the summer."

"I'm sorry I interrupted your lunch," he said, nodding toward my un-eaten sandwich.

I automatically glanced in the direction he was indicating. Sure enough, my sandwich was still there. It hadn't grown legs and walked off, but I still stared at it like an idiot.

"Oh, no big deal." I bit my lower lip.

"I'll make it up to you. Come to dinner with me tonight, and I promise not to freak you out."

I blushed, heat rushing to my cheeks. Nervous again, my palms began to sweat, and I prayed silently that he was as unobservant as the guys in my high school.

"Tonight?" My voice was unnaturally high. I took a deep breath.

Relax.

"Yeah, I mean, if you're not busy." He shoved his hands in his pockets, giving me a sexy half-smile.

Oh, wow.

Of course I wasn't! I had no reason to tell him I couldn't go, but I also wondered if I could hold myself together. Thus far, my stats weren't looking so hot.

"No, I'm not busy," I said in my best got-it-together voice. My nails bit into my palms hard enough to make me cringe.

He quirked an eyebrow. Gorgeous. "Does that mean I can pick you up at six?"

"Six-thirty?"

Hold it together, Carrie, at least until he gets out the door.

"Six-thirty it is."

"Here?"

"If that works for you." He paused, a distant glint flashing across his face. Narrowing his eyes a little, he took a few steps backward, away from me. "I'll see you later." A small smile lit his face as he turned on his heel and made the bell ring on his way out.

I pinched myself to make sure I wasn't dreaming. Lucas seemed interested—should I be? Suddenly, I couldn't figure out why I'd told him I'd go. Really, it wasn't a good idea. In Sherman, a much bigger city than Villisca, I would have said no; it was dangerous to be alone with someone you just met. But here everything seemed safe. Strange, yes, but safe.

The more I thought about it, the more I wondered if I should cancel, though he didn't leave a number or any way to get a hold of him. A thought crossed my mind to stand him up, but it left just as quickly as it came.

I rubbed the back of my neck with both hands, taking slow breaths. I closed my eyes then opened them and stared blankly at nothing. All of my random thoughts began to cluster in my head, unable to sort themselves out.

Did I say I'd go just because he was movie-star gorgeous? I hoped not. That would make me extremely shallow. Or because Stacy had told me to? That, I thought, made me desperate, which I wasn't. Maybe because I wanted to avenge my parents by acting out and dangerously agreeing to see a guy who was no more than a stranger. Possibly. Or because I was a glutton for embarrassment? I considered this option the longest of any of them, and my conclusion—I was an idiot.

And what about Mike? I liked him too, and yet I had more easily convinced myself that nothing could happen there. Why was Lucas different? He *was* different, though. The fainting dizziness I felt with Lucas, and the electricity that shot through my veins when he touched me, was nothing compared to Mike.

As soon as the last customer left for the day, I gathered my things and told Grandma I'd see her at home. Ever so slowly, I wandered to my car. I cranked the air on and stared out the windshield, allowing my thoughts to continue.

Why had Lucas come in to ask me to dinner? Paranoia creeping in again, I pondered the looks he gave me as we talked. The way he searched my eyes, my expressions, my body language, made me shiver. Not in a bad way, but still, what was he trying to figure out about me? Something familiar? Something off? Something … enticing?

Then it hit me—was I going to dinner with a lunatic? Some crazy person?

Pfft. Even if he is, it's not that much different than going to dinner with myself right now.

Okay, yeah, I'd go, but with a can of pepper spray and the police on speed dial. Now I had to figure out what say to my grandparents. I didn't want to lie, but the truth was definitely not a consideration. First off, they'd tell my parents. Secondly, they didn't know Lucas, so I wondered if they'd even let me go. Which brought me to number three: why date someone I don't know when Mike was right there. I had no logical answer to the third reason.

I went inside. No one was home yet, so I went upstairs to take a shower. I dressed as quickly as I could in my super-hot room. I chose my favorite jean capris and a sleeveless top. After grabbing my brush, hair dryer, and make-up bag from my bathroom, I headed for the cooler downstairs bathroom to finish getting ready.

I gave myself a once-over in the mirror and sighed; no amount of time was going to make me as beautiful as Lucas. And degrading myself wasn't going to help either, so I snatched my purse, took a deep breath, and walked into the kitchen.

Still having no idea what to say, I smiled at Grandma. She was busy heating up leftovers in the microwave. By the look on her face, I'm sure she assumed she'd only have to warm enough for two.

"You look nice. What are you up to, tonight?"

"I just thought I'd go out. Maybe see a movie in Red Oak or something." Half-lie.

"By yourself?" Her face was skeptical. Then it softened and her confused look faded into a smirk. "Or with Mike?"

I knew that's what she'd think. Reason number three. I shook my head. "No, by myself." I shrugged, trying to make it all seem inconspicuous.

"Hmm." She pursed her lips together and studied me, probably trying to decide if I was lying and actually meeting Mike secretly. "Okay. I'll keep a light on for you. Have a good time."

"Thanks, Grandma. I will," I said, grateful she wasn't asking any more questions.

The evening was beginning to cool off, but not enough to make it comfortable. Opening my car door was going to be the easiest part of my night.

As I drove into town, I took my hand off the wheel and pinched my forearm—hard. Was I dreaming or was I *this* crazy? I held it for almost ten seconds before I cringed in pain and realized that I was actually driving to our pre-determined meeting place. The pain lingered, reminding me of my stupidity.

There were more people in town, driving and cruising the sidewalks, than I'd thought. Good, we'd be in public. I circled the square twice, telling myself to breathe and stay calm.

I parked in between a Caravan and a Town & Country as both seemed as unlikely as the other to belong to Lucas. After two more deep cleansing breaths, I grabbed my purse—a can of pepper spray included—and stood by the store windows. I scanned the other cars parked alongside either side of the street trying to decipher in which one I'd be riding to my doom.

My watch said six twenty-six. I bounced up on my tiptoes each time a car turned on to the square, analyzing it. An ancient orange Chevy truck, a forest green Saturn, a navy Caravan, a tractor, and a rusted multi-colored Ford—none fit Lucas, confirmed by none stopping. I slipped my purse from my right shoulder to my left for something to do.

Six twenty-eight. Time could *not* go any slower.

Before, I was kicking myself for even considering coming. Now I was worried that he wouldn't show. I bit my lip and stared at the sky; it was an airy shade of blue. I intertwined my fingers and played restlessly with my own hands.

Was this a sick joke made up to see if I was gullible enough to show up? He and the rest of his gorgeous friends were probably watching from a window laughing it up.

Another car, a new black Toyota pick-up. Not him.

Six twenty-nine.

I shifted my weight and sighed, wondering how long I should wait. Another car, a blue Stratus. I raised my eyebrows, hopeful. It didn't stop. I slumped back against the window. As I considered the foolishness of the whole situation again, a new shiny red Pontiac G8 rounded the corner and turned into the only remaining spot on this side of the street. I looked up, half-hoping it was Lucas and half-hoping I'd been stood up.

I checked my watch; six thirty, exactly.

Lucas sauntered toward me, a smile spreading across his perfect face. He didn't just walk; he glided across the sidewalk.

I'd never seen someone look so good in such simple clothing. Loose-fitting jeans accompanied the long-sleeve white button-up shirt with light blue pinstripes—the sleeves rolled up. His short dark hair was gelled into soft spikes on top, and his emerald eyes sparkled. I could have sworn my heart stopped beating.

"Hey there," he said.

I'm in love with the sound of his voice. Just keep talking, please.

"Hey," I choked out, finally remembering I needed to exhale. A cold breeze passed through me, but I barely noticed; my eyes were glued on Lucas.

"You look nice tonight."

"Thanks." I blushed. "You too."

He chuckled under his breath and flashed me his heart-stopping, crooked smile. "Ready?"

"Um, yeah. So, what are we doing tonight?"

I'd told Grandma I was going to Red Oak, but now that I thought about it, he never actually indicated a place.

"Well, you're new around here and probably have yet to try Dan's famous tenderloins. I thought we'd start there."

He was right; I hadn't been anywhere in town for food other than The Coffee Shop and my grandparents' house, which hardly counted.

Lucas put his hands in the pockets of his jeans and nodded in the direction of the restaurant. He took a step away from me, making sure to not walk too close.

He watched me as we made our way down the sidewalk; I kept my eyes ahead of me. Finally realizing the frigidness of the air, I shivered, hugging myself. Lucas glanced toward the street, muttering something under his breath, and inched away from me.

What's his deal?

I turned away to check my breath. Minty.

So far, our date felt more like an uncomfortable visit to the dentist. Maybe I'd loosen up some once we were at the restaurant.

The front of Dan's Bar and Grill had strips of logwood running across it, giving it that rustic, country feel that Iowans seemed to like so much.

Lucas held the door open, and I stepped in. The walls gleamed, lit with honey-colored wood wainscoting. Booths with plastic teal covers lined the left-hand side of the restaurant.

"Two tonight?" A young girl with brown bouncing curls held menus and waited for us.

"Please," Lucas replied.

She led us to a booth against the wall and handed us the tri-fold laminate cards, eyes pinned on my date.

"Can I get you something to drink?" Would she ever look away from him?

Lucas lifted his eyes to me, prompting me to order first.

"Pepsi please."

"I'll just have a glass of water, thanks."

"Ok. I'll be right back." She bit her lip and sighed before walking away.

Lucas seemed oblivious to how she checked him out again over her shoulder.

"So, a tenderloin, huh?" I asked, trying to ignore our server.

"If that's what you want."

"Sounds fine." Instead of continuing the conversation, he just watched me. If he wasn't so damn handsome, it would've put me on edge.

When he finally spoke, his shoulders relaxed. "I wasn't sure if you'd show up." He stared at his hands on the table.

The honesty caught me off guard, and I really, truly liked it.

"Really? Why's that?"

He sighed. "I mean, how weird is it for me to walk into a store and ask out someone I don't know?" He laughed. "Ironic, since I promised you I'd try not to freak you out tonight."

I smiled.

"I'm happy you decided to come, Carrie."

Yeah, this is much better.

"I considered not coming," I told him, surprising myself.

"I'd have understood." He offered a nod and turned up the corner of his mouth. "Why *did* you decide to come?"

I wasn't sure if I had an answer—at least not one that I wanted to share or that made any sense.

"I don't know," I said. If he wasn't crazy, I definitely didn't want him to think *I* was. "Curiosity."

As soon as I said it, Megan's voice rang in my mind. '*Curiosity killed the cat, Carrie.*'

I wiped my palms on my jeans, trying to shake the thought.

"Curious?"

The waitress arrived and set our drinks in front of us. Thankful for the interruption, I contemplated what to say.

"Have you decided what you want?" she asked,

shooting Lucas her best smile.

"Two tenderloins with fries, please," he said.

"With everything?"

"Yeah."

"Thanks," she said, picking up both menus and leaving us to our conversation.

Lucas looked at me with his eyebrows raised, waiting expectantly for my answer.

I swallowed. "About you."

"What about me?"

I circled my finger around the rim of my soda, insecure. "You just seem…um…different."

He sat back in his seat and rubbed his hand over his chin. "Different, huh? Is that good?"

"I think so."

Lucas seemed satisfied with my conclusion. He grinned, leaning forward with his arms crossed on the table. "Whatever your reasons, I'm happy you're here."

"Me too," I said as I shivered again.

"Are you cold?" he asked, biting his upper lip.

"It's a little chilly in here, but I'll be fine," I answered. "So, why are you looking for a fireplace mantel?"

"Oh...that. It's a…a gift." He cleared his throat, furrowing his brow. "Do you like working there?"

Strange how quickly he changed the subject. I shrugged it off.

"It's actually my grandma's store and her hobby. I don't mind it; it's a pretty cool way to meet people." I smiled, feeling more comfortable.

"That it is," he agreed. "So, why are you visiting all summer?"

My stomach knotted at his question. I wasn't sure how much of myself I wanted to disclose to a stranger, but somehow, he was making it very easy. I twisted awkwardly in my seat and glanced away. He noticed my hesitation, and his expression softened.

"Problems at home," he stated.

I toyed with my hands. "It's not something I want to talk about."

"I get it."

Our waitress arrived with our dinners and sat one plate of food in front of each of us.

"Anything else I can get you?" I watched as her eyes drifted to Lucas, and she tightened up.

"Carrie?" he asked, nodding in my direction.

"More Pepsi please?" I asked.

We both waited, but she didn't move.

Lucas nodded at her. "Another Pepsi would be great."

As if broken from her statuesque pose, she jumped. "Oh, no problem."

In disbelief, I watched as the girl hurried away. Part of me was jealous that she was so mesmerized with my date, and the other part relieved that Lucas had the same effect on others as he did on me. I turned my attention back to him. He was staring back at me, a jocular smirk on his face.

"What are you thinking?"

"Oh, nothing," I lied.

He didn't buy it. "Nothing? Come on, I can't read your mind."

I rolled my eyes. "Have you not noticed how our server reacts to you?"

"I'm not *completely* unobservant. She acts…" he chuckled, "like you did yesterday."

My eyes widened as the blood drained from the rest of my body and flowed directly to my face, making it hot. Hoping to hide, I took a drink, slurping what was left at the bottom.

"It's okay. It was cute coming from you," he said, carefully studying my reaction.

I almost choked. *Cute? Coming from me?*

Words slowly made their way from my brain to my mouth. "Do you usually have this kind of effect on people?"

He shrugged nonchalantly. "Some."

Our server set a new glass of Pepsi on the table and hurried away.

"Eat. Your dinner's getting cold," he instructed.

He hadn't touched his food either, but he watched as I put extra ketchup on my bun and placed it neatly on top of the giant tenderloin. I picked it up and took a bite.

"Hmm. It's good."

"I'm glad you like it."

Every so often, Lucas would pick a small piece of lettuce or tomato from his plate and put it in his mouth.

"Aren't you hungry?" I asked, feeling somewhat awkward that I was eating and he wasn't.

"Not really," he said. "But go ahead. I'll take mine home."

"Where exactly is home?"

"I have a place in Red Oak," he said, not offering more.

"Do you go to school there?" He couldn't be

much older than me.

He twitched in his seat, in uncomfortable movements.

"I'm finished. How about you? Do you like school?"

"Yeah, it's okay. I'll be a senior next year."

The server came back and stood at the edge of the table "Can I get you anything else?"

"A box and the check, please," he told her.

I finished my food as a Styrofoam box and the check were quickly laid on the table. I smiled to myself as the young girl scurried away.

Lucas dumped his food in the box and slipped some money into the black leather folder.

We left the restaurant and emerged into the fresh evening. It hadn't cooled off much, but there was a chilled draft stirring through the skies. We could hear the reason for the bustling of people on the square. Jazz music filled the air, and people had gathered in the courtyard with lawn chairs and blankets.

"Let's walk," Lucas suggested. "Tell me about life."

"What do you want to know?"

"Anything. Everything. Tell me about your friends, favorite classes, teachers. Whatever."

I sighed, deciding where to start. "Well, I go to Sherman High School, and I guess it's like most of the other high schools. I like literature, and I hate math. I'm not athletic, but I enjoy watching football. I'm not artistic, but I appreciate art. And I'm not musical, but I do love music."

"That can't be all."

"Yeah. Pretty much."

I paused. He looked at me, wanting more.

"Getting you to talk is proving very difficult. Why is that?"

"Why are you so interested?"

"You're interesting." He grinned.

I smiled back, flattered.

"I grew up in Texas, and I've never called anywhere else home. My two best friends, Jessica and Stacy, couldn't be any more different from each other." I giggled at a sudden memory.

"You miss them?"

"Every day."

"If you were at home, what would the three of you be doing right now?'

"Hmm. Anything, really. We'd probably be at Stacy's house, though. Her parents travel for work all the time, so she's home by herself a lot. Their housekeeper checks in on her often, but only during the day. Tonight, we'd be in her pool, under the waterfall, sipping strawberry daiquiris and listening to the new Fall Out Boy CD."

"Saw them in concert last month," Lucas mused.

"Jess would be totally jealous. She missed them when they were in Dallas, and her parents wouldn't let her drive to Houston."

"What about after school? Any plans?" he asked, walking closer to me now.

"I'm not sure yet. Maybe be a literature teacher."

"Ah yes. 'To be or not to be, that is the question: Whether 'tis nobler in the mind to suffer the slings and arrows of outrageous fortune—"

"I'm impressed! Most people can't get past 'To

be or not to be.'"

"*Hamlet* is, uh…enlightening."

"Huh. Because he's trying to decide if it's better to live or die? The answer is a bit self-evident, I think."

The corner of Lucas's lips turned up, and he let out a puff of air. "Yeah, it is."

"How about you?"

His eyes lifted. "Me what?"

"What interests you? Other than contemplating life and death."

The sounds in the courtyard faded and most of the crowd cleared. The intense heat of the day dissolved, replaced by the sweet scent of nightfall.

Sucking his lip into his mouth, he nodded. "How about if I show you. Want to take a drive?"

"Sure," I said, wishing the evening would never end.

Approaching his G8, he guided me to the passenger side and held open the door.

Before I knew it, we were speeding north on Highway 71 past the Villisca Country Club. I gripped the side of the door. Stacy didn't even drive this fast. He glanced in my direction and apparently guessed my nervousness and slowed down.

"Sorry."

"Where are we going?" I asked, refusing to let go of the door.

"Not too much further," he answered, flashing me an incredible smile.

Not three minutes later, Lucas slowed and turned onto another paved street going east. Soon after, he turned again on a small gravel path, not large enough to be a road. On the right-hand side, a wooded area of trees and shrubs towered to the sky. On the other lay a hay field.

"Where are we?" I looked to the woods and then out to the open field. The street was silent and darkness enclosed us, not a house in sight. No one around. I swallowed.

Terror struck my insides, causing me to tremble. My eyes darted from the car to my surroundings. He'd catch me easily if I ran. I shuddered and reached for my purse, ready to grab my pepper spray.

Lucas watched me incredulously and tilted his head to the side. "Are you okay?" He snickered.

I shot him a glare, shocked at the lightness of his laugh. My lower lip quivered. I took a deep breath and wondered if I should be running instead of staring aimlessly at the way his lips curved up.

He sighed and shook his head. "You think I brought you out here to hurt you?"

I loosened my grip on the pepper spray still in my purse, perplexed. His eyebrows rose in bewilderment. I didn't know what to say, so I chose nothing.

"Carrie," he started. "I'm not going to hurt you. I'd never hurt you. I brought you out here because it's quiet and away from all the lights in town. It's the best place to look at the stars. They're beautiful tonight."

Something about the way he said it made me believe him. I felt foolish; Lucas had been nothing but remarkable all evening. Studying his soft face, I offered him a timid smile.

"I'm sorry."

"Come on," he said, shrugging it off.

He reached for the blanket in the backseat before opening the door. He spread the large quilt over the hood of the car, smoothing it out.

"Hop up." He extended his hand.

I took it hesitantly, half-thinking of my dreadful behavior and half-considering it was a trick. The evening was warm, but his hand was cool. I remembered his touch when he'd introduced himself. Because of the odd sensation of having met him before, I hadn't thought anything of it. Yet, this time I was taken aback, expecting his skin to be warm and firm. But there was something else about his hand, something other than the temperature. I felt his skin and bones, yet, his hand felt almost hollow. I looked at him stunned. The glint in his eyes said he made a mistake by extending this gentlemanly gesture. As soon as I was up, he quickly withdrew his hand and leaped up next to me in one swift, fluid motion.

I sat beside him with my legs up to my chest and my arms wrapped around my knees, gazing up into the glittering sky. Lucas sat with his legs extended in front of him, leaning back on his elbows, his gaze far off. I watched him for a few moments trying to decipher why I already felt connected to him. He never looked up.

"Lucas," I whispered.

He turned his head to me. "Yeah?"

I stared into his eyes. They were soft now, not as intense as they had been during the daylight. But they had weariness to them, almost sad and exhausted. I longed to reach out and touch him.

"I'm sorry if I offended you," I murmured. "I—"

"You have nothing to apologize for." His eyes searched mine, and I couldn't look away. He lifted his right hand and pushed back the lock of hair that had fallen in front of my face. His cool, light-as-air hand slid down my cheek to my shoulder and gently down my arm. I held my breath, memorizing his touch. Though his skin was cool, the traces left by his fingertips left a path of warmth. Tremors ran up and down my spine.

I barely knew him; these tantalizing feelings I was having should *not* exist. Still, with him, somehow the pain and emptiness that had consumed me since my mother's announcement faded to almost nothing. Something invisible seemed to be holding Lucas and me together. Like a magnet, I was being pulled to him, not against my will, but against everything I thought was right. Whatever that something was, it only moved to intensify my feelings for him.

When his fingertips reached my hand, he dropped his behind him. His eyes never left mine. At that moment I wanted to feel his lips pressed against mine and his arms wrapped around me.

Lucas shook his head. "I'm the one who should be apologizing to you." He averted his gaze, his shoulders slumping.

I bit my lip. "For what?"

Time stood still for a few moments before he answered. "For not finding you sooner."

Chapter 6

"Here kitty, kitty, kitty," Megan called from the front porch of the Moore House. "Here kitty, kitty, kitty."

A black cat jumped out from the bushes and landed in her arms. She turned to me, and I screamed. The cat's eyes shone blood-red in the moonlight.

My teeth chattered in the tunnel of cold twisting around me. The cat hissed.

"I warned you, Carrie" she said, stroking the cat's head. "Curiosity kills, my dear."

"I don't know what you're talking about." My voice quivered with the rest of my body.

Megan laughed, throwing her head back, her auburn hair catching in the breeze. "Secrets, Carrie. Secrets."

I shook my head. "I don't have secrets."

"Come on, we all do. You. Me." She scrunched up her nose at the cat. "Lucas."

"What? You said you didn't know him."

Megan ignored me, her heels clacking on the

wood. She pulled a knife from under her black dress.

"I told you to be careful." Megan pointed the tip of the blade under the cat's chin. The cat writhed in her arms, hissing and clawing. "Some secrets are lethal. Isn't that right, kitty?"

Megan glanced up at me as she jabbed the blade into the cat's throat, and the ice-cold air around me turned into fire.

I bolted upright, panting. Covering my face with my palms, I breathed into them until my heart rate slowed. Why did Megan keep making appearances in my dreams, or rather, my nightmares? Why in front of the Moore House? And what the hell was wrong with that cat?

I fell back against the pillows. Really, there was no point in trying to decipher the dreams. Dreams were just ... dreams. Not real. All in my head. My overactive imagination.

***

After I'd fallen back asleep, the dream of Megan had been replaced by visions of Lucas. I dreamt of the feel of his skin, the softness of his smile, and the glisten in his eyes. I still couldn't figure out exactly how I felt about him, but I couldn't fathom missing a day without seeing his breathtaking smile. Luckily, I didn't have to.

Grandma called from the store the next day asking if I'd bring by the invoices she'd forgotten on the kitchen counter. Secretly hoping I'd see

Lucas in town, I agreed. After I dropped them off, I walked outside and my heart leaped out of my chest. Sure, I'd wanted to see him, but I really hadn't expected him to be perched on a park bench across the street. He focused on me and grinned. I had to hold myself back from running into his arms. Instead, I gave him a little wave and a flirty smile and walked to my car without taking my eyes off him. He rose to his feet and shook his head slightly, summoning me to him.

I let out a soft giggle, bypassed my car and headed for the park. When I couldn't stand the slowness of walking, I picked up the pace.

"What are you doing here?" I asked, standing in front of him, shivering.

"Waiting for you."

I ran my fingers through my hair. "You'd have been waiting a while if my grandma hadn't forgotten some stuff at home. I'm not working today."

He grinned, the dimple sinking deep into his cheek, and swept a strand of hair out of my face. "That's the best news I've heard all day. Let's get out of here, shall we?"

We drove to a nearby town and spent the whole day talking and laughing. I never grew tired listening to him laugh. Being with him was so easy; I wasn't sure why. Even when we sat next to each other, saying nothing, I loved it.

We played a round of mini-golf. Lucas's hands covered mine as he showed me the proper grip. He wasn't hesitant, and he didn't pull away immediately. His hands lingered over mine, sending ripples of waves through my body. He let go too soon.

The next day I received a text from him first thing in the morning.

Any plans today?

A smile danced on my lips.

Not yet.

Meet me at the park in an hour.

I jumped out of bed, racing to the bathroom to get ready for another amazing day with him. We spent the day at a park in Red Oak. He'd packed a picnic lunch and a deck of cards. As we played another round of Hearts, he reached for my hand, and this time, he didn't let go. His skin was still cool, but my body seared with fire. There was just...something about him. When we got back to Villisca, he walked me to my car, still parked on the square.

"Tomorrow?" he asked, still holding my hand.

"Absolutely."

Butterflies filled my stomach as he leaned closer. His breath smelled like spearmint. I felt his other hand slide its way from my shoulder, down my arm, and into my hand. My eyes closed automatically, waiting for what I yearned for. I didn't have to wait long. Lucas's cool lips brushed lightly over mine. It only lasted a second, but it was the longest second of my life. I went to bed that night still feeling his kiss on my lips.

More eager than I knew I should be, I met Lucas in town the next evening, where we had dinner at Dan's Bar and Grill again before heading out to watch the stars.

With a blanket on the ground in the middle of nowhere, Lucas lay on his back with me cuddled up in his arms. Another blanket wrapped around me, shielding me from the cool evening air.

"And see that one?" Lucas reached toward the sky, pointing with my hand. "It starts here." I did a one-eye squint and followed our motion as he traced the constellation above us. "Goes over here, makes a box with the little triangle on top. See that?"

I laughed. "Not at all!"

Lucas kissed the top of my head. "And the tail? No?"

"I got nothing."

"It's like 'connect the dots.'"

"There's way too many dots!"

He hugged me tighter. "You're impossible!"

I giggled, folding my hand on my stomach and lifting my eyes to the sky. My head rose and fell with his chest.

"It's called Ophiuchus, The Serpent Holder," he murmured, the sound buzzing against my ear.

"Another mythology thingy, right?"

Lucas chuckled. "You catch on fast. We've only been out here for an hour."

"Oh, shut up!" I nudged him, unable to stop my grin.

"You see, Asclepius had great healing abilities. He was the son of Apollo, the god of medicine.

After his mortal mother died in childbirth, Apollo saved him and sent him to live with Chiron, a centaur. Chiron trained him in the art of healing. Well, Asclepius got so good at it, he began bringing the dead back to life, angering Hades, the god of the Underworld. So, Hades had a chit-chat with his brother, Zeus, and Zeus killed Asclepius with a lightning bolt, forever sending him into the heavens." Lucas's voice got softer as he spoke.

I followed Lucas's gaze. The stillness of the night settled around us. Lucas combed through my hair, gently weaving it around his fingers.

"How do you know all this?" I asked.

"I don't know."

I rolled onto my stomach, facing him. "What do you mean, you don't know? You learned it somewhere, right?"

Lucas's jaw clenched. "Um, yeah. I guess I … it fascinates me, so I read up on it."

I rested my chin on his chest. "Why didn't you just say that in the first place, silly?"

Folding my arm around his waist, I reached for his hand, lacing my fingers with his.

"Want to share my blanket?" I asked, tugging at it.

"Nah, I'm good."

"Your hands are cold."

Lucas sighed. "I'm always cold."

When he dropped me off at my car, he cupped my face and brushed his lips over mine. The kiss was light and short, making me long for more.

***

At night, I couldn't stop thinking about him. He filled my dreams with his smile, his eyes, and I felt each touch all over again in my mind.

What is he doing to me? I can't think of anything else. I don't want to.

The next week passed with Lucas waiting for me in the park during my lunch breaks. He rarely ate anything but always had a lunch for me. Our afternoon dates always ended with a kiss, usually light, and each time, I wanted to pull him into me. He never spoke of himself or of his past. He stayed guarded, and honestly, the mystery made me crave being with him even more.

Thursday night, we stargazed again. We mostly laid in silence, holding each other on the hood of his car. He stroked my hair, running his fingers through it continuously. I relished his touch, hungering for more of him. When he stopped combing, he turned my face to him. That sad expression that I hadn't seen for a while filled his eyes. He caressed my cheek with his fingertips, peering thoughtfully into my eyes.

Turning up the corner of his mouth, he leaned in. I felt his arms tighten around my back before our lips touched. Expecting the same brush, my eyes flew open when his lips separated over mine. My heart beat faster, and I closed my eyes, accepting the kiss with enthusiasm. And maybe a little too much. He pulled away, his tongue moving over his lower lip. Without saying a word, he ran his fingers over my cheek and kissed me again, holding me closer.

***

Lucas dropped me off at my car at eleven. He brushed the back of his hand against my cheek and gave me a smile that made my heart flutter. The way he touched me was so tender, so delicate, and so deliberate.

Every part of me needed him, and I hated the seconds that ticked by without him with me. With him, I felt … whole.

Looking into his eyes, dread filled me. Was this love? If so, how could I love someone I barely knew? My parents were in love once. And that fell apart so easily. What if…

"Do you want to come by my grandparents' farm? Around two? We could go for a walk," I suggested.

He considered it for a moment. "I'll see you at two."

"Do you need directions?"

"Nah, small town. See ya tomorrow."

He turned and started walking toward his car. A few paces in, he turned and flashed an enticing grin my way.

"Bye," I whispered. Tomorrow couldn't come soon enough.

***

The porch light barely illuminated the front door of the darkened house. I flipped the switch down and locked the door before going up to my room. A soft buzz hummed at the window, and I noticed the new air conditioner Grandpa had installed. I dropped my purse on the floor and slipped into pajamas, rubbing warmth into my arms with my hands. The room was freezing, instantly reminding me of Lucas.

When Lucas had left, I felt…strange. Off. But when he was around, it was easy to forget the world around me and all the pain my parents had caused me.

I threw down the covers and climbed in. Fighting the sudden urge to cry, I drew the blankets up to my neck, closing my eyes, inviting Lucas to fill my dreams. I wanted him with me all the time.

Morning came sooner than I wanted. In fact, I was angry at the sun for waking me from my blissful night of all Lucas and no Megan. I groaned, glancing at the clock sitting on the nightstand. Nine-thirty; everyone was gone for the day.

I hadn't checked my email in a while, too preoccupied with Lucas, and I knew Jessica had responded. I decided to wait to tell her about him, just in case it was all an amazing dream and I'd wake up soon.

I picked up my laptop from the bench in front of the window and plopped on my bed. Ignoring the junk and email from my mom, I opened Jess's.

Wow! I researched Villisca, and I can't imagine what you must be going through. I'll bet you get shivers and goose bumps all the time. You can't help being paranoid; it's in the air.

So, those strange feelings you're having is your supernatural sense in

overdrive! Carrie, do you realize you're surrounded by ghosts? They're probably everywhere and you don't even know! How cool is that?

You've already felt a ghost—that cold breeze on a warm day? That was a ghost floating by you. Don't worry, though, it won't hurt you; unless you give it a reason to … you haven't, have you?

Megan obviously knows the ghosts are there. What she meant was that whenever a place of murder is restored or renovated back to its originality, the spirits are released back inside.

You are NOT paranoid. You are simply allowing your Extrasensory Perception to surface. I'd give anything to be there.

Tell me more about your Mantel Guy. It may be coincidence, but in that town, it's more likely something else. Don't do anything yet…

Now Mike, well, he's been around for a while. Your grandparents trust him. You don't get any whacked-out vibes with him, maybe you just need to drop this other guy and stick with the safety-net guy.

BE CAREFUL
Jess

I wasn't sure what Jessica was getting at. Did she think we are all born with telepathic abilities? I knew I wasn't. And why did she need more information on Lucas? She couldn't seriously believe that he was a ghost or something. That's ridiculous.

She's obviously watched one too many episodes of The Ghost Whisperer.

I stared at her message and read it one more time before hitting "reply." Unsure of what to say, I let my fingers do the work for my brain. I started and deleted the email three times before deciding to humor her.

Jessica,

The Mantel Guy's name is Lucas. And he is amazing! Too amazing. We've been seeing each other for a while now. We went out last night, actually.

We've gone to dinner a few times. He barely eats anything, saying he isn't hungry. When he asked me why I was spending the summer here, I didn't tell him. I'm still trying not to think about it, myself. I think he was okay with it; he doesn't talk much about home either. He asks me questions about myself, he says I'm interesting. Weird, right? Me?

Anyway, whenever I'm cold around him, he wraps a blanket around me or lends me a jacket. It's so flipping sweet! He loves stargazing. We've gone out to a field a few times, just to watch the night sky. He knows all the constellations and the names of stars. Now, whenever we're together, the first thing he does is reach for my hand. It used to bother me, how cold his hands are, but not anymore. I love

how soft and smooth they are, almost
hollow.

His eyes are the most beautiful
sea-green color. I wish they didn't
look so sad. It's almost like he's
hiding something, but then again, so
am I, right?

Everyone has secrets. Anyway, he's
so wonderful. I can't stop thinking
about him. I want him with me all the
time. I don't know what to do.

Talk to you later,
Carrie

My mind was flustered. I desperately needed
something to distract me from my thoughts. With
my iPod on, I started cleaning the kitchen. My eye
caught the time on the microwave; I still had three
hours—I cleaned the microwave.

Grandma kept all the cleaning supplies in the
cupboard over the washer and dryer; I took the glass
cleaner and the wood cleaner. Every piece of
glass—mirrors, pictures, vases, knick-knacks, and
lamps—was cleaned. Next, I dusted each piece of
wood. When I finished, I still had two hours before
Lucas would arrive.

After lunch, I stretched out on the sofa, enjoying
the downtime. Before I knew it, there was a subtle
knock at the front door. I jumped up, looking at my
watch. Two o'clock exactly. Lucas had impeccable
timing.

I scrambled for the door, almost tripping over
my own feet. He was standing on the step looking
as radiant as usual.

So gorgeous.

"Hey there, beautiful," he said, the corner of his lips curving up.

I stepped out into the sunny day. I breathed in the fresh air and closed my eyes. The scent of hay and Lucas's cologne filled my senses. Ah, he smelled so good!

I opened my eyes and gave him a sly smile. He took my hand, kissing the back of it. Even though his expression was happy, something about him didn't seem right. He held my hand too tightly, his shoulders were tense, and his eyes...the sadness behind his eyes was apparent.

Beyond the house, past the sheds and the barn, we arrived to a field Grandpa had left fallow.

"Thank you," I finally said, breaking the silence. "I don't remember if I told you I had an awesome time last night."

He glanced up. "I always have an amazing time with you."

We continued walking, and I peeked at him. Lucas had his head bowed, his lower lip between his teeth. I wondered what was bothering him, but I didn't want to pry. If he wanted to tell me, he would.

"So, why Red Oak?" I asked.

"Huh?" His head jerked up, one eyebrow lifted.

I giggled. "I asked why you chose Red Oak. Do you like living there?"

"Um." His gaze drifted to the open field in front of us, his brow furrowed.

I waited. He didn't answer.

"Uh, where do your parents live?" I pried, against my initial intentions. His hesitancy had my mind reeling. "Any brothers or sisters?"

He pushed his hand through his hair. "Can we talk about something else?"

Suddenly I felt aggravated. I stopped walking. "Why? Why can't I know anything about you?"

Lucas shot me a stare. "You haven't told me why *you're* in Iowa. There are things I don't want to talk about either."

"I'm not asking you to share your deepest, darkest secrets, Lucas. I'm just asking simple stuff."

"I can't, okay?" His voice rose, startling me.

"Wow! Well, how about you tell me something real, at least. Something easy. Like, when's your birthday?"

Lucas stared at the ground, his jaw clenching. I waited, but he didn't answer.

"How old are you?"

More silence. Finally, he murmured, "It doesn't matter," and started to walk away.

I frowned, shaking my head.

What's he hiding?

I grabbed his hand, stopping him. "Really? How hard is it for you to give me a number?"

"Why, Carrie? Is this a test? Right and wrong answers? If I come from the wrong place, or have the wrong birthday, or I'm too old for you, do you walk away?"

What in the world is his problem?

I glared at him. "No, of course not."

"Then it doesn't matter."

I pursed my lips, studying him. No, I didn't want to drop it, because it did matter.

"How can I know you, without really knowing

83

you?"

"You do know me."

"Yeah, but…"

"Carrie." Lucas sighed and pulled me into him. With a hand, he threaded his fingers through my hair. "I'm sorry, I…some things are…"

The stupid dreams with Megan weaved into my thoughts.

"Secrets," I muttered.

"What?"

I took a small step back. "Look, if it's too hard to tell me the simple stuff about your life, how will we ever move through the hard stuff?"

Lucas reached for me, holding me tight, his chin resting on the top of my head. "We can't."

I nodded against his chest, a lump forming in my throat.

"Hey," he said, stepping back to examine my expression. "Come on."

He folded my hand in his, the lines on his face fading. Taking a deep breath, he said, "Alright. Something real about me."

The lump dissolved immediately. I nodded.

"Before I came to Red Oak, I lived in Southern California. Before that, Colorado. I even spent some time in Las Vegas."

I glanced up at him, and he grinned at me. "Why so many places?"

"I guess I was trying to find myself."

"Then, where's home?"

Lucas squeezed my hand, stopping us. "Here. With you."

How did he do it so quickly? Make the hurt go

away and replace it with warmth?

I reached up, running my fingers over his cheek and down his chin, barely noticing the coolness of his skin. He took my hand off his face and held it in his against his chest where his heart was.

Mine must be beating so hard that I can't feel his.

He pressed his forehead against mine and sighed. Dropping his hands from my face and hair, he placed them around the small of my back, wrapping me snuggly to his chest. His cheek rested against the top of my head. He hugged me closer, mumbling something that sounded like, "This is wrong."

Just as softly, almost inaudible, he said, "God, I don't want to lose you. I love you."

Sure he hadn't meant for me to hear the words, I didn't respond. And I didn't know if the waves crashing in my stomach meant I loved him back.

My fingers clenched onto the back of his black t-shirt. I never wanted to let go. Being with him felt so … right.

His body tensed before he pulled away. He kissed my forehead. Taking my hand, he led me out of the field. As we approached his car, his grip on my hand tightened. Glancing at him, his eyes squeezed closed, and his eyebrows furrowed. I looked away.

When we got to his red G8, he forced a smile and kissed me on the cheek.

All of a sudden, Goldie let out a loud neigh. She stood by the fence facing Lucas and me. Her tail thrashed, and she waved her head back and forth.

Her behavior reminded me of the night of the storm. She stood up on her hind legs and whinnied again.

Lucas stared at the ground, shuffling his feet in the gravel.

"She's been acting strange lately. Mike thinks there may be a mountain lion in the area," I told him.

He tucked a loose lock of hair behind my ear. "I'd better go. Looks like you should take care of her. I'll see you later." His full lips, forming a straight line across his face, almost trembled. His eyes delved deep in mine, showing me the war behind them.

"Soon?" I asked, feeling somewhat responsible for his confliction. Reaching his face, I traced his lips with my finger.

He took my hand and held it to his mouth. "Soon. I promise."

He flashed his crooked smile, got into his car, and drove away. I watched until the red dot disappeared out of view.

Goldie shot out another neigh and started a full-out run down the field. I jogged down to the fence, unsure of what to do about her. The last time, Mike opened the barn door and she went inside by herself.

I crawled over the gate, landing none too gracefully on the ground. The barn door was ajar, so I swung it all the way open, hoping Goldie would go inside by herself again.

Quickly, I jumped back over the gate and tapped my nails on the metal pole, waiting for Goldie to return. My mind drifted back to the words Lucas had mumbled. *'This is wrong.'* Yeah, he was on to something. How could I know him for so short a time and still be so enamored by him? Why did I need him so badly?

Out of the corner of my eye, I saw Goldie trotting back toward the barn, breaking my thoughts. She'd calmed down, acting like she'd just needed a run. I reached out my hand to her as she got closer. Stopping at the gate, she allowed me to stroke her nose.

"What's gotten into you, girl?" I asked. "What's out there that has you so scared?" I sighed, patting her until I heard a car pulling into the driveway.

"Hey, Care," Grandma said, stepping out of her truck. "How was your day?"

I shrugged, walking toward her and stealing a glance back at the barn. "Not too bad. Goldie was acting strange again."

"Maybe Rob needs to call the Iowa Department of Natural Resources, see if anything's been reported."

"Can I help with anything?" I grabbed some grocery sacks from the back of the pickup.

"That would be wonderful. Mike and Rob are working late tonight, so they'll both be in for dinner."

"Oh. Where was Mike last night? I noticed his truck wasn't here."

"John Roy's cows got out again, so Mike went over to help. They're making up for it tonight." We walked into the kitchen. "Carrie! You cleaned in here. It looks amazing. Thank you."

I shrugged. "No problem. It's what I would have

done if I were home." Home. What was that? Where was that?

In Lucas's arms.

The guys weren't due in for another hour, and dinner was in the oven, so we went to the living room and turned on the news. I sprawled out on the sofa, staring at the TV with my mind focused on Lucas. I smiled to myself remembering the touch of his hand and softness of his kiss. I could still feel the warmth on my face where his fingertips had been. The thought of seeing him again would have to be enough to get me through the night.

I was so engrossed in my thoughts that I didn't notice when Grandma got up at the sound of the buzzer. It wasn't until I heard the door open and close, followed by Grandpa's and Mike's loud voices echoing into the living room, that I jumped up and ran to the kitchen to continue with my neglected dinner duties.

"I'm sorry," I said as I entered the kitchen.

"Don't worry about it." She took the milk out of the refrigerator.

She had already set the table and was pouring everyone drinks. Since there was nothing left for me to do, I sat in my chair and waited for the guys to wash up. I didn't have to wait long before Mike took his place.

"Hey, Carrie," he greeted. "Thanks, Renae. This looks delicious."

I could tell he was trying to be more talkative, unlike our first dinner together. As I looked at him, I realized all my earlier feelings for him had disappeared. Before me I saw a friend. And that was all.

He sat down and drank his whole glass of milk, just like the first time we'd met. When he sat it down, Grandma was there pouring him more.

"Carrie," Mike said, spooning out the steamed vegetables I had cut up earlier. "Are you doing anything on Sunday afternoon?"

"I don't think so," I answered, glancing at Grandma for confirmation.

Grandma shook her head.

"Apparently, I'm free." I secretly hoped I'd have to cancel to see Lucas again.

"I thought we could have a riding lesson."

"Yeah," I said. "That'd be fun."

Mike winked at me, and I bit my lower lip, wondering if my response was too enthusiastic.

After Mike and Grandpa headed back outside, I helped Grandma clean up.

"I think I'm going to crash early tonight," I announced. "I'm pretty exhausted."

"Okay. Just make sure to be at the store by eight. Megan has the key."

To be honest, I wanted to escape to my room to avoid any human contact the rest of the night. My walk with Lucas had only been a few hours earlier, but it felt like a lifetime. I replayed the afternoon in my mind before slipping into a pair of shorts and tank top.

It was too early to sleep, so I grabbed one of the few books I brought and propped myself up on the pillows. I turned to the first page and realized I'd chosen *The Hobbit*. It was one of my favorites; I had the first few pages almost memorized. I flipped on the lamp beside my bed and started to read. *In a hole in the ground there lived a hobbit.*

I'm not sure when I fell asleep, but when I awoke, I was freezing, and it was past midnight. I got up, turned off the lights and put my book on the nightstand. The blankets were warm and in no time, I was asleep.

The woods were dark and the large trees stood so close together it was impossible to see around them. But it didn't bother Lucas; he glided over the lumpy ground and tree roots effortlessly. His face was grave and his eyes somber.

The dark hooded figure was waiting for him and he didn't know what to tell her. Today had confirmed what he wanted to do, and it wasn't what he knew he should do. The last thing he needed was for her to make this more difficult. But that is why she'd called this meeting, to remind him that he had crossed the line. That he needed to let it go before someone got hurt.

The mistakes kept piling up.

She didn't understand, though. He couldn't just walk away. He was too involved, and it would hurt him too much. Nothing had gone as he'd expected or hoped. And in some ways, it was better. Much better. He'd felt almost human, whatever that meant. A part of him wanted to give up his quest now and keep a hold of that wonderful feeling. Until now, he hadn't even realized he was capable of those types of feelings. He was torn, and it ate at him. Eventually, the decision would have to be made, and he dreaded making it. He wanted more time. Desperately.

"Lucas." Her voice chimed in his head as he approached her. He stared at the ground, lost in thought. "I know this is hard for you. But you have gone too far. You know this."

He nodded. "Yes."

"You can't do this. You have no choice. You must leave and never return."

"I can't," he whispered.

"You must. For you and for her. You must!"

"There has to be a way." Lucas struggled to get the words out.

"It's too dangerous."

"I have to be with her."

"Lucas! If you love her, you have to let her go. She could die. And you could be lost forever."

"She doesn't have to. I could tell her. I could tell her everything. Let her decide. I don't care about myself. Just one day feeling alive with her is enough to last an eternity."

"Don't be stupid. You cannot tell her. It may put her in even more danger. And you, you have no idea how long eternity is."

Lucas was silent. He looked around the ground as if searching for an easy answer; there was none. Deep down, he knew the hooded figure was right. He'd have to go. Vanish. Forever.

"I don't want to make this choice," he said.

"Don't be selfish, Lucas."

"I will hurt her if I leave," he said.

"You may kill her if you stay." The hooded figure's voice softened. "Keep searching, Lucas. There is no life for you here. And not for her either.

This relationship is impossible. You have to go. She'll get over it."

The hooded figure held out her hand and rested it on Lucas's shoulder. After a moment, she dropped her hand and walked into the shadow of the looming trees. Lucas stood by himself, eyes closed.

He knew it had to end but he didn't want it to end yet. If she loved him... maybe she could help him. It could work.

No, he was already in way too deep. He'd already made too many mistakes. This decision had to be made tonight before someone else got hurt.

She was right. It had to be done. This one decision would change the course of both their lives.

Chapter 7

The dream disturbed me on so many different levels. The first one was strange enough, but the second was disconcerting. I wasn't much for believing that dreams meant things, however these were different: familiar and vivid, unlike the nightmares with Megan. Not only could I hear them speak, I knew their thoughts. The dreams were burned into my memory as if they had actually happened. I hadn't given much thought to the first one, passing it off as a strange dream, but this one led me to believe there was something more. And it had to do with me.

At least I knew that Lucas was half the mystery duo. But the woman? Who was she, and what did she want with him?

I thought back to the first dream—the one in the alley. Neither Lucas nor the woman seemed happy about meeting. Lucas had wanted to do something, but the woman warned him to not even consider it. That it would expose them, and that it was dangerous for him and whoever else was involved.

Me?

According to Lucas's thoughts, he went through with his plan, and something had gone wrong. However, he wasn't upset about it. In fact, he was ecstatically happy. Which was…problematic?

The figure told him to leave, but if he chose to stay, I could die. Oddly, this idea wasn't the most disturbing part of the dream, although I knew it should have been. The most outlandish parts were the eerie references to Lucas's being.

With me, he felt *human*. It also made him feel *alive*. The hooded figure said Lucas would be lost forever, not die—his fate would be different than mine.

Now, he had a decision to make. Without me.

No matter how hard I tried, and truthfully I wasn't trying that hard, I couldn't put the dreams behind me. They were too weird…if I considered they were real. *If*, being the big question. If it was real…then what?

It makes me a crazy person, that's what.

I sighed and looked up from the book I'd been pretending to read. It was just after noon, and Megan was eating her lunch at the counter, Kindle in hand. The store had been busy all morning, but no one had come in since after eleven.

"What are you reading?" I asked, trying to break the silence.

Megan glanced at me as if sizing me up. She thought for a few seconds. "*The Salem Witch Trials*." Then she went back to her book without another word.

Okay. I wasn't in the talking mood anyway.

I set my book down and glanced out the window. The sun blazed, and the skies were a beautiful shade of light blue without a cloud in sight. Earlier, people had been out doing errands, riding bikes, taking walks, and otherwise enjoying the summer morning. But as the afternoon wore on and the heat intensified, they'd all disappeared into the coolness of their homes.

As I stared out at the empty sidewalks, my mind drifted to Lucas who had yet to drop by. I checked my phone. No calls. No texts. He hadn't said he'd come to the store, per se, but I assumed he would. He promised to see me again soon, and I was relying on him keeping that promise. Each time the bell over the door rang, my heart sunk to see just another customer.

"You anxious about something?" Megan asked over the top of her tablet.

"Sort of."

"What's going on?"

I thought about it for a few moments; her sudden interest in me made me weary. Plus, I was unsure of how much I wanted Megan to know. Her odd behavior over Lucas hadn't warmed me. I didn't even consider the nightmares, which really, I couldn't hold her accountable for.

"I guess I thought someone would be coming in to see me today."

"Ah." She put her Kindle on the counter, clearly intrigued. "Does that 'someone' happen to be a guy? Mike Carson, maybe?"

I cocked my head to the side. "You know Mike?"

"Oh, honey, *everyone* knows Mike. Everyone loves Mike."

Of course, they did.

"Well, it's not Mike."

Megan rested her elbows on the counter. "Who is it?

"You've seen him. He came in a couple weeks ago looking for a fireplace mantel."

I waited for her expression to change. It didn't, but it took her a second too long to answer.

"Oh, yeah. He was pretty cute."

I nodded, studying her closely.

Megan quirked an eyebrow. "Do you like him?"

I hesitated. Should I tell her? Can I trust her?

Oh, what the hell. They were just stupid dreams.

"I do…a lot."

"Like, a lot a lot?"

"Yeah."

Her voice deepened. "Well, be careful. You barely know him."

'Be careful, Carrie. Some secrets are lethal.'

I stared at her.

The store door opened. I jumped up, startled, until I recognized Mrs. Taylor.

"Good afternoon, girls," she said.

"Good afternoon," I replied.

"Hi, Mrs. Taylor. How are you?" Megan greeted.

"Good, dear. I was wondering if you would be able to come by after work today and have some tea. I could really use your talents in my garden."

"Yeah. No problem."

"Thank you so much. I'll see you later. Nice to see you again, Carrie."

"You, too," I said as she walked out the door. "You have gardening talents?"

Are those like your water dumping skills?

"She wants my help tilling. It's hard on her back."

The phone rang, and Megan went to answer it. I turned around, and out of the corner of my eye I saw Lucas standing outside the window. Rushing to the front of the store, I couldn't stop smiling. By the time I got to the front, he'd disappeared.

My eyes darted around. Maybe I was hallucinating.

Sounds about right.

A short, bald man swept past me into the store, asking if we had any crocks. Still preoccupied with the empty sidewalk, I led him to the back wall. My eyes stayed glued to the door, though. After a few moments, he chose six. Carefully, I wrapped the smaller ones and sat them inside the larger ones like Russian nesting dolls without their heads. Then I helped him take them to his car.

I stepped back to the curb, distracted. "Have a great day," I said to myself as he drove off.

My eyes flitted up and down the sidewalk. Nothing. I glanced across the street and a sense of relief consuming me. Sitting on a bench in the courtyard, was Lucas.

I waved excitedly and opened the store door to tell Megan I'd be right back. When I turned around, he'd vanished—into thin air. There was no one in the courtyard, no one on the streets, and no one on the sidewalk. I shook my head and blinked several times.

Not possible.

No one could get up and leave that quickly. I glanced around again; there wasn't a soul in sight.

"I think I need glasses," I muttered, stumbling back inside.

Megan paused from her phone call to shoot me a quizzical stare. I shrugged and slumped back into my chair. I picked up my book but didn't read it.

What if Jessica's ghost theory's correct?

The prospect made me shudder.

***

My mind swirled as I drove up the gravel road toward to my grandparents' after my shift ended. I glanced out the window, remembering when life was simple. To the east of the quaint farmhouse lay a small forty-acre cornfield where I used to pick corn when no one was watching. I liked to peel back the husk and play with the silk between my fingers.

I sat in my car for a few minutes, trying to enjoy the nostalgia. Until *Superstition*, the Glee version erupted from my phone. A text from Jess.

Call me. ASAP. We need to talk.

I groaned and stuffed the phone in my back pocket. Knowing Jess, she'd probably add something else to my cluttered mind.

The bird-calling clock in the living room read a quarter after five. Deciding now would be as good a time as any to call, I took the cordless off the cradle and dialed Jessica's cell.

"Hello?" Jessica's voice sounded confused.

"Hey, Jess, it's me."

"Hang on. Let me go to my room."

Less than a minute passed before she said, "I'm back."

I plopped down on the love seat. "Yes?"

"Carrie, I think you have a problem," Jessica stated matter-of-factly.

"And that is...?"

"Don't you think there's something strange about him? Lucas, I mean. Granted, he sounds sweet, but don't you think murderers are nice and sweet to their victims before they go in for the kill?"

"You think he's a murderer?" I asked dryly.

"I think he's a monster. His end goal is to kill you."

I rubbed my forehead. *There's no way this conversation can get any crazier.* "Go on."

"Don't you see? He doesn't eat. He refuses to talk about himself. He wants to know everything about you—for information. He's inhumanly beautiful. His body temperature is not ninety-eight degrees, and he's drawing you in by his malicious powers."

"You watch too much TV."

"He's not human, Carrie. He's something else."

Note to self: Don't tell Jess what I saw, or didn't see, today.

"I'll bite. What is he, then?"

"I'm not sure. Do you sense any...evil about him?"

"Uh, no."

"How about fear? Does he scare you, or does your hair stand up on end when he's around?"

"If that answer was 'yes', don't you think I'd try to avoid him?"

"You can physically touch him, though?"

"Yes. He looks as human as I do. Except for his eyes. It's like they glow. They're beautiful."

"Not a ghost then. Weird in that town. Um … huh. Is he hairy?"

I was wrong. This conversation just skyrocketed out of crazy and was heading straight for eccentric.

"You've got to be kidding me? Jess, are you serious?"

"Werewolves are human, Carrie—for most of the month."

"A werewolf? You realize they don't exist, right? That you're nuts?"

"Just go with me here."

I scoffed. "Fine. What kind of creature is he, then?"

"Hmm. He doesn't seem to fit entirely into one category. Unless, of course, he's an angel. I guess I hadn't considered that. That would be good, 'cause then he's not out to kill you." She paused for a few moments. "Unless you're going to die soon anyway, and he's waiting to escort you to the afterlife. You know, that might be your best bet."

I rolled my eyes, happy Jess couldn't see through the phone to comment. "Really? The best you've got is that I'm going to die? Jess, all of the stuff I told you before can easily be explained. He took home his dinner 'cause he wasn't hungry. That's normal. And he has talked about himself. No offense, but I think you may be trying to find drama in my life and honestly, I don't need any more."

I waited for an answer, hoping I hadn't offended her. Thirty seconds ticked by in silence. "Jess?"

"I'm thinking," she responded. More time passed in silence before Jessica spoke. "You might be right. It's just, in that town, you should expect paranormal activity and not be surprised about it. I'm just worried about you, Carrie. I've been having strange dreams."

My breath caught. "What did you say?" I bit my lower lip too hard, drawing blood.

"Uh...that I was worried?"

"No, no. After that."

"My dreams?"

"Yeah. What are they about?"

"Well, you...dying."

Death. There is a parallel with my dream and Lucas. Coincidence?

"How do I die?" I asked, holding onto the phone too tightly.

"At the mercy of a vampire, I think."

Oh, thank God. It's Jessica who's crazy.

I sighed, relieved. "You mean Lucas? You think he's a vampire? Really?"

"I don't know. Does Lucas have yellow-blond hair and turquoise eyes?"

"No. Lucas has dark hair and green eyes."

"Oh, good. Then it's not him who kills you."

Um, yay?

"Jess, dreams don't come true. They're just random synapses firing in your brain," I said, half-impressed that I'd actually remembered something from my Psychology class.

"I've never had a dream with this much vividness. Does that make sense? You know, it's probably nothing. I'm worried, so my mind's playing tricks on me."

Vivid dreams, the same as mine. The similarities were beginning to scare me. Shaking my head, I brushed it off. No point in making Jessica either more worried or more superstitious—if *that* was possible.

"It's okay. Hey, let me know if your dream changes. I'd really rather not die!"

Jessica chuckled on the other end. "I'll do what I can. Just stay away from handsome blond guys, okay?"

"I can do that," I said smiling. "So, tell me. In these dreams of yours, how do you die?"

"My dream isn't as clear on that, but it doesn't look like I ever die. I turn into a unicorn and prance happily over a rainbow." Jessica giggled.

"Good to know." I sat up and peered out the window. "Hey, I just heard a car pull up. I think my grandma's home. I'd better let you go. I'll talk to you later, 'kay?"

"Okay. Just be careful…for me."

"Will do," I promised.

After helping Grandma carry in the groceries, I went back into the living room. I opened my laptop and searched the web, somewhat intrigued by Jess's dreams. Not that I believed there was any kind of link, but my curiosity won out.

My research on dreams came up fruitless. Most of the hits were of people suffering from bipolar disorder, diabetes, other diseases—physical or mental—or side effects of medications. Since I was fairly sure I wasn't suffering any of the above disorders, except maybe insanity, I closed my computer and wandered into the kitchen.

My mind stayed so focused on the dreams, Jess, and Lucas that it barely registered that my grandparents were bickering during dinner about artificially inseminating the cows.

Um, ew.

Excusing myself, I ran up to my room. My nails clicked on my teeth as I paced the floor. I hadn't seen Lucas all day, and it bothered me more than I wanted. I checked my phone again. Nothing. He'd promised to see me soon. What did 'soon' mean? Obviously, it didn't mean he'd see me the next day, because he hadn't. Had he told me he was doing something today? Crap, I couldn't remember. Walking in circles around my room, trying to figure it all out, started to make me dizzy.

Then it hit me. Like conspiracy theories, you never really ponder them until after the conversation with a crazy person. Had I not spoken to Jessica, I may have missed it completely. The promise wasn't that we'd see each other; it was that *he* would see *me*. I had only assumed that meant I'd see him, as well. If Jessica was on to something— and I hoped with every ounce of my being she wasn't—the omission in his words meant…what?

The endless and ridiculous possibilities ran one by one through my mind. An angel? A vampire? A ghost? A demon? Something else? None of it made sense. It was…it had to be…impossible. Lucas was human. I kicked myself for even flirting with any other option, but…but what if? Putting both hands on my head, I paced faster. Could my wacked-out superstitious friend be right? Was Lucas human?

What if?

Admittedly, I didn't know much about the undead, other than what was portrayed on TV and movies. Those theories had to come from somewhere, right? I took each impractical creature one by one.

I've gone over the deep end. Thanks Jess.

Vampires. Usually evil. Sometimes dead, sometimes not. In most movies, have fangs, turn into bats, and sleep in coffins. Not to mention, they sucked the blood of humans. Vampires were beautiful, like Lucas. Although, unlike Lucas, they wouldn't have left me alive. And we were outside in the daylight. Vampire—not likely.

Hmm, ghosts. Save one, all ghost movies have haunted houses—the Moore House?—and the ghosts seek payback on unsuspecting, stupid humans. They were invisible or transparent. The only good ghost I could recall was Patrick Swayze, and even he was out for revenge. Again, not Lucas. What would he want with me?

Demonic beings. Very, very evil. Nothing good came to mind as I considered this one. I felt stupid for acknowledging any of them, but this one most of all. Moving on.

Werewolves. At this thought, I could have slapped myself. Wondering if there had been a full moon since I'd met Lucas, I walked over to the window and peered outside. Then I checked the calendar hanging on the wall; we wouldn't have a full moon for almost a week.

Good God, I've lost it.

Angels. Angels were good beings sent from Heaven to help humans. They usually had wings and halos in Heaven, but maybe not on Earth. This, by far, was the most likely option. Aside from Lucas just being human, of course. If Jess was right about him possibly being an angel, then my dreams made more sense. Sort of. So then, why would being with him be dangerous for me, or him?

Searching my purse, I found a pen and grabbed a notebook from the dresser. I sat back down on my bed, crossed my legs, and began to write. Every tiny detail I could recall from the first dream filled up the first page. It surprised me how much I was able to remember.

Like I was there.

Then I proceeded to the dream I'd had the night before.

I sighed and set the notebook on my lap. Biting my lip, I stared at my closet as if it held the answers I so desperately wanted.

I allowed my eyelids to fall. Deep within me, I knew that the connection Lucas and I shared was more than mere attraction. I loved him, with all my heart and soul. He was all I could think about; all I could see.

Loving him was so easy, and it scared the hell out me. I didn't want to need him so badly—that meant he'd have the power to break my heart into a thousand tiny pieces. But the damage was done. I had fallen too hard and *way* too fast.

Oh, God. What have I done?

My heart sank; emptiness filled my stomach. I stood up and walked to the window. As I peered out into the darkness, I imagined Lucas's face reflecting back at me.

"Lucas, where are you?" I paused, breathing slowly.

I stared out the window, holding my arms across my body. If my dream was real, then he was out there somewhere thinking of me. Trying to decide. A choice he would be making by himself, but one that would affect me either way. And I had nothing to say about it. My life was in someone else's hands, as seemed to be the case lately.

Shivering, I closed my eyes and ran my fingers through my hair.

"Good night, Lucas. I love you," I said, wishing I had told him earlier.

Chapter 8

"Lucas!"

Standing on the porch of the Moore House, I leaned over the rail, panicking.

Where did he go?

"Lucas!"

I ran to the stairs, ready to dart out into the yard, but a large rush of heat blew me backward. Air flew out of my lungs as my back hit the wood floor. I lay there, staring at the ceiling, trying to breathe.

Heels clacking on the wood vibrated in my ears. I lifted my head to see Megan standing over me.

"It's useless, Carrie."

Shuffling my legs, I backed up against the door, standing. "Where is he? What did you do with him?"

Megan scoffed and took a step back. "Nothing."

I pulled myself to my feet, glaring at her. "I don't believe you."

She shrugged.

The doorknob dug into my back. I reached

behind me, turning it. "Is he inside?"

Megan's eyes narrowed. "Nothing's inside, Carrie. Nothing you want to get involved in."

"You brought me here, remember?" I flung the screen open.

Megan's hand shot out and grasped my wrist. "Do not go inside that house." Then, she let go, her eyes softening. "Please."

My eyes fluttered open, daylight streaming through the window. Megan might know more than she let on.

Is Lucas really gone? And what's inside that house?

I groaned, annoyed with myself.

"This is ridiculous," I muttered out loud and headed to the bathroom.

***

Twenty minutes.

I threw my church clothes on the bed and opted for a pair of jeans and a sleeveless shirt. They seemed like good horseback riding clothes. I checked myself out in the mirror and made one change: sweeping my long brown hair up into a claw clip on the back of my head. My heart raced, and I hadn't even made it downstairs yet.

Fifteen minutes.

Grandma and Grandpa were fixing themselves lunchmeat sandwiches. It took me five minutes to scarf down my turkey and ham.

Ten minutes.

I tapped my fingers on my knee and stared absently at the television. Assuming I'd hear Mike's loud truck as he pulled in, I almost toppled to the floor when I heard the door open and his voice calling my name.

"Hey, Carrie!"

I jerked my head around to see Mike, dressed in jeans and a T-shirt—yay!—standing in the doorway.

"Ready to try this?" he asked, rubbing his hands together like an evil scientist.

I laughed. "Definitely."

Mike went outside, and I slipped on my tennis shoes since that was all I had. Excitement bubbled through me until I stepped outside and stopped dead in my tracks. Instead of Mike's old, rusty truck, he'd brought a large dark brown horse and parked her right outside the back door. I gasped in surprise at the size of the massive beast. The horse looked much larger than Goldie. It was beautiful, though, with a shiny black mane and tail. Mike held onto the reins, a childish grin on his face.

"Wow!" I said. "Did your truck break down?"

"No. This," he patted the giant horse on its side, "is Roxanne."

"She's gorgeous…and large."

"Roxanne is a draft crossbreed. She's very strong. And very gentle. I brought her because she's the perfect learning horse."

"Huh? You want me to learn with her? Not Goldie?"

"That's the idea."

I was speechless for all of ten seconds. "Mike," I

said, letting out a nervous laugh. "Do you realize that's a long way to fall?"

"You're not going to fall. I've taught kids much younger than you to ride. And they all start on Roxanne."

"How...young?"

"Seven."

I swallowed. Bravery was not one of my strengths. In fact, I considered myself an all-out wuss. I hadn't expected learning to ride a horse would be dangerous, but as I stared at Roxanne, I discovered how wrong I'd been.

"Don't worry, Carrie." Mike reassured me. "You'll be fine. I promise. Now come on."

Um...

Walking a safe distance next to Mike, I shuffled my feet along the gravel. When Mike stopped, I stood back a ways, analyzing the situation. In the barn, Goldie wasn't threatening. Out in the open, however, with Roxanne, I couldn't force myself forward.

"Animals can sense fear. You need to relax. Go pet her, talk to her first. Let her smell you and get used to your touch."

Taking a few cautious steps forward, I stole a glance at Mike. He nodded his approval with his eyebrows raised and a smirk on his face. When I finally made it to the horse, I started stroking Roxanne's nose. She snorted at my hand, spraying horse boogers on it. I took an instinctive step backward, pretty sure she could bite off my fingers.

"She's not going to hurt you," Mike said, taking my damp hand and guiding it back to the horse's nose. "Just let her sniff."

I stood perfectly still as Roxanne examined me. Mike reminded me to relax. He kept a hold of the reins with one hand and patted her with the other.

Mike let go of my hand. "Are you ready to mount?"

"I don't know. Is she ready?"

"Yeah, she's ready. It's kind of her job." He laughed.

I sighed, looking the horse over again. She seemed tame enough, but I knew she could flatten me in a heartbeat if she wanted to. Not to mention I'd need to stand on a ladder in order to get up on her back.

"I'll mount first and talk you through it. Then I'll help you. Okay?"

I nodded and gulped.

"Always approach a horse from the left-hand side. Place your left foot in the stirrup. Make sure it's secure so you don't slip out, okay?" He looked at me, making sure I was paying attention. I nodded, and he continued. "Both hands go on the horn. This piece." He patted the small erect part of the saddle. "Are you good so far?"

"I think so," I said, watching carefully.

"Okay. Now, take all of your weight and put it on your foot in the stirrup. Then jump up and hoist yourself up, swinging your right leg over the seat." In one swift motion, Mike did exactly what he had just finished explaining. "And you're on. Easy, right?"

"Oh, yeah. Uh-huh. Piece of cake…for *you*!"

Mike chuckled. "You'll be fine. Come on. Your

turn." He dismounted with the grace of a platform diver.

This is going to be embarrassing.

"I'll hold onto the reins, so don't worry about that. Stand up next to her. Good."

I attempted to do each task as he said it. I put my left foot in the stirrup, and he adjusted it. The horn was difficult for me to reach, and I nearly lost my balance. Mike told me to grab hold of the belt piece instead.

"Ready?" he asked.

"I can do this," I encouraged myself. I took a deep breath and let it out slowly. "I'm ready."

"On the count of three, push off with your left foot, okay?"

"Yeah."

"One…Two…Three!"

I stepped into the stirrup until I was standing straight up in the air like a soldier. I moved my hands onto the horn and started to swing my leg over. As I kicked, my foot hit something hard.

"Ow!"

I looked down and saw that I'd kicked him in the head. "Oh, I'm so sorry." I dropped my foot back down. On my way to the ground, I remembered Mike hadn't told me how to dismount. I toppled onto my already-injured teacher, my foot stuck in the stirrup. Roxanne didn't move an inch, probably laughing inside.

"Oh, Mike. Sorry. Sorry!" I exclaimed. "My foot's stuck!"

He crawled out from under me and laughed. "Not bad."

Removing my foot from the stirrup, he held out his hand to help me to my feet.

"I'm sorry!" I said again.

"I've had worse. At least you're not wearing boots. Come on, let's try again."

"No, no. I think I've inflicted enough damage for the day," I said, backing away.

Mike grabbed my hand. "Not yet, you haven't. It's going to take more than a knock in the head and a fall on my ass to get me to give up."

I grimaced.

"Foot in the stirrup," Mike encouraged. "There you go."

Perfect. I am all set to give Mike a concussion.

"Now, swing your leg over *as* you step up," he instructed. "One…Two…Three!"

This time he ducked as he helped lift me onto Roxanne. In less than five seconds I was seated on top of the oversized beast.

I was aghast. "I did it! I did it, and you are still standing!"

"That's the idea. Good. Do you want to try again?"

"Sure…How do I get down?"

Mike shrugged. "The same way you got up. Just reverse it."

"Make sure I don't fall on you."

I swung my left leg over and landed safely on the ground, Mike's hands securely around my waist.

"Not bad," he said, taking a few seconds too long to let go of me.

We practiced four more mounts and three dismounts. Each one was better than the last and each with less help from Mike. On the last try, Mike handed me the reins.

"Now we ride," he said. "Scoot up a little bit. I'm getting on behind you."

I wanted to object. Mike riding the same horse, directly behind me, meant he'd have his body pressed against mine with his arms around my waist. I tensed as Mike scooted up behind me.

"Relax," he said. "Take each rein in one hand. There you go." He put his hands over mine. Unlike Lucas's hands, Mike's were warm. They felt strange, unfamiliar. "We just want her to walk. So with the heel of your feet, give her a light kick."

"Excuse me? You want me to kick your horse?"

"Yeah, lightly. I don't want to fall off the back."

"O...kay."

I did as Mike instructed, and Roxanne continued to stand in place like a statue.

"Harder."

I dug my heels in a little deeper. Nothing.

"You're not going to hurt her; you saw her build. Put some power in that kick, she has to be able to feel it."

I took a deep breath and kicked, digging my heels hard into Roxanne's side. She threw her head back and started to move forward.

"There you go," my instructor said. "Now, guide her with the reins. If you want to go left, take them both left. If you want to go right, pull right."

"Easy enough," I said. I tried each direction with Mike's guidance, and Roxanne followed. "Cool."

I was proud of myself. This was something I'd never have done if I were still in Texas. As Mike and I rode around the open field, I felt a sense of freedom. Something *I* was controlling, instead of everything controlling me. *I* set Roxanne's pace. *I* told her which way to go. *I* told her when to stop. Unlike my life—my mom was moving, I was following. I was told I *had* to come to Iowa. And Lucas, possibly, was somewhere out there making some decision that affected my life without knowing what I wanted. Yes, I was in control now. I liked it.

I glanced back at Mike; he winked.

"Wanna try trotting?" he asked. "We'd go a little faster than turtle pace."

"How much faster?"

"Oh...maybe like a waddling penguin."

I thought about it for a moment. "Hmm. *If* I wanted to trot, how would I do it?"

"Kick her again."

"That simple?"

"That simple."

"Okay." I sat up straight. My legs went out, then I dug my heels into Roxanne's side. Immediately she picked up her speed. It wasn't bad. Nice, actually.

"Good job."

We trotted around the outer rim of the field, bouncing on Roxanne's back. She never missed a beat. Her black mane shined brightly in the hot sun, shimmering in the glory of the rays. I looked up to the sky, letting the moment sink in.

Mike released the reins, giving me full control. He moved his hands and held me around the waist. My body tensed at his touch. He squeezed tighter and leaned in until his lips were next to my ear. My heart beat faster, pounding behind my ribs. His mouth was so close.

"Roxanne needs a drink. How about we get Goldie saddled up, and you can try this by yourself? I'll ride right next to you." His low voice hummed in my ear.

"Yeah, sure." I turned Roxanne around, almost too fast, and headed to the barn. Mike jumped off Roxanne like a pro and held up his hand for me.

"I can do this!" I said, motioning him away.

Mike shrugged, taking a few steps backward. I dismounted, less stylishly than Mike, but I didn't fall on my ass, which was good enough for me.

"See?" I said, crossing my arms.

Mike rolled his eyes. "Fancy."

"Yeah, but I did it."

He took the reins with a smirk on his face, leading Roxanne through the gate into Goldie's field.

"Come on," he said. "You can help me saddle up Goldie."

After an enjoyable ride, we guided the girls back to the barn. I dismounted, this time tripping over myself and stumbling into the fence.

Mike looked amused but suppressed his laughter. I ignored him.

He patted Roxanne on the side. "I need to get Roxanne home before it gets dark."

"Oh, well, thanks for today. I had fun."

"You know, I don't help Rob on Monday mornings. I could bring over a movie tonight and we could pop some popcorn?"

I hesitated. I didn't want to lead him on. On the other hand, I wasn't ready to be alone quite yet with Lucas having yet to make an appearance.

"Sure," I agreed.

Mike's eyes sparkled as he grinned. "Great. I'll be back around nine."

He mounted Roxanne and led her to the gravel road. At the end of the driveway, he waved.

What have I gotten myself into?

Grandma and Grandpa were nestled into their recliners—Grandma knitting and Grandpa reading. They didn't seem to notice me come in. I walked across the room and sat on the sofa.

"Mike's coming over later to watch a movie," I announced, unsure as to whether I should state the fact or ask permission.

"All right. How was your riding lesson?" Grandma asked, looking up from her work.

"Good. It was fun."

"Your dad called," Grandma said. Grandpa glared at her. She glanced over at him. "What? I just thought she'd want to know." Grandpa shook his head and went back to his reading.

Again, Dad? Anger boiled inside my veins. Thinking about him and what he was doing to our family made me want to scream. Why did she even bring him up?

"I think I'm going to go shower. Get the horse smell off." My tone was harsh and edgy. Neither of them said a word.

***

Mike arrived at a quarter to nine.

"Hey, Rob! Good reading?" he asked as he walked into the living room.

Grandpa Robert nodded. "It's all right. I'm about done, so you kids can have the livin' room to yourselves."

"No hurry." Mike plopped down on the sofa next to me. "What are you reading?"

"*The Hobbit*. It's a classic. One of my favorites."

"Never read it. But I've seen the Ring movies."

I raised my eyebrows. "You don't like to read?"

"Not really. I read what I have to and no more."

"Huh," I said and went back to my book.

"Hey, bookworm!" Mike said, flicking my book.

"Yes?"

He gave me a "don't-read-I'm-here-talk-to-me" look.

"Let me get to a good stopping place, okay?"

"Fine." He slumped into the sofa.

I ignored him.

Grandpa rose from his seat. "Well, goodnight, you two."

A few minutes passed in silence until I placed my bookmark between the pages and set it on the floor.

"So," I said.

"So what?" Mike answered.

"What movie did you bring?" I asked, looking at him sideways. I didn't know what type of movies Mike enjoyed, and I was somewhat concerned. I could, however, be fairly sure it wasn't a Nicholas Sparks adaptation.

He flashed a wide smile while holding up two

black DVD cases. The cover of one was black with two odd-looking characters in front of a black castle, while the other just freaked me out. "Nineteen sixty-three version of *The Haunting*, and my personal favorite, *Young Frankenstein*. You pick."

I looked at him skeptically. "*Young Frankenstein*?" I licked my lips then pursed them together.

Maybe I should have gone to bed.

"Oh!" Mike stood up looking insulted. "No! No. Please don't tell me you've never seen *Young Frankenstein*?"

I shook my head. "Sorry. No."

"You have got to be kidding me. Talk about your classics! Gene Wilder. Gene Hackman. Peter Boyle! A Mel Brooks movie!"

I shrugged.

Mike started to sing ... and dance. "I ain't got no body! And nobody's got me!"

I stared at him, my hand clamped over my mouth.

"I-gor?" he tried again, his eyebrows lifted so high they almost touched his hairline. "This is the best movie ever made!"

I shook my head, trying to repress the laughter. "Sorry. Still a no."

He gave up. "Well, after tonight, that 'no' will become a firm and definitive 'YES!'"

"Let's go get our popcorn before you break out into more song and dance."

He looked playfully hurt. "It wasn't that bad."

I tossed the popcorn bag into the microwave.

"What do you want to drink?"

"Pepsi."

I grabbed two and set one in front of him. Picking up the rejected movie, *The Haunting*, I turned it over in my hand to read the back. I took a sip of my soda and wondered what Mike thought about the Moore House and the supposed haunting there. Would he react like Megan? Surely not.

"What do you think of the Moore House in town?"

He shrugged. "It's weird, I guess. I've never been there, but I know people who have. They say there's something there."

"Like ghosts?"

"Something." Then he flashed a mischievous smile. "Want to go? Check it out for yourself?"

I bit my lower lip, contemplating Mike's suggestion. Dream Megan's warning to stay away just made me more curious. "When did you have in mind?"

"Friday afternoon? We'll leave here around two?"

"Sure," I shuddered. Making plans to visit a haunted house and learning to horseback ride all in one day made me a daredevil in my mind.

Oh, yeah!

Mike and I sat on opposite ends of the sofa with the popcorn between us. Mike took control of the remotes. He grinned like a lunatic, excited to be sharing one of his all-time favorite movies with me.

When it was over, Mike worked me over wide-eyed.

"I laughed like a crazy person! Doesn't that

answer your un-asked question?" I said, wiping the laughter tears from my eyes. "I enjoyed it."

"Told you!" he said playfully.

"Don't rub it in."

Silence hung in the air as Mike stared at me. I sucked in a breath and glanced away. Clumsily, I reached for the empty bowl, knocking it to the floor. We went for it at the same time, our fingers touching. I jerked my hand back.

"Thanks," I said. "We'd better get this stuff put away."

I heard Mike's disappointed sigh. "Yeah."

"Thanks for everything," I said. "I guess I'll see you later?"

He grinned. "Later."

"Right."

Awkward silence settled in the room.

Now it's uncomfortable. Nice.

"I'll walk you to the door. I need to lock it anyway," I said.

He stood for a moment at the doorway, hands in his pockets.

"See you later," he said, his gaze cast downward.

"Good night, Mike. Thanks again."

He nodded. "Good night, Carrie."

After a slight hesitation, he walked out the door. I closed it behind him and leaned back against the wall.

Just great.

***

The week slinked along at a snail's pace. Each

day I waited for Lucas to turn up. Each night I'd go to bed disappointed, listening to blaring music to help me sleep. He didn't show up in my dreams, either. Nor did Megan or the hooded figure.

I went to bed that night feeling empty. Giving up on Lucas was out of the question, but I had begun to lose hope that I'd ever see him again.

Deep inside I didn't want to admit he'd left, or that my dreams were more than just random brain activity. I couldn't fathom that he had made his choice, and the hooded figure in my dreams had won. Every time I considered this, tears welled up behind my eyelids, but I fought them. If I admitted he was gone, then it would be true.

I sat in my pajamas on the cushioned chair in front of my window. The full moon, large and bright, illuminated the dark sky. In the stillness, I allowed my mind to wander. I didn't have the energy to fight my emotions any longer. I was torn; my heart physically hurt. That night, for the first time, I allowed myself to cry over Lucas.

Chapter 9

I paced the living room floor, rolling my nails over my thumbs. First off, I was going out with Mike again, and I didn't want any of the time we spent together to be weird. Secondly, we'd be exploring one of the scariest places in the country—supposedly—today.

The night was difficult. Lucas invaded my dreams, and I woke often, sometimes even thinking I'd seen him in my room. In an effort to remember what I'd dreamt, I tried to write them down. It didn't work, though. I couldn't remember anything but the perfect features of Lucas's face: his dark, disheveled hair; intense green eyes; high cheekbones; kissable, soft lips. My dreams may be the only link I had to him now, and that notion left the empty void in the pit of my stomach duller.

Nothing hurt more than the idea of Lucas separated from me forever, making the hollowness of my parents' divorce feel like mild menstrual cramps. Though I hadn't known him long, we shared a connection that I'd never before experienced. He was the missing piece—the other part of my soul.

A loud engine and spinning tires against the gravel driveway broke my thoughts. Gulping, I peeked through the curtains. Sure enough, Mike's truck sat in front of the house. Now that we were going, I was having second thoughts. I was paranoid enough; would this trip make it worse?

What would I find behind the door, anyway? All this talk of ghosts was just because the crime had never been solved. If it ever was, no one would pay attention to the old house.

Nicely thought out there, Sherlock. You're a freaking genius.

Mike didn't knock, letting himself in. "Ready?"

I spun around to face him. "Yeah. Let's go."

"No spooky stuff ever happens during the day." He glanced at me sideways, a boyish smirk appearing on his face. "You scared?"

"Of what? A house?"

His eyebrows rose. "Your face is red."

I sighed. "I'm fine."

"The tour starts at the museum. Let's go."

I climbed up into Mike's truck and slammed the rusty door. With my hands placed neatly on my lap, I continued to fidget with my nails. Mike slid behind the wheel and gave me a sly look before starting the engine. He didn't say much on our short drive to the town square, probably amused by my anxiety.

The museum sat just a few buildings east of The Coffee Shop, on the same street as Renae's Antiques. The building was brick, painted white. A large red door stood between the two sets of black-lined windows, and 'Villisca Museum', set in large black letters, graced the canopy that extended across the whole building.

Mike jumped out of the truck while I stared at the white building, glued to the seat. A tiny chill ran its cold, bony fingers up my back. Shivering pricks of ice cascaded down my limbs. When Mike opened the door for me, I shook off all the rational urges to run away.

Why did I feel this way? It's just a museum, nothing to freak out about.

Come on, Carrie; pull yourself together.

"Are you okay?" Mike asked again, sensing my hesitation.

"Of course," I said, and to prove it, I smiled.

The building was much larger than it looked from outside. Covered in murals of Villisca in early 1900, the walls boasted a quiet farming community. Pictures hung on the walls, along with old rakes and period clothing. In the middle of the room, an old Coke bottle machine stood beside a support beam like best friends. I thought that if I had a nickel, it might dispense me a bottle of Coke—all I needed was the straw. The truck, Mike informed me, was an incredibly rare Maxwell from 1924—whatever that meant.

Everyone in the museum began gathering around the counter just before two o'clock. The tour guide, the owner of Lot 310, waited at the far end. He was an older gentleman with short, silver hair and large glasses. He wasn't unusually tall or stout, but his presence was confident, his chin held high.

"Good afternoon. I'd like to thank you for coming today, and I encourage you to ask whatever questions come to mind. I hope you've had adequate time in the museum, as the tour will last close to two hours, and the museum will be closed by the time we return."

Before we left, he handed each person a small map of Villisca and a packet of all the sites, explaining that we should read each one as they came up in the horrific tale.

Mike and I hopped into the truck to follow the caravan of vehicles out to the Villisca Cemetery. He swiveled his head my way, and I grinned back.

"I'm fine," I assured him. "I'm actually kind of excited now. Not at all scared."

He chuckled. "Whatever you say."

We toured the cemetery and drove by the prominent places in town before ending up at Lot 310.

Mike parked alongside the street in front of the house. I shivered for about the thousandth time that day.

"Still okay?"

"Yep." I nodded, staring at the white farmhouse. "For now, anyway," I mumbled under my breath.

I rounded my eyes over at Mike, giving him a slim smile before opening the truck door and getting out. We walked to the front of the house where everyone gathered around the owner.

A new red barn stood on the property beside the house. I saw no signs of supernatural activity, but I also didn't know what to look for. The neighbors' house was close, and I wondered why anyone would live there. No matter how normal the house seemed from the outside, it was creepy. I inched closer to Mike.

The owner began telling the history of the house built in 1868. Joe Moore was the second owner and moved his family in 1903. The home passed to seven different owners until purchased by our tour guide and his wife.

I scanned the property, half-listening to the historical overview. My eyes flashed around, scrutinizing each and every detail of the house and surroundings. An odd feeling of extreme anxiety overcame me.

I shouldn't be here.

My hands began to shake. I threw them into my pockets, not wanting Mike to notice.

Even though the afternoon sun beat down on the property, shadows lurked in every corner. A chill raced down my spine, making me shudder. Laced with fear, a terror of unknown, unmistakable evil, it shook me. I hadn't noticed it across the street when I'd left Mike's truck, but now, on the actual grounds of the house, it was eminent. Forcibly, I turned my attention back to our guide.

"Now, the house has no electricity or indoor plumbing. This is exactly how the house was when the Moore family lived here."

Along with the strange sensations overtaking me, the dreams of Megan and me on the porch clouded my mind. Maybe this was a bad idea. Maybe I should heed dream Megan's warnings, turn around, and never look back.

"No, I've never seen any ghosts in or around the

house personally. But as I said before, there *is* something in there," the tour guide said.

No matter how hard I tried, I couldn't focus on what was said and only able to catch bits and pieces. My arms broke out in tiny bumps that felt like sandpaper on my skin. Each breath was a forced action. My shallow gasps for air went unnoticed by Mike. I glared at the ground, telling myself that it was just my imagination. All in my head. Ghosts don't exist.

The owner answered, "There were only a few reports of odd things happening in the house before the restoration. Unfortunately, though, since it was used mostly as a rental property, it's been impossible to track down everyone who's lived here."

"So why has so much happened since the restoration?" someone asked.

"There are many theories. One that most paranormal scientists quote is that after a renovation, the energy within the walls is released and calls for the spirits to come back. They have returned to what is familiar."

The word was said so nonchalantly, like the meaning was implicit. Megan had used the term "they" in reference to the house when we'd first met. She said, "Released them". Jessica mentioned the same thing the guide was talking about: spirits returning to a house that was renovated. "They." Ghosts? Spirits? Something more terrifying?

"I've never stayed at the house during the night. Those who have tell tales of objects moving across the floor by themselves, doors opening on their own, and voices of children that don't exist," the owner said.

Ghosts weren't real. Why was I even considering the possibility? Just because Jessica believed in them, and apparently Megan did, too, didn't make it true. All of the stuff the owner had explained could be other things. Anyone could build a haunted house and make it realistic.

I shuddered. My body tensed, and my gaze scurried in every direction.

That, however, I can't explain.

Our tour guide answered another question, which I hadn't caught. "Orbs, EVP audios, and lights have been captured on tape and film on the grounds, but only when taken on the property itself. Photos taken from across the street, for instance, have never shown anything out of the ordinary."

I stepped closer to Mike. He glanced at me, smiling. I returned the gesture, reassuring him that everything was great, even though my insides were turning to mush. I ran my fingers through my hair, trying to steady them.

"If there are no more questions, let's go in," the owner suggested, leading the group forward.

Everyone followed him onto the front porch. He took the key out of his pocket, all the while continuing to answer the endless stream of questions. Mike and I were last to enter.

"Ladies first," he said, holding out his hand.

I sighed, my psyche fighting me with every step I made. Evil was stronger here, and I assumed, even stronger inside. I stood on the porch, contemplating my next move. Mike waited patiently. I stepped one foot over the threshold and felt a cool breeze pass swiftly beside me. I froze. Slowly, I turned my head toward Mike, my eyes wide.

"Did you feel that?" I whispered.

"Actually, I did." He gave a sly grin. "Spooky, huh? Maybe it was just a hidden fan somewhere." He winked.

Mike stepped inside behind me. The door closed with a click. Our tour guide continued talking about the room we'd just entered—the parlor.

I shivered, this time not out of fear, but because despite the heat, I was actually cold. All of my previous hesitations disappeared, and I felt at ease. Cold, yet comfortable. No longer tense, and for the first time since I stepped onto the grounds, my muscles relaxed and the shaking steadied. My mind cleared, and I could easily pay attention.

The parlor walls were white and mostly bare except for a few framed photographs. White lace curtains covered two windows on the far wall, separated by an upright piano. Smaller pieces of furniture lined the perimeter of the walls: a wooden chair, a small table, and a hand-carved bench. Across from the door where Mike and I stood sat an old wood stove—the heat source for the house. The dark wood floor creaked when anyone moved.

Next, we all huddled into the blue room off the parlor. The murderer made his final blows to the Stillinger girls in this room. The one window in the room was closed, yet, again I felt the cool breeze brush by me. I gazed around the room to see if anyone else felt it. One guy rubbed his arms. Another girl visibly shuddered. The guy with spiked hair suddenly shot his head up at the ceiling and then around the rest of the room as if searching for something.

"I feel like I'm being watched," a blonde-haired woman said, nudging her husband.

Everyone felt it, something invisible in the room. I didn't feel like something was watching *me*, though. I was just cold. My edge vanished, although the rest of the group had now acquired one.

The group followed the guide into the kitchen and then upstairs to the kids' and parents' rooms. Lastly, we checked out the attic where the killer was said to be hiding until after the family went to bed.

In this small space, drops of sweat formed at my brow. I wanted more than anything to escape. All of my comfort evaporated in the heat. My heart began to pound, thudding against my ribs. Adrenaline surged through my veins, convincing my muscles to flee. No one else seemed to be bothered.

I closed my eyes and concentrated on breathing, but as my lids fell all I wanted to do was scream. All around me was red and scorching. I saw flames and blood. I heard shrieking; shouts of pain, of undeniable terror. Fire burned in large pits with atrocious blazes. Souls trapped inside the heat of orange and blue, screeching in terrible agony. Their voices echoed in my ears. Their hands scratched and clawed, trying to get out of the pit; writhing and slashing, but they couldn't escape. The smell of sulfur stung inside my nostrils.

Time stood still. I couldn't escape. My fingers curled into a fist and began to dig, deeper and deeper until blood dripped from my palms. I tried to scream, but nothing came out. Hot, boney hands clenched around my throat, squeezing and burning my flesh. As soon as a tear formed in my eye, it vaporized in the heat. I watched in horror at the trapped souls. No one could help them, not even me, frozen in place. They would cry out and claw at the pits, burning alive, but never getting the sweet relief of death.

I tried to think of Lucas, to picture him in my mind. But I couldn't. I couldn't remember his smile. How he smelled. Or the color of his eyes. His image faded, replaced with the thrashing souls fighting to free themselves. The heat rose, crawling up my arms, ready to consume me.

My eyes flew open, wide in terror. My mouth was dry and blazing with the fire I'd tasted. I let out a faint squeal and started to run. Mike caught me in his arms. He gazed down, staring into my eyes. His widened when he saw the fear in mine. My mouth quivered as I struggled to hold back the screams.

"Hey," he whispered urgently. "Are you okay? You're pale."

I stared at him, unblinking, my hands still balled into fists. I uncurled them and looked down. Both of my palms bled from where I'd sunk my nails and broke the skin.

"Come on." He took hold of my wrist and guided me out of the attic and out the front door.

In the yard, I sat on the grass to refocus and breathe. Mike slipped off both of his shirts, peeling them apart, and ripping two strips from the white one. He reached for my hands and began wrapping the material around them.

Outside, with the sun blaring down, I shivered, but the panic was gone. The memory of the vision, however, remained. So real. So close.

I stared blankly at the ground. Mike put his hand on my back. The strong images, no matter how hard I tried to suppress them, haunted me even in the broad daylight.

"I think I'm all right," I finally said.

"Are you sure?"

"Yeah, yeah, I'm fine," I answered, forcing a smile.

"What happened up there?"

"I'm not sure." I took a deep breath. "I thought I felt something, and I freaked. It was probably nothing." If Mike knew the truth, he'd think I was crazy, and that was the last thing I needed. "The house is creepy. I think it may have gotten to me. I…I'm fine now. Thanks."

Mike looked at me sideways. For a second I wasn't sure if he bought my lie.

"Really, I'm fine," I assured him.

He bit his lip and rapped his fingers on his knee, seemingly annoyed at my lack of honesty. "No. I saw it in your eyes, Carrie. You were scared stiff. Look at your hands!"

"I can be very paranoid," I said. "Like I said, I…I thought I felt something. That's all. My mind just took off with it."

Mike sighed. His shoulders dropped, and I knew I'd won.

"You sure you're okay? 'Cause you had *me* scared."

"Mike, I'm fine. Really."

"All right." He put his arm around my shoulders and squeezed me next to him.

All of a sudden, a cold breeze circled us, then gusted away. Mike jerked his arm back. I shot my head around, but there was nothing except grass.

"Wow," Mike said. "That was the third time I've felt that."

I continued scanning the area. Then I stood up and walked around, waiting for the breeze to return. Something about it made me want it to return. It didn't.

"What?" Mike asked.

"Um, nothing. Paranoia."

A few moments later we heard voices around the back of the house. We got up and rejoined our group in the backyard. No one asked where we'd gone or what happened, as if the whole thing was normal.

After a walk through the back premises, the owner led us into the new red barn. Mesmerized by the signatures and messages written across the beams inside, I stared at the walls. Visitors made their permanent condolences and best wishes to the family—a memorial.

Rest in Peace – with Love, Joshua & May Smith

My heart was touched by your story. I pray that you all find a place to rest and can spend eternity with each other as a family.
Erik & Linda McLea

The Spirit

The LORD is my Shepherd, I shall not want.
Psalm 23:1
Rest in Peace.
Elva Lewis

Through Love and Devotion, we are spared a life of loneliness and despair. To have someone to love so greatly and have someone love back so deeply is the only way to live a life of Happiness and Joy. Even in death, you can still Love in a way that brings Life. Wishing you all the best in the second life.
Ethan & Lisa Hobbs

I ran my fingers over the words. Perfect and touching. I pulled a pen out of my purse and jotted it down on the back of the Villisca map.

"The tour is over," Mike said, walking toward me.

"Just a sec." I took my pen, and under the lovely inscription, I wrote a simple message.

Thank you for sharing your life and your death.
You will never be forgotten.
Carrie Reese

Mike grinned. "May I?" He held out his hand. I gave him the pen and under my name, he added:

Farewell- May you find your comfort in death.
Mike Carson

We walked back out to the rusty truck across the street. As soon as I climbed in, all rigidity left. I felt normal again.

"What did you think?" Mike asked, cranking up the AC. "I mean, other than your outburst."

"Pretty cool," I said, though most of the time I hadn't heard much of what was being said. I enjoyed seeing the house for what it was back when. And when I wasn't freaking out, the murder stuff had been interesting—of what I'd caught, anyway. "How about you?"

"Very informative." He glanced over at me. "Do you think it's haunted?"

"Oh, I don't know. Do you believe in that stuff?"

"Totally. I had a girlfriend who stayed the night here once. She swears she saw a child crouched in the corner of one of the bedrooms. Besides, with all the stories of hauntings all around the world, I find it hard not to believe."

"Really?" I asked, intrigued. "Like where?"

"Ah. You want to hear ghost stories, huh? Think you can handle it?"

It wasn't that I wanted to hear ghost tales, but after today I knew there was something in that house—something evil and desperate to escape. Were there more evil places like this tucked away? "Yeah, I've never believed in ghosts."

"How about if I come over after dinner and tell you ghost stories all evening?"

"Why after dinner?"

"Two reasons. First, it'll be darker, which makes it scarier. And second, my parents may not remember they have a son if I don't come home once in a while."

***

Mike and I sat on the porch swing, the sun beginning to set. I placed a wooden crate in front of the swing and a bowl of chips and two glasses of lemonade on top.

"Let's start in Fall River, Massachusetts, in the early 1890s," Mike began. "It was another axe murder—Andrew and Abby Borden. On the morning of August 4th, 1892, Andrew went to town to run errands. He had visitors in his home— family—but they were away for the day. The only people at home were his wife, Abby, his daughter, Lizzie, and the housemaid, Bridget Sullivan. After only half an hour at home, Lizzie found her father on a sofa in the sitting room. Bridget, the maid, ran to Lizzie after she heard the screams. Lizzie went to the neighbors, and that's when Bridget found the body of Abby in the guest bedroom. Both of their skulls had been smashed in, Andrew with eleven blows and Abby with almost twenty."

"Oh." Instinctively, I covered my mouth.

Mike continued, "Lizzie was the only person ever arrested and tried, though she was eventually acquitted due to lack of evidence. But some evidence was kept from the courts. The house is now a bed and breakfast. People who've stayed there report a woman weeping in the night, shoes walking across the floor, a woman tucking them in at night, and the ghosts of Andrew and Abby wandering the halls."

Mike grinned, raising his eyebrows.

"That's horrifying."

"Next we have Sarah Winchester in 1881. Sarah's husband William owned Winchester Repeating Arms Company—they made guns, Winchester Rifles. The couple had one daughter, Annie, who died just weeks after birth. Sarah melted into a great depression and never had more children. William passed away in 1881, leaving her with over half of the company, allowing an extraordinary income.

"After his death, Sarah believed her family was cursed by spirits. So, she found a medium to tell her what she should do. Sarah was told she and everyone who had died by a Winchester Rifle cursed her family. The psychic also told her to move west and build a house for herself and all of the ghosts, and if construction on the house ever stopped, she'd die.

"So, Sarah moved to California and bought a farmhouse. She began remodeling and adding to it, using her massive income. For thirty-eight years, every hour of every day, she had workers remodeling and building onto the home.

"Sarah was also obsessed with the number thirteen. The number is incorporated into every room of the house. The place is insane. There are corridors that lead nowhere, windows that open to walls, and random staircases.

"She did die, eventually, at the age of eighty-three after a séance with the spirits living with her. Today, footsteps are heard everywhere in the house, and windows shatter in the night. It is said that the spirits continue to call Winchester House their home, as does Sarah herself."

Mike waited for me to respond. I bit my lips together. "So everyone who died lived with her?"

"Yeah. Or she called them to live with her. Who knows?"

Did I think it was crazy for Mike to believe this stuff, or that I was starting to believe it, too?

"Did they kill her?"

"Don't know, but in most ghost stories, ghosts never kill, they just haunt."

"How does one become a ghost?" I asked. "I mean, do you have to be murdered or commit suicide or something? Or be the murderer?"

"I think so. The death has to be a tragic event of sorts. A death that torments a person so they can't rest peacefully, making them stay trapped here."

"None of your stories have a theme of revenge, though."

"Maybe the Lizzie Borden one. Most ghost-type revenge stories are Hollywood made, like when they try to kill people who live in their home or seek out and torture the killer. These things don't really exist in real life."

"What about the Amityville one?"

"All made up." He shrugged. "It probably happens a lot. People enjoy ghost stories. They like the crawling under their skin. So they make them up and put them out there as true."

"But you believe these ones?"

Mike nodded. "Yeah."

"How do you know these are real and not made up?"

"Well, first of all, no one has died visiting these places. No one has claimed to be injured by these ghosts. Secondly, they seem like normal hauntings. Little things: ghosts wandering around, things moving. Nothing incredible happens that's way out there, you know."

"Things moving and dead people walking isn't 'incredible' enough?"

He chuckled, spreading a crooked smile across his moonlit face. "I mean, people are not being tortured in any way. I don't think ghosts are here to wreak havoc on human kind."

"Why do you think they're here?"

"I think they're lost. They don't know where to go, so they go to a place that's familiar to them. But they are still plagued by their death. They're restless."

"Hmm. I guess that makes sense," I said. "Is that all you have?"

"No, but that's all for tonight. I've got weights at six tomorrow morning, so I'm going to leave you to your nightmares."

"Oh," I grimaced, thinking about the attic. "Thanks."

Mike stood up. "I'll see you later."

"Thanks for the fun day."

He nodded. "Again, you're welcome. I like spending time with you."

I gave him a friendly jab on the shoulder. "You're a good friend."

His expression was unreadable. "Good night."

***

The AC in my room had been on high all day. It felt good, though. After today, I came to the realization that when I was cold, somehow, I was calmer. At peace. I changed into a pair of pajamas and set my alarm.

Lying in bed, my thoughts traveled back to the fact that my parents had betrayed me, and Lucas was gone. The hole in my heart continued to grow. I knew why my parents' divorce bothered me so much, but why Lucas? I barely knew him.

I missed him more and more each minute of the day. Although, I did well this week, keeping my mind occupied enough so that he wasn't a constant thought in my head; I had to work at it.

It wasn't just him, it was me. Like a part of me was missing.

I thought about what Mike had said. He believed ghosts were lost. I was lost. Were the ghosts lost before they died? Were they empty inside?

I glanced around my dark room. The pit of my stomach lurched as I pictured Lucas. It brought me some comfort as I drifted off to sleep, that maybe the two of us were lost together.

Lucas's eyes weren't focused as he paced the dock. He sighed and ran his fingers through his hair. Why did this have to hurt so badly?

"This is what I wanted. This is the choice I made…even though I didn't exactly leave. It was the best option. This is how it has to be. The way it should be. She's safer without me."

Trying to convince himself of his thoughts, Lucas lifted his eyes to the sky. He would much rather be with her tonight. Holding her, kissing her. Being without her was driving him mad. But being with her…how could he do that without exposing the truth?

His body faded to transparent for a split second before returning back to normal.

He sat down on the floating dock bouncing with the water. The reflection of the stars made the water look like glitter. He skipped a rock across the water's rippled surface.

All week he'd watched her from a distance. She was trying so hard to preoccupy herself with other things, but he knew she was hurting. Somehow, he felt her pain inside of himself. And he couldn't do that to her. What if something happened? He couldn't bear the thought of her living the life he lead now. Death would be better.

He sighed again, burying his head in his hands. His green eyes were sunk back into his skull, and heavy, dark circles shadowed around them. He was pale and limp. He gazed over the water, thinking about her: the way she smiled, her laugh, how she touched him. How could he give all that up?

Yes, he needed her. More than he should.

His mind was made up. He'd tell her everything. Let her decide what she wanted. It wouldn't be easy, and she'd probably be scared, but she needed to know the truth, and all the costs.

Chapter 10

The auction didn't begin until nine, but according to Grandma, it was 'customary to be early and scope things out.' We parked alongside Highway 59, north of a little town called Harlan. The former owners were auctioning everything: the farm machinery, vehicles, even the house. Already at eight, crowds of people sauntered around the property.

Since Grandma drove and I wasn't alone, I hoped it would be safe to sleep in the truck. I tucked a pillow under my head and leaned against the window.

"Still tired?"

"Yeah, I couldn't get comfortable last night."

I'd dreamt of Lucas the night before; I'd expected to have a peaceful night. Unfortunately, I was wrong. The vision in the Moore House attic coupled with Mike's ghost stories plagued every one of my dreams. Each one was different, but they all ended the same—me, burning in a pit of fire with blood pouring out of every orifice of my body, while Lucas watched helpless from the sidelines.

I tried to fight for control, tried to run to Lucas and away from the flames engulfing me. He was so far away; I couldn't make out his expression. I reached out for him, cried for his help. He didn't move. Then he vanished, leaving me alone to suffer and burn.

My heart raced each time I opened my eyes and bolted upright, safe in my own bed. I got up, went to the bathroom for a glass of water, and stared at my reflection in the mirror. Wet hair stuck to my neck. Peeling it off, I raked the strands into a ponytail and tossed cold water over my face.

I tried to think solely about the vision of Lucas coming back to me, but the fire kept creeping into my thoughts. With all the lights on in my room, I got dressed.

Grandma interrupted my thoughts. "How long did Mike stay?"

"Huh? Oh, not long. He said he had to get up early and lift this morning."

She nodded with a faint grin slowly appearing on her face. I assumed my grandparents enjoyed the idea of Mike and me spending time together. Neither of them knew about Lucas. If he happened to reappear into my life, I hoped Grandma wouldn't be too disappointed.

I liked Mike, definitely. But I loved Lucas. Big difference.

"Feel free to wander around," Grandma said as we crossed the road. "Let me know if you see something promising."

"Specifically?"

"Not really. Oh, but keep an eye out for kerosene lamps for Mrs. Taylor."

Grandma wandered into the garage first, and I decided to check out the house, not that I was in the market or anything. Most people were using the back door, so I followed suit. The door let into the kitchen. Black-and-white tiled flooring with wood cabinetry and white boomerang countertops "decorated" the empty space.

An open staircase with carpeted risers that matched the living room floor curved to the second floor. I followed them up. Six doors lined the rectangular room: two on the right-hand side, one in front of me, and three on the left.

I walked into the master suite and peered out of the north window. More cars now lined the street. Most were trucks, but out of the corner of my eye, I caught a glimpse of a bright red Pontiac G8. I closed my eyes and shook my head.

It can't be.

When I opened them, the car looked like a speck on the highway, getting smaller as it continued driving north. I sighed, disappointed, and shuffled out of the room.

I sulked back downstairs without searching behind the other doors. It didn't matter anyway.

Back outside, I moseyed by the countless number of tables, each filled with similar items. I browsed the one directly next to the back door. It held picture frames, photo albums, and vases. One thing caught my attention: a beautiful crystal picture frame. Glass angels danced around the outer edges in a circle of iced wings. Lucas's face would look even more exquisite inside the crystal—if that was possible. I made note of the frame in the notebook Grandma had given me.

When I finished wandering around and taking notes of items for the store, I hunted for Grandma. A small table placed outside the back door acted as the central command station. Behind it sat a mousy-faced woman with short hair and rimless glasses. Grandma stood third in line.

"Hey," I said, walking up to her.

"Ah, Carrie. Did you find anything?"

"A few things—two lanterns."

"Yes! I saw those, too. Mrs. Taylor will be pleased."

"So, what are you doing here?" I asked, motioning to the table.

"Getting a number and card for the auctioneers to keep track of the items I buy." She filled out her card and handed it back to the woman. Then she took her number, pinning it on her shirt. The auctioneer, a heavyset balding man with thick glasses, tested his microphone next to the first table.

Slowly, it began to warm up to blistering hot, and the crowd made the heat worse. The clouds had fanned out and the sky took on a blissful shade of blue, tinted in streaks of white.

The auctioneer stood by the table of picture frames and glass figurines. He held up a small box and began speaking—if that's what you call it. The words blurred together so fast I wondered how anyone understood what he said. He pointed his fingers out into the crowd and as he did, the inflection in his voice perked.

"SOLD!" he yelled. "Number 23."

The auctioneer moved quickly to the next group of items. We waited among the crowd and watched as item after item was sold to different numbers.

It wasn't long before the angel frame came up for bidding—being auctioned by itself. I nudged Grandma.

"Could you bid on that for me?" I asked. "And let me know how much you're bidding?"

"Sure," she said, and raised her hand. "Six-fifty."

"Eight."

"Ten twenty-five."

"Twelve."

"Seventeen."

I grimaced. I didn't know how high it would go.

"Eighteen."

I examined the crowd to see who else was bidding, not that it mattered. It wasn't like I was going to go over to them and ask them to stop because a picture—that I didn't even have— of my…whatever Lucas was to me—who I haven't seen or spoken to in over a week—would look perfect in it.

Yeah, that's a conversation I'd love to be a part of.

"Nineteen-fifty."

I winced. Grandma peeked at me. "You tell me when to stop, okay?"

I nodded.

Stop bidding, people!

"Twenty-two."

I bit my lower lip. Grandma remained silent.

"SOLD. Number 51."

I smiled. "I got it?"

"It's yours," she said.

"Do I go up and get it?"

"No, they'll have it for you at the front table. We can wait and pick it up with the rest of our stuff."

We waited for the next round. More household items and a few things I remembered from the barn were next on the list. Nothing that interested Grandma.

"Hey, I think I'm gonna go wander around some more, if that's okay."

"Sure, sweetie. Go right ahead." Grandma patted my shoulder.

Escaping the swarm of people, I went to the front yard and sat under a shade tree. More buyers made their way up the drive carrying purses, pushing strollers, or pointing out specific objects of interest. The house, backyard, and outbuildings teemed with people. Some took their time while others dashed around like honeybees.

My attention turned back to the street. Cars lined the road, facing in both directions. I scanned the rows and suddenly my eyes widened. This time parked, facing south, less than a thousand yards from the house, was the red Pontiac G8. I rose to my feet, focused on the conspicuous car. It couldn't be his. And yet, I found myself moving toward it.

Voices of people died out behind me with each step I took. Had I been back in Texas, I probably wouldn't have given the vehicle a second thought. But here, in the middle of nowhere, the car seemed out of place. I shook my head and sucked my lips between my teeth.

I stopped halfway there. What was I thinking? Even if I did go over and peek into the windows, it wouldn't tell me if the car belonged to Lucas. Though I was no expert in the matter, I was pretty sure a black interior, red Pontiac G8 was a fairly average car, even if it didn't belong out here. In an effort to make money, GM probably made more than one.

More than likely, someone from Omaha or Council Bluffs had driven it here. It wasn't Lucas. And besides, there was no way he'd know I was here.

I sighed.

So pathetic, Carrie.

I wanted so much to talk to him that I was willing to walk up to some stranger's car and peer through the windows. I rolled my eyes, annoyed with myself.

This is crazy!

I shook my head again and pivoted to go back under the tree. Instead I ran face-first into the person standing behind me.

"I'm s-so s-sorry," I stammered.

As I raised my head to see whom I'd attacked, my mouth went dry. Frozen in place, I stared at Lucas. He grinned, his gorgeous dimple sinking into his cheek.

"Careful, Carrie," he said.

The way he spoke my name sounded more like a string orchestra than someone simply speaking. I gaped at him in utter disbelief.

He grinned wider. "Breathe."

I sucked in some air. Lucas took my hand and led me to the south side of the farmhouse. Blindly, I followed. It was quiet there; everyone had congregated farther back in the yard. He faced me. Still unable to process my thoughts to form words, I gawked at him. I had enough trouble remembering how to exhale.

His smile was more gorgeous than my memory. His face more perfect. And his voice, I had forgotten how it made me melt. I couldn't even break a grin. Instead, I just stared, taking in every feature, memorizing it, just in case he left again. Here, now, I wanted—no, needed—him to stay.

"I missed you," he said.

A mass of emotion filled me as he said the words I'd been imagining since our walk in the field. I kicked at the grass, my muscles tensing. Admittedly, I missed him like crazy, but now I seethed with anger. Anger for lying to me, for leaving, for not saying goodbye.

I didn't know where to start. If I opened my mouth, I'd probably spit out something stupid or incoherent. I wanted so much to throw my arms around his neck and never let go. But I also wanted to scream at him for hurting me. Instead of succumbing to either, I just stood there, unblinking, looking like an idiot.

"Say something," he said, reaching out and tucking a stray lock of hair behind my ear. I flinched at his touch.

Breaking my gaze, I opted to watch my own feet. "I don't know what to say."

"Say what's on your mind. Whatever it is. I want

to hear it all. Good, bad—everything."

I thought for a few moments. "You lied to me."

"What about?"

"You said you'd see me again soon, and you left."

"We're seeing each other now, so technically, I didn't lie to you."

Whatever, just kiss me.

"Where have you been?" I demanded, the anger taking over.

"I had to go away for a while. I'm sorry. I should have told you, but it came up so fast. I didn't have time. I promise it won't happen again."

He didn't answer my question, and I *did* notice. I didn't want to start an argument in public, though. And I was still fighting the urge to press myself up against him. I didn't want to drop it completely, yet I couldn't resist the involuntary smile spreading across my face.

Lucas cradled my cheeks between his hands, forcing me to lock onto those breathtaking eyes that made my heart flutter. He leaned down and brushed his lips over mine.

"Am I forgiven?" he asked with such childish innocence, I couldn't help giving in.

"Don't do it again," I said with narrowed eyes.

"Agreed."

I threw myself at him, wrapping my arms around his neck. He staggered back a couple of steps, not expecting my sudden burst of enthusiasm. He gasped a laugh and enveloped his arms around my waist. I breathed him in. He smelled fresh, like springtime at twilight.

"I missed you, too," I said, leaning my head against his shoulder.

I held him tighter, not wanting to let go. Lucas gave an impish laugh and ran his cool hands up my back and over my bare arms until they rested around my wrists.

"I'm not going anywhere," he said, gently unclasping my arms and stepping back. "I'm staying with you...for as long as you want me."

"Stay," I whispered. "Stay with me always." I stepped closer to him and rose to my tip-toes.

He bent down and crushed his lips against mine, folding me close to his body. My knees went weak. It didn't last long enough before Lucas pulled away and kissed my forehead.

"I love you, Carrie," he said, holding my gaze.

My heart knocked into my ribs. It was the first time he'd said the words and meant for me to hear.

"I love you, too," I answered. "I've been lost without you."

"Please don't say that."

"Why not? It's true."

"It's one thing for me to be in love with you. It's completely another thing for you to be so enamored by me. Don't give me so much power. You are a perfect, whole person without me."

"No, I'm not."

Lucas gazed down at the lawn. His shoulders rose and fell.

"We need to talk," he said.

My heart stopped. Panic began to run like lava through my veins. "You said you weren't leaving again."

"Oh, Carrie," he said, drawing me into his chest. "I promised I'd stay as long as you want me. I'm not going back on my word."

I nodded, my head buried into him.

"I have to tell you something, though. Something I should have told you a long time ago. I was selfish; I still am. I can't see past wanting to be with you."

I glanced up at him. He stared off into the distance as if lost in another world. "You can tell me anything. What is it?"

All of a sudden, the dream from last night echoed in my mind.

Not possible. It was just a dream!

"Not here," he said. "Tonight."

"Tonight?"

"When do you think you'll get home?"

"I don't know. I'm not sure how long these things last," I said. "How did you know I was here?"

Lucas sighed. "I just did."

"How?" I repeated.

"Ask me again tonight."

"Fine."

Why doesn't he just answer?

"I'll be parked by your grandma's store at seven. Make it when you can."

"What if I can't be there until eight?"

"I'll wait until eight. However long it takes," he answered. "We're having a picnic. You'll probably be out late, so you'll need to tell your grandparents something."

"Should I tell them about you?"

"Wait," he said. Then he sighed and touched his hand to my cheek. "You may change your mind about me after tonight."

Lucas looked into my eyes as if he were gazing into my soul. His pupils moved back and forth—searching for something deep within me.

"Nothing you say can make me change my mind about you," I murmured.

Lucas squeezed his eyes shut and pursed his lips together. "I need to go. I'll see you this evening."

"You're leaving?"

"I have to."

"No!" I'd heard something like this before and then he'd disappeared.

As if reading my mind, he answered, "I *will* see you tonight. I promise."

He flashed me a quick reassuring smile. As I watched him leave, anxiety overpowered me. Part of me wondered if I would see him tonight, or if something else would come up, keeping him away.

Lucas climbed into his car, the one I'd seen, and drove off.

I went back to the tree and gazed over at the bidding crowd without seeing them. Instead I tried to figure out what Lucas was going to tell me, and why I had to wait for tonight. Other than the questions he avoided today, the look in his eye told me he'd tell me everything.

Megan's words repeated in my mind. *'Everyone has secrets. Some are lethal.'*

I didn't know what he was going to say, but I knew whatever it was, he'd finally be free of his demons. The pain behind his eyes would disappear.

He was finally letting go, releasing everything that tormented him.

No matter what he told me tonight, all I wanted was him. To be with Lucas forever. My dream reminded me of the danger. I wasn't afraid of death. He was giving me the choice I wanted. Death may be waiting for me after tonight, but so was Lucas.

Chapter 11

Lucas was leaning against the side of Renae's Antiques, hands in his pockets. I ran over and threw myself at him. He wrapped his arms around me and held me against him. I breathed in his white t-shirt, allowing his scent to linger in my mind. He pressed his lips against the top of my head.

"If you want to go, you're going to have to let go of me." He didn't loosen his hold.

"I don't want to let go."

"Me neither, but we have to," he said, pulling back. "You look amazing tonight."

I rolled my eyes. "Nothing compared to you. Have you seen you?"

Lucas chuckled. "Come on." He took my hand and led me to his car. Like a perfect gentleman, he opened the passenger door and kissed my hand as I slid in.

He walked around the front of the car. I couldn't take my eyes off him, afraid he'd disappear into thin air if I did.

"Where are we going?"

"A little place I found out in the country."

"Are you answering questions yet?" I asked, hoping to get that out of the way.

The smile on Lucas's face faded into a hard line. "Let's have a nice evening together first. Before I ruin it."

"You know that's not possible, right?"

"We'll see."

"Yes. We will," I said smugly. "So, can you tell me where you went this afternoon?"

"I went back home to get ready for tonight." His jaw clenched, and I figured there was more to it than that, but I didn't push.

The smile he gave me was darker than usual, saddened. I trembled both from a sudden chill and from the overwhelming sensations his fingers laced in mine sent through me.

As he shifted his attention back to the road, I peered out my window, watching the town pass into the background. I folded my free arm around myself, trying to keep from shivering.

"Are you cold?" Lucas asked, staring straight ahead.

"A little."

He let go of my hand and turned down the air, returning his hand on the steering wheel, leaving mine empty. His expression hardened. I wondered what I'd said or done to deserve this response. Wrapping both arms around my body, I stared forward, trying not to think about his indifference.

For the rest of the drive, neither of us said a word. Nerves probably held him back, but his uncanny silence almost frightened me. For the first time, I felt uneasy with him.

More than anything, I wanted him to get everything out in the open. I thought he did, too, but as I watched him drive, his eyes gazing rigidly at the road in front of him, I realized it would hurt him either way. He believed I would let him go.

Before long, Lucas pulled off the main road onto gravel. Ten minutes later, he turned and parked, facing a wooded area in the middle of nowhere. It sort of reminded me of our first date, without the pepper spray.

"We'll have to walk a little ways," he said, grabbing a blanket and picnic basket out of the back seat.

We set off into the woods. The sun still gleamed in the sky, getting ready to set in a couple short hours. Having no path to follow didn't seem to be a problem for Lucas, he knew exactly where he needed to go. Beauty surrounded us—greens and browns with spots of purple, red, and yellow flowers poking up from the earth.

We didn't have to walk far before the trees opened up in front of us. Nestled within the thick wooded area, a small semi-circle clearing with a hay field beyond it sat tucked among the trees.

Two large weeping willows stood in the center, swaying in the summer breeze. Each tree cast its own shadow over the ground, but together, they formed a large canopy of shelter from the setting sun. We sat at the base of the trees, the overlapping branches cascading between with small beams of sunlight breaking through, making stars of light dance on the ground below. Sparrows filled the evening with sweet music.

I closed my eyes, inhaling the scent of pine and wildflowers mixed with the breeze. The aroma of newly cut hay and alfalfa filled the air. I could hear the distant buzz of a tractor baling hay at the far end of the field.

Lucas, who had been watching me enjoy the scenery, stood up and spread a large rectangular blanket on the ground in front of us, placing the packed wicker picnic basket in the center. His mood had reversed, his eyes glancing up at me. He worked diligently, filling each plate with a sandwich, potato salad, and Doritos. Next, he pulled two mugs of iced tea out of the basket, set the purple one beside my plate and kept the blue one for himself.

"Hang on. I'll be right back." He sprung up and gave me a quick peck on the tip of my nose before disappearing into the trees.

He returned all too quickly, holding a bouquet of wildflowers. He grabbed a glass vase out of the basket and placed the bouquet in the center of the blanket. When he finished, he sat down in front of his plate and beckoned me to join him. Through the happy expression, he was still unable to fully conceal what I saw behind it—fear.

"This is perfect," I said, noting his fingers tapping against his knee.

"I'm glad you like it."

"You seem anxious."

"I know. And I'm sorry. I'll try to do better." Then he kissed my cheek. "Eat."

"Did you do this all yourself?" I asked playfully,

hoping to lighten the mood.

"Yep, with the help of the local grocery store," he answered. "I packed it all by myself."

I laughed. "And I'm sure that took a lot of extra effort."

Lucas snickered, flashing me those sexy greens.

I took out my camera. Now that I had the stunning angel frame, I needed the face of an angel to put inside of it.

Lucas studied me. "What are you doing?"

"Just in case," I said, snapping a couple pictures.

Lucas crawled to my side and placed his face next to mine. I held out the camera in front of us and captured the moment.

"My turn." He snatched the camera and started shooting away.

"Stop!" I exclaimed. "I don't want pictures of me!"

He threw his head back and laughed. "No, but I do." Handing me back the camera, he kissed me, soft and subtle, making me yearn for more.

He picked up his iced tea and took a swig. I did the same before sinking my teeth into my sandwich. Lucas, like last time, only picked at his food.

"Are you not hungry again?"

"Just distracted. I know I said I'd do better. I guess I don't have much of an appetite right now." He stared off into the distance.

We—well, I—finished eating, and Lucas placed two flashlights on the blanket before repacking the basket. He set the basket aside and lay on the blanket, facing me.

"Come here," he said, opening his arms for me.

I crawled to him and nestled in, my back pushed up against him. He wrapped his arms around my stomach. The coolness of his skin sparked goose bumps on mine as I ran my fingers up and down his arm. My head rested in the crook of his elbow; I kissed it. His skin was so smooth against my lips.

Lucas inhaled my hair and kissed the top of my head. He sighed, and I could sense his conflicting emotions. It was hard to ignore, but I wasn't going to hassle him. Instead, I enjoyed the comfort of his arms and watched the skies over the field. As dusk approached, I began to have second thoughts about Lucas revealing his secrets. I wanted the evening to stay as perfect as this: Lucas holding me while I relished in his tender touch. This important yet bound-to-be painful conversation could wait for another night.

Lucas laid his head against mine and slowly dropped down toward my ear. He kissed me just below my hairline as he cinched me closer. Tenderly, his lips made their way to my neck. All of my inhibitions began to fade. My heart beat wildly. I lifted my arm behind me and folded it around his neck. I took it all in, his touch and his kisses. My fingers entwined through his hair. His lips moved across my neck, and he nibbled on my ear. I let my eyelids fall and concentrated on his caresses. He slipped his hand under my tank top, sliding his fingers lightly up and down my side.

Unable to take it anymore, I turned my head to face him. His lips found mine quickly. I rolled on my back as his arm tucked under me, pressing hard against my back. Both of my arms reached for him as I pulled him closer. My lips parted under his, and he accepted the fervor of my kiss. I moaned as he tugged on my lower lip. Nothing compared to this moment. Even in my dreams, I couldn't invoke the burning path the trace of his fingers left over my skin.

Breathless, Lucas's lips left mine, and he began kissing my cheeks again. I stared up into the starry sky through the elegant fountain of silk branches, gasping for air, yet wanting him to take it all away. My nails clawed at the back of his shirt as he ran his tongue over my neck. His mouth moved lower onto my chest before making his way back to my lips. He kissed me more passionately than ever, and I melted into him. His arms tightened around me, drawing me in. Urgency flowed through me, wanting him, needing him, in ways I had only imagined.

I yanked up the back of his shirt, feeling his bare skin. He groaned. Excited to illicit this reaction from him, I drew my hands forward to caress his chest and stomach. That his whole body was the same cool temperature as his hands didn't stop me from burying my fingers into his skin. I arched my back and pressed my hips into his. In response, he crushed his mouth into mine, massaging his tongue with mine.

As quickly as the last kiss began, it ended. Lucas threw himself back.

"I'm sorry," he breathed.

"No, it's okay," I said, wishing he hadn't stopped.

"We can't do this." Lucas slipped his arms out

from under me. He sat up and ran his fingers through his hair.

"What do you mean?"

He gazed at me and curved up the corner of his mouth. "Because it's not fair."

"Why don't you let me decide what's fair for me?" I retorted.

"Fine. Decide. But after I tell you what I need to say."

"So, talk," I said, preparing myself. This was it. The moment I both looked forward to and dreaded.

He didn't move nor did he take my hand. Feeling rejected, I crossed my legs and waited.

"I never really left you," he said. "You just couldn't see me."

He glanced up at me to see my expression. I gave nothing away. His words didn't make sense, anyway.

"I never broke my promise. I told you I'd see you again, and I have. I've seen you every single day since the first day I laid eyes on you. From the moment I first saw you, you captivated me. I couldn't stay away. I knew I had to be with you. That's how I knew where you were today. I heard you talking to Megan about it at the store."

"How? Were you there hiding?" I stared at him, searching his face for something that might give me a clue.

"Um…no. Not like that. Well…not exactly." His eyes narrowed and closed. He squeezed them tighter. "This is so hard," he muttered to himself. His lids opened and he looked at me, his face pained. He reached out his hand and touched my cheek. "I love you. So much. I can't..."

"I don't...I don't understand." Thoughts ranging from "Was he married?" to "How many people has he killed?" raced through my mind.

Lucas sat, his focus fixated on the ground, biting his lower lip. The hum of the tractor in the field and the crickets chirping wafted about the air. Speaking softly, just over the noise, he said, "Being with you has been the best thing that's ever happened to me. You make me feel more," he swallowed, "*alive*...than I ever thought possible."

My eyes narrowed, and my breath caught in my throat at his familiar words from my dream.

"Alive?" My head reeled. "You're not...human?" The last word barely made any sound. Time stood still as it echoed in my ears.

His jaw clenched. "I used to be."

"Used to be?"

"Yes," Lucas whispered. "Before...before the accident." He took a deep breath and lowered his head. "Before I died."

A lump formed in my throat, making it hard to breathe. Shivers raced up and down my spine in quick, sporadic movements. I blinked several times trying to comprehend what Lucas had just said.

When I was little, I crawled up on top of the counter and took one of the knives from the butcher block. Thinking I was grown up enough to cut my own apple, I sliced into it. The first cut didn't go through the fruit all the way, so I tried again, this time harder, and sliced into my other hand. I knew what had happened. I saw the blood. But full realization of it didn't hit me until it started to hurt.

This was like that.

"You're a...a..."

This was what he wanted—no—needed to say. The secret that haunted him plagued whatever life force that kept him here, couldn't make it past my lips.

'Some secrets are lethal.'

Inhaling a deep breath, I let it out slowly. Now I understood why he'd been so worried about telling me. I *was* scared. Nothing could ever have prepared me for hearing this. Not from his mouth, anyway.

"You're a...," I swallowed again. "A ghost," I managed in a barely audible whisper.

Lucas kept his eyes on mine but withdrew his hand. "Are you afraid?"

I allowed silence to surround us. The breeze blew through my hair, sweeping it across my face. Lucas held out his hand to brush it away, but as he reached, he hesitated. He sighed and placed his hand back on his lap.

"You don't have to be," he said.

I didn't answer. The pain hadn't hit me yet.

"I can go. Or take you home if you want."

Staring at the ground, lost in my own thoughts, I shook my head. "No," I said. "No, I don't want you to go." Having him there made his words more real, easier to deal with, although, part of me *did* want him to go. His words cut like the knife through me.

He can't be dead. He can't.

"Okay."

I was still unsure of what to say, and I didn't want to come across rude, or worse, stupid. Questions flooded my mind. What I really wanted was for everything to go back to the way it was ten minutes ago, when the only thing I thought about was how his lips fit perfectly over mine.

Lucas was amazing, wonderful, and flawless. But that was before I found out he was dead. *Dead.* Now I didn't know what to think. The numbness had yet to wear off and allow the pain to overtake me.

We sat in silence for what seemed like hours. The sun had set, and the stars were twinkling in the night sky.

Lucas sat next to me, patient.

"You won't hurt me, will you?" I knew it was a dumb question, but I didn't know what else to say. I stared straight ahead of me at nothing, too nervous to look at him.

"I'd never hurt you, Carrie. Never."

"How can I see you?" I kept my eyes down, afraid to see him, yet more afraid he'd disappear again.

"Because I want you to."

A normal response would be to run away screaming for my life, and honestly, a part of me wanted to. The only thing that held me in place, aside from the fact he'd easily catch up to me, was, despite my fear, I loved him. He completed my life. I pursed my lips together.

Silence.

"I don't understand any of this," I said at length.

He nodded. "I know. I'll tell you anything, just ask."

I exhaled loudly. "Lucas," I said, the pain finally washing over me. "I'm not sure if I even *want* to know. This is all so…so strange. This shouldn't be happening! You should *not* exist!"

He didn't respond. He just sat next to me with his hands folded neatly in his lap—a blank expression on his face. I searched his eyes to no avail. I hugged my knees to my chest and buried my face into my arms, wishing they were his. Lucas placed his hand on my back.

"I'm so sorry," he said. "I never meant to hurt you, but I couldn't bear you not knowing."

"Why? Why, Lucas?" I sobbed, looking up, my face wet. "Why did you tell me? Why do I have to know?"

He was quiet for a moment. "I think deep down, you already knew. I only confirmed it for you."

"Yeah, well, ignorance is bliss," I retorted. Was I angry he told me?

"Really? You're telling me that this is something I should've kept to myself?"

"I don't know." I laid my head back into my arms. "I guess not."

"Maybe I'm being selfish for wanting to be with you so badly. I don't know why, but from the moment I first touched you at The Coffee Shop, you drew me in. I had to appear to you just to see what was there." Lucas brushed his hand across my cheek and tucked it under my chin, lifting my face to his. "I had no idea I would fall in love with you. I didn't even know it was possible. I know this doesn't make sense. Honestly, it doesn't make much sense to me, either. I don't want to lose you, but I'll understand if you never want to see me again."

He removed his hand, and I wished he hadn't. No matter what I was feeling, his touch was comforting.

It was so quiet, I couldn't even hear him breathing. As I watched him, I noticed his chest wasn't rising and falling as it should've been.

Why would it? Breathing isn't necessary for dead people.

A breeze swept through the trees carrying the faint smell of hay. I lifted my head to feel the coolness brush over my wet face. There were no words, no way to feel, no appropriate response.

Lucas stared into the woods, obviously hurting. I couldn't help but pity him. I knew all along he was tormented at the idea of telling me, and now that he had, the ending was up to me.

"Lucas," I whispered. "I think I need some time."

"Take what you need."

He stood, packed up our picnic, and folded the blanket. Then he handed me a flashlight and tucked his back into the basket.

"Don't you need to see where you're going?" I asked.

"No. I can see perfectly well in the dark."

"Oh."

Of course he can.

We started walking through the woods. After what I'd heard tonight, the darkness frightened me. What if other ghosts existed that *would* hurt me? My eyes darted in every direction, and I jumped at every little sound. Lucas noticed and put his hand on my shoulder.

"Don't worry. It's only us out here."

"Um, so when you left, you said you really didn't leave?"

Do I want these answers? Can I handle them?

"No. You just couldn't see me."

"So you were haunting me."

My comment surprised him. "Uh, I knew where you were." He sighed. I couldn't see his expression, but I felt him tense. "It's hard at the farm house because of your horse."

"Goldie?"

"Yeah. She doesn't like me there."

My breath hitched. "What? You're the reason she's been going crazy."

"Yeah. I wanted to make sure you were okay. Lately, I've stayed on the south side of the house."

I stopped and shined my flashlight into his face. "Your eyes. I saw you the night of the storm. You were watching me through the kitchen window."

"I was worried about you." He paused as he looked at me, trying to read my expression. "Are you mad?"

"I'm not sure," I answered. Was it sweet that he was worried about me? Or creepy that he was actually haunting me?

"I saw what my absence was doing to you. How hurt you were."

"Were you in my room?" I asked, sounding more upset than I actually was.

"No. Only outside your window."

"When I first came to town, I saw you at the Coffee Shop, standing in the doorway. Then you disappeared."

"I told you, you captivated me from the beginning."

We made it to the car and climbed inside.

"Mike seems like a nice guy," Lucas said, the look on his face giving him away. He was searching for information.

"He is."

"He likes you."

"I know," I said, a little too smug.

Lucas kept pushing. "Do you like him?"

"He's alive," I retorted.

"Yeah. Yeah he is," Lucas replied quietly and said nothing else.

We drove in silence, cutting through the darkness surrounding us.

I kept thinking about my dreams. Maybe it was just my subconscious trying to reveal the truth to me slowly. It knew I couldn't handle knowing about Lucas all at once.

Lucas was right, though. I did know. Deep down, I knew his secret. But knowing and believing were two different things.

In my dreams, my mind had given it all away. He vanished into thin air. He made eerie references to his being. I even saw him in his ghostly glory on the dock. Even without the dreams, I think I knew. It was in the look in his eyes, in the hollowness of his touch, in the coolness of his skin and the hunger in his kiss. I tried so hard to fight the truth. I wanted to bury it under all the excuses I'd made to myself that he was real. Hell, even Jess knew he was dead. I just didn't want to believe it.

I glanced over at him as he parked next to my

car. "I'm sorry. This is just a lot to take in."

"I know."

"Goodbye, Lucas," I said and got out of the car knowing exactly what my last words meant.

I figured he'd stay until after I left, so I got into my car quickly and backed into the street. My mind spun in circles as I drove. I was so deep into my own thoughts that I didn't notice Lucas's headlights behind me.

I pulled into the driveway at home and saw Lucas stop. Refusing to acknowledge him, knowing he could see every movement I made, I grabbed for the knob and jutted into the house before he could see my tears.

Alone in my room, I completely lost it. I fell onto the bed and buried my face into my pillows. The only release I welcomed was the intense sobs, muffled by the pillows. All of the feelings I'd been hiding for weeks about the divorce and all of the duplicity I felt from Lucas shot to the surface and began to explode. The emptiness spread a thousand-fold. I had no more energy to try and contain it. My parents had abandoned me and now Lucas, my love, my soul-mate, had handed me the ultimate betrayal.

The love of my life didn't exist. He'd never be mine. I had to accept reality—it was the only truth that made sense. Although, what was logical about any of this? I couldn't be in love with someone who wasn't real.

My tears flowed faster as I contemplated the situation. I never felt for anyone the way I felt for Lucas. He was mine—at least he used to be. Now it wasn't humanly possible. He'd been dead ever since we met. From the beginning, our relationship had been doomed. He knew it, and yet, pursued it anyway.

Lucas.

Lucas with his sweet words, his perfect features, his soft skin, his mesmerizing eyes.

How was I going to move on? He shouldn't exist, and yet, he does. In some form, he was out there. I didn't know how, or if, I could live without him knowing that he loved me.

My heart lurched, and my sobs grew louder. *Lucas.* He cared about me more than anything in the world. I saw the torment in his eyes as he told me his secret. He trusted me. He wanted me to stay. I couldn't see how we could be together, but I also didn't know how we could stay apart.

I couldn't breathe, gasping for air. I clutched my pillow tighter and curled up into a ball on my bed. My chest heaved, my heart shattered, my mind made up. I couldn't be in love with Lucas. He was dead.

The pillows were drenched with tears by the time I finally fell asleep, just as the sun began to rise.

The dream was simple.

Lucas and the hooded female sat on a log, staring out over a lake. The stars and moon reflected off the water like crystal. Neither looked at each other, and as the minutes ticked by, neither spoke. The only sound was the occasional fish nipping at the water's surface. Both knew what brought them together again, and both believed they knew the ramifications of Lucas's decision.

"You told her," the hooded figure stated, staring over the rippling water.

"I did."

"As soon as she accepts it, you must take her to Susan. Precautions must be taken."

"Will she accept it?"

There was a short silence before the unknown woman spoke, "I don't know."

Lucas nodded, his eyes pained. He'd made the necessary sacrifice; the rest was no longer up to him.

Chapter 12

Grandma knocked on my door early. The words caught in my throat, unwilling to be released. I rolled over and curled into a ball. Grandma knocked again.

"Carrie," she hollered. "Time to get up."

My head pounded, and the sound of Grandma's voice combined with knocking made it worse. I smothered the pillow over my head, hoping it would drown out the noise. There was no one I wanted to see, no one I wanted to talk to. I didn't even want to see the light of day. Nothing in the universe could take away the hurt, nor did I want it to go away. The more it hurt, the more I knew it was real.

Grandma opened the door and poked her head inside.

"Carrie?" she said. "Are you okay?"

I took a deep breath before I answered. I didn't want her to know how upset I was. My head remained under my pillow. "I'm not feeling good today," I said, trying to keep my voice steady.

"Do you have a fever?"

"I don't know. My body hurts." Not a lie, that's for sure. Inside and outside, I felt like exploding.

"Should I call a doctor?"

"No."

"I hope you're not coming down with something," Grandma said. "I'll check on you when we get home."

I heard the door click and waited for her to go downstairs before breaking down again. I wound my fingers in my hair and twisted as I shrieked into my pillow.

Lucas's words ran on replay in my mind. The numbness from the night before had faded away. By this morning, his admission crushed my soul. My heart floated in my body, broken into tiny little pieces.

I squeezed the pillow tighter against my chest. Lucas had taken my heart with him, and I didn't want it back. It belonged to him anyway. The only place it would be happy. Complete.

He was dead, and I was alive. That difference alone made our relationship impossible. We couldn't be together, no matter how we felt about each other. I had to let him go.

It hurt. It hurt so much I couldn't stand it. I had to find a way to move on, even if it meant I had to leave my heart and soul behind. Eventually the pain would numb my insides, and I'd stop feeling anything. Already I longed for that day.

I stayed in bed, crying and sleeping, telling Grandma I was sick for the rest of the week. I quickly forgot the difference between night and day. I didn't care. For me, it was always dark. Black and empty.

My favorite Coldplay song rang so many times on my cell that eventually I stuffed it in a drawer until the battery died. Besides, what would I say if I answered?

There was nowhere to go, and no one I wanted to be with. It was easy to let the pain take over. I didn't have to think or feel, I just had to hurt. That was easy.

On Friday, I got up, showered, and crawled back into bed for the rest of the morning. At noon, I decided to get dressed and go downstairs, taking my laptop with me. The tears had run dry. Zombie-like, I wandered around the living room and kitchen before grabbing a can of Pepsi for lunch. My stomach ached. I ignored it. Eating would physically fill me up, some satisfaction I didn't deserve.

I flipped on the TV and curled up on the sofa. Listening to the fuzz of the carbonation, I opened my computer and waited for it to boot up. Jessica and Stacy would be worried about me. Only that morning had I recharged my dead cell phone.

Stacy sent an email and a text each day this week, and Jessica sent two of each. They all said the same thing, just in different words.

Carrie, where are you?

Carrie, what's going on?

Carrie, are you okay?

Carrie, what happened with Lucas?

Carrie, what's happening with you?

Carrie, what did he tell you?

I needed to let them know what had happened, but I didn't want to tell them the truth. It was too much for me to handle, and it wasn't my place to tell Lucas's secret. There was a reason people like him didn't go around telling everyone they're dead.

Stacy and Jessica,
I'm sorry for taking so long. I know you've been worried. It's been a long week. Things didn't go well with Lucas Saturday night. I've decided it's not going to work out with us. We're two very different people from two very different worlds. I'm not sure what I was thinking anyway. I'll be in Texas again soon, and he'll be here. I was stupid to even consider we could be anything but friends. And now, we can't even be that.

I wish you were here. I haven't exactly been handling this well. Today is the first day I've even gotten out of bed. Pathetic, I know. I told my grandma I'm sick.

I miss him so much. I can't stop thinking about him. I assumed I'd cry for a little while (not a week), and then move on. But that's not happening. I have no energy, no motivation, no anything. It's like my

177

`life has been taken away, and the`
`worst part is, it was my choice! I`
`wanted to leave. Not him. Me. I`
`thought if I was the one ending it, it`
`wouldn't hurt as much.`

`I can't go back, though. I think`
`I'm going to go back to sleep. I get`
`to see Lucas in my dreams and I don't`
`have to feel the nothingness in my`
`heart and stomach. He's gone. And I`
`really, really, don't want to deal`
`with that.`

`I hope all is well with you two.`
`Carrie`

After finishing, I did exactly as I said I would. I yanked a blanket over my head and fell asleep on the sofa.

***

"Carrie? Carrie?"

I groaned. It took a second to remember where I was. The room looked unfamiliar and bright. Grandpa Robert stood over me holding a bowl of hot soup. Steam rolled off the surface of Grandma's famous chicken noodle.

"It's good to see you out of bed, Care Bear," he said as I sat up and rubbed my eyes. "Are you feeling better? You've gotten too thin."

I forced a laugh. "Yeah."

I didn't feel better, but if I didn't start acting normal soon, they'd either call my parents or rush me to a hospital, which Grandma had threatened the day before. Neither sounded like something I wanted to deal with on top of everything else. I put a fake smile on my face and sipped at the soup.

The broth tasted good even though I still didn't have an appetite. I sipped a few more spoonfuls and set the bowl on the end table. Grandpa sat in his recliner, feet up, flipping through *The Farmers' Almanac.*

"Mike asked if you would call him when you got up," Grandpa said. "His number's by the phone whenever you want to call."

"Thanks." The idea of talking to Mike was tempting. He'd done a great job of keeping my mind off Lucas last time. He might be a good start to moving on.

"How was your week?" I asked, trying to make conversation.

"Good. Looks like harvest will be good this year," he replied.

"Where's Grandma?"

"She took some homemade bread over to the Young's house. She'll be back later. I figure she'll visit for a while."

Already tired of trying to converse, I glanced to my open laptop. I moved it to my lap and checked to see if I had any replies. I half-grinned when I saw Stacy's name.

Oh, Carrie!
I'm so sorry. I dumped Ben. I'm a little upset about it, but not really. He wanted more than I was willing to give. The bastard tried to seduce me Saturday night in his car! It was

revolting. And now I have to see him every single day at work. He disgusts me!

Sorry. This is about you.

Lucas seemed so sweet. What did he say that made you change your mind about him? Was it really that terrible, or are you just overreacting? Don't get mad, but you do that, you know.

I understand the mileage difference, but those things can be worked out. If you like him so much, you can find a way.

I wish I were there to eat a pint of ice cream with you. I know you vowed once to never do that, but this sounds like an emergency to me! Go get some mint chip. I think it works the best to freeze the pain. Although, I can honestly say, I don't think I've ever been that upset about a guy. Go figure, right?

BTW, how's it going with Mike? A rebound may be just what you need!

Stace

I sighed. It wasn't what I wanted to hear, but then again, I didn't know *what* I wanted to hear. Ice cream sounded good, though. Never mind. The coldness against my skin would remind me of Lucas. I squeezed my eyelids together.

Why can't I forget about him?

I shut my laptop and stood up. "Where did you say Mike's number was?"

"By the phone," Grandpa replied without

looking up.

I padded to the kitchen and dialed. A few moments without the desperate feeling of loneliness wouldn't be so bad.

Please be home.

Being a Friday night, it was probably a long shot.

He answered on the second ring.

"Hi Mike. It's me, Carrie."

"Hey. How are you feeling?"

"Better," I replied. "Grandpa Rob told me you wanted me to call."

"Yeah. They said you were pretty sick."

"I got out of bed today, so that's a good sign, right?"

"Totally."

Silence.

"Are you busy tonight?" he asked suddenly.

I smiled. It was exactly what I hoped he'd say, except in the back of my mind I knew I'd rather have heard it from Lucas.

"No," I replied.

"Do you want me to bring over a movie? You're not contagious, are you?"

"I don't think so. A movie sounds great." I paused before adding, "Oh, and can you bring some mint chip ice cream? Half a gallon?"

What am I doing?

Mike laughed. "Sure thing. Give me half an hour."

True to his word, Mike walked through the door thirty minutes later, holding several movies and a half-gallon of Stacy's favorite. I dipped out two bowls and handed one to him. His hand grazed mine, and I jerked it back. The warmth of his touch felt...strange.

We sat on the love seat in the living room, slurping our ice cream and trying to pick between the movies Mike had brought.

"Comedy. Definitely," I said.

Mike scrunched up his nose. "Really? We did comedy last time. Action?" He held up a DVD and shook it hopefully.

I scrunched my nose. "An oversized green guy, a man in a glorified tin suit, and a chemically imbalanced patriot fighting an egotistical god with daddy issues doesn't really interest me."

"That was a mouthful." He tried to hide a snicker. "How can *The Avengers* not interest you? It's *like* a classic."

I rolled my eyes. Mike and his "classics".

"Fine. Drama?"

I had enough drama in my life. I shook my head, reaching into the pile. Again, our hands touched, and I swept mine back to my lap.

Mike glanced at me for a second before he picked it up. "Sci-fi?"

"Yeah, that's fine." I wasn't even sure what the movie was about.

He slipped it into the DVD player, stepped over the pile on the floor, and settled in beside me. Close. I tensed, gave him a slight grin, and scooted away. I felt his eyes on me.

Halfway through the movie, I asked Mike to pause it so I could get a refill of ice water. When I returned, I plopped down on Grandma's recliner.

Mike cocked his head to the side. "What's going on, Carrie?"

"What do you mean?"

He sighed. "You seem, uh…jumpy."

I bowed my head, not knowing what to tell him.

I want to be honest, but…

His eyes narrowed. "Why did you ask me here tonight?"

"I…I wanted," my voice trailed off, and I looked away. "I just wanted some company," I mumbled.

I felt Mike's eyes boring into me. "Company?"

I shifted in the recliner, trying not to meet his gaze. "Yeah. After being sick and…"

In the time we'd known each other, every time we'd been horseback riding, every dinner, every movie night, I'd never seen him lose his temper. But as I got the courage to glance over at him, I saw his eyes boiling. "That's bullshit, Carrie."

I dropped my head, swallowing a lump in my throat.

"Look, I thought we had something. I guess I was wrong."

My eyes met his. His lips were pulled tight, his arms crossed. Bad sign.

"I'm sorry, Mike. I…" I sighed. "You're a good friend."

Mike didn't move, nor did his expression change. "And the ice cream? Why do I have the feeling you weren't just craving a bowl of mint chip?"

I had a hard time keeping eye contact. He deserved my honesty. I didn't want to lose him as a friend.

"I met a guy at Grandma's store." My gaze dropped to my bowl as I spoke. How could I face Mike *and* tell him the truth? "We hung out, a lot. And…" I sighed again, chickening out a little. "And now it's not going to work out."

His voice calmed, and he unfolded his arms when he spoke. I relaxed a little. "I may be a guy, but that doesn't mean I'm dumb. You're pale, your eyes are sunken in, and you sound like you're trying too hard."

I shrugged.

Mike clenched his jaw.

I gave in. "Yeah…I'm completely in love with him." When the words were out, I looked up.

He shook his head and averted his gaze, staring out the closed window. I bit my lower lip. The last thing I wanted was Mike's hurt feelings stacked on top of Lucas's. I didn't deserve either of them.

Mike took a deep breath. When he turned his head to face me, his eyes were filled with anger and pain. He nodded at me, and then he stood up and walked toward me.

He paused in front of my chair, opened his mouth as if to say something, but closed it. He stared at me for a few seconds, shook his head, and walked out the door, leaving me alone.

I bowed my head and shuffled over to the television, stepping over the movies still strewn over the floor. After turning off the TV, I shoved Mike's movies in the corner of the living room. He'd probably never want to see me again. My track record was a solid oh-for-two. I felt like King Midas, just the opposite. Everything I touched turned to dust.

Not bothering to pick up our empty ice cream bowls, I ran to my room and threw myself on my bed.

Carrie,
What did he tell you?
And ARE YOU CRAZY? If he means as much to you as you say he does, WHO CARES? Whatever he is, he's not out to hurt you. And yeah, I agree. I mean, how often does someone find their soul mate? I think that's a once-in-a-lifetime thing. Whatever he told you, think about it. Is he worth giving up? Can you really live without him? What about that connection you talked about? You told me you couldn't lose him and now you're the one walking away. Just do me a favor. Think about it. Hard. Because I don't want you ruining something you feel so strongly about. Besides, it is kind of romantic. Movie romantic, even. I just want you to be happy. So, stop over-reacting and get him back.
Jess

Hey Carrie,
I talked to Jess, and as usual, she convinced me. If you found someone who makes you laugh, who completes you, someone that you care so deeply about that you would risk anything for them, what can be so huge that you're willing to throw it away? I wish I

**could find that. You're lucky and you
don't even realize it.**
　Stacy

Interesting. For once, they were on the same wavelength, but both were wrong. I envisioned them sitting in Stacy's backyard pool, drinking strawberry daiquiris and discussing my love life. They were right—if Lucas was alive. He's not, though, and I couldn't tell them *that*.

The days were hard. I got up, showered, and went to work. I barely spoke to Megan, but she acted fine with that. The distance was nice because I didn't have to talk about Lucas out loud. I could try to pretend he never existed when I worked.

I plastered a smile on my face around my grandparents and did my normal routine. Mike didn't stay for dinner on Tuesday with the lame excuse of having a dentist appointment that evening. He avoided me on Thursday. On Sunday, I didn't even dress for our usual horseback riding session. It wasn't like he would show, anyway.

Lying on the mattress in my room, I busied myself with my book, trying not to think about Lucas or Mike. Just a couple of weeks ago, I had two guys interested; now I'd hurt them both.

"Hey."

I jerked my head around, startled. Standing in the doorway to my room, Mike's hands were stuffed in the pockets of his faded blue jeans.

I sat up, knocking my book to the floor. "Hi."

The corner of Mike's lips turned up for only a second. Neither of us said anything for a few moments.

"I'm sorry about the last few days," he said.

I crossed my legs in front of me, watching him. He looked kinda cute when he apologized.

"May I?" He nodded toward me.

"Yeah. Sure." I followed him with my eyes as he walked from the doorway to sit next to me on my bed.

He scooped up my book and sat, facing me. A ticking noise rapped on the window. We both turned, but saw nothing.

"Probably just the air conditioner," I said, glaring outside. It stopped.

"Well, I just want to say that I would really like to hang out for the rest of the summer together."

I nodded, giving him a half-smile. "Yeah. I'd like that, too."

Mike grinned. "Good." He leaned over and kissed my cheek. Right then, a large gush of cold air sprung from the window unit, encircled us, and evaporated.

I stared down at my hands, a lump forming in my throat.

Mike rose from the bed and examined the air conditioner. "Does it do that often?"

I shook my head.

"Hmm, I'll let Rob know. Might be a problem with the compressor."

Mike stayed late after dinners on Tuesdays and Thursdays from then on, watching movies with me. We rode horses on Sunday afternoons. Sometimes he came over on Fridays when I didn't have to work, just to keep me company. I enjoyed his friendship.

Nights were bad, though. I was alone in my room with my thoughts. In the silence, tears were inevitable. Some nights I crawled under my blankets and succumbed to the pain. Others, I sat by my window with my hand on the glass. I couldn't feel him, but part of me knew he was out there, his hand on the other side. Imagining him outside my window brought a strange feeling of comfort and despair. I couldn't—didn't want to—let him go.

The dreams of Lucas and the nightmares of Megan both stopped. Now, only the flames of Hell from the attic corrupted my sleep. I'd wake up, drenched in sweat, and clinging to my duvet. Most mornings, I had to stifle the screams by burying my face in a pillow.

The Fourth of July came and went. I spent the day with Mike since the store was closed. We went to Red Oak, watched some bands on the square and hung out at the small carnival. Mike played the basketball game and won me a brown, stuffed bear with a large red bow. We rode some rides and ate funnel cake and cotton candy. When the sun went down, we watched the fireworks at the park. Mike reached for my hand a few times, and I let him.

Even with Mike by my side, I could feel Lucas near. It was the cold breeze that swept by or lingered in the air. Each time I felt it, the pain inside distended. His face imbedded itself in my mind.

Still, I couldn't bring myself to take Stacy and Jessica's advice. It didn't matter how I felt about him or he about me. Life separated us; death couldn't be undone.

Each day my heart ripped apart more than the

day before. Jessica was right; I was doing this to myself. I imagined his arms around me, his lips pressed against mine, his eyes piercing me. But it wasn't real. Because *he* wasn't real.

I developed the pictures of him I took the night of the picnic. A part of me was surprised that he showed up in the pictures at all. He did, and he was beautiful. On the back of my favorite one, I wrote the lines I read on the barn at the Moore house. Then I put it in the frame I bought at the auction. His face made the angel frame seem so ordinary. It sat on the table beside my bed during the day, and I held it in my arms at night. I longed for things to be different, wished for another ending—one where we could be together and ride happily into the sunset. It was impossible, I know. We met at the wrong time.

A few nights, I didn't know if I could handle it anymore. I whispered his name in the dark and wondered if he'd given up on me.

A month passed. All of my laughter, all smiles, were fake. I knew I wasn't getting over him. And yet, even with the pain killing me, I couldn't convince myself to return to him.

The first week of August came with intense heat and intolerable humidity, making the thick Iowa summer unbreathable. Lucky for the farmers, it had been a great summer for crops. The corn was full and tall, the soybeans deep green and leafy. Grandpa stayed busy tending to the cows and baling hay, and Mike began football practice for his senior year.

That night I went to bed and cried myself to sleep, as usual, holding the angel frame with

Lucas's picture against my chest. I woke in the middle of the night freezing cold, my arms still wrapped around the frame, but a sense of comforting arms wrapped around me. I stared at the clock, breathing steadily. I closed my eyes and sobbed.

He was there. I could feel him all over my body. Consoling me and crying with me.

"Lucas," I whispered.

I couldn't take it any longer. I needed him. I needed his smile, his comfort. I *had* to give in. I *had* to see him again. Feel him again. As I said his name out loud, the emptiness began to slowly fade away.

"I'm right here," he murmured in my ear.

I cried harder, and suddenly his solid arms pulled me close, hard to his chest as his body appeared next to me. My hands instinctively found his.

He kissed my wet cheek and buried his face in my hair. He inhaled deeply, breathing me in. I faced him. Even in the dark, I could see his eyes.

I could see him and touch him. That made him real. And that was enough.

"I'm so sorry," I said.

"Don't." He kissed me, his lips cool and soft.

"Lucas," I started. He put his index finger to my lips, making me forget what I was going to say. He brushed the back of his hand across my face and ran his fingers through my hair, just as I had imagined so many times before.

"There's nothing to forgive."

"Don't leave me," I said, touching his face. Through the coolness of his skin, I felt his warmth. His realness.

"I'm here. Forever."

I smiled a real smile for the first time in over a month. I nestled my head on his shoulder. The tears stopped as Lucas held me all night. The fear was gone, the pain fading. My life with Lucas had begun. He was with me. *Forever*, he said. It wasn't long enough.

Chapter 13

Golden sunbeams poured through the curtains, casing a soft glow over my bed. I smiled to myself, relishing in the cool draft settled beside me.

Lucas kissed my forehead. "Good morning, sleepyhead."

As I gazed into his eyes, I saw Lucas for who he was, not *what* he was. Beyond his perfect features and pale skin, I saw his life force. Whatever piece trapped him here didn't seem missing. Next to me, his complete being shined through the truth. He was real *because* he existed.

I rolled into him, caressing his arm with my fingertips. "How long have you been awake?"

"A while."

I studied him, arching an eyebrow. "Why did you appear to me last night?"

He curved the corner of his mouth, showing off his dimple. "I couldn't stand by while you destroyed yourself. It was too hard seeing you suffer."

"Why didn't you come sooner?"

"Would you have let me?"

I pondered his question for a moment and shook my head. "Probably not."

"So I waited."

"But you knew I'd come around." I traced my index finger over his full lips, over his cheek, and down his chin.

"I hoped."

"How did you know it was time?"

He grinned playfully. "I have my ways."

My eyes widened. "Tell me!"

Lucas laughed. "Well, I had this … dream. More like a vision really."

I eyed him skeptically. "Yeah?"

"It was so vivid that I knew it was actually happening. It was night before last, you were asleep, and I slept by the window."

"How often have you been in my room?" I interrupted him.

"Not as much as you think. Last night was only the third time."

I shook my head. "No, I've seen you more than that."

"Only in your mind. Anyway, I saw you open your eyes and bolt upright. You said nothing, but I heard your thoughts. You wondered what life would be like if you never saw me again. You couldn't bear it and broke down. Then you thought that you'd do anything to take it all back. When I woke up, I sat next to you. It was then that I knew what I had to do."

I leaned back against him. Did Lucas believe his dream actually happened? He did call it a 'vision.'

I considered my first dream, discarding the ones of Megan, which had a completely different feel to them. Lucas came into the store that Wednesday. I didn't know his name then, but I dreamt about him that night. I hadn't recognized him because I didn't know him. The dark figure didn't want him seeing me. Did she know what was going to happen? That he'd fall in love with me? Was that the danger?

The second dream happened after he told me he loved me. Lucas was distraught about the decision to leave me. To him, it was the safest choice. He didn't want to go, but he didn't mean to fall in love with me. It tormented him because loving me meant danger and death.

Dream three. Lucas was sitting on a dock looking less than glorious. He wanted to be with me, to tell me the truth. When did that dream happen?

I stifled a gasp. I saw him. Really saw him, doing what he was actually doing the night before the auction.

I perked up as it dawned on me. My dreams, Lucas's dream—they weren't dreams at all. They were real. Visions of each other when there was something at stake. But, what did it mean?

"Carrie?" My eyes shifted from the ceiling to Lucas. "You okay?"

I let out a deep breath. "Yeah. Uh, why didn't I see you that day, then?"

"I wasn't sure how you'd react. Plus, there was something I needed to do first."

"What?"

Lucas sighed. "Someone I had to talk to."

"Who?"

"Why don't I let you get ready? We'll go to the lake today. You can ask me all the questions you want."

I glared at him. "Hmm. And you'll *answer* my questions?"

Lucas chuckled, "Yes." He got up and faced me. "I'll come in an hour to pick you up. Is that enough time?"

"Where are you going?" I just got him back, I didn't want him leaving again so soon.

"I have to get my car. You can't exactly travel the same way I do." He covered his lips over mine. "One hour."

Then he walked out my bedroom door.

As soon as the door closed behind him, my smile disappeared. I ran to the door, throwing it open. Lucas was gone. I paused at the doorway before making a mad dash for the stairs. Nothing, no sign of him.

I slumped against the wall.

I must be crazy.

Before I allowed myself to believe I'd completely lost my mind, I got ready. Exactly one hour later, the doorbell rang. I almost yelled to Grandma and Grandpa that I'd get it, then I remembered it was Saturday. Grandpa had gone out to the fields before sunrise, and Grandma had driven to Mills County for an auction.

I rushed out the door, nearly tripping over my feet. A quick toe-to-head scan of Lucas, and I hoped I didn't have drool dripping from my mouth.

Damn, he looks good in swimming trunks.

I wrapped my arms around his neck. "That took way too long."

His laugh vibrated against my chest.

He opened the car door for me, and I slid in. In the back seat lay a green mesh bag with two beach towels and a red cooler. Lucas pulled out on the gravel and started driving toward town.

"Where are we headed?" I asked, excited to be spending the whole day with him.

"Corning. Icaria Lake is just north of there. I already reserved a boat. It'll be waiting for us at the dock."

"Can I start my questions now?"

"Haven't you anyway?" Lucas cocked an eyebrow.

"What's in the cooler?"

"That's a really intense question, Carrie. I'm not sure if I can keep up!"

"Ha, ha," I said. "I'm working up to them."

How did it happen?

No, no. I couldn't go there yet. Did I even want to know?

"Soda, bread, lunchmeat, ice, chips, and carrots."

"Why bring so much when you barely eat?"

"I brought less. Most of it's for you."

"Since you're...you know," I inhaled, not wanting to say it.

"Dead," Lucas finished.

"You say it so nonchalantly," I muttered.

"No use covering up the obvious. Secret is out. Might as well deal with it."

I sighed. I definitely wasn't ready for *that* yet. "Why do you eat at all? I mean, do you really need it? Can you even digest it?"

"Why do you eat food?"

I rolled my eyes. I hated that he answered my question with another question. Lucas just smiled at me, awaiting an answer.

"Because I'm alive."

"You eat for energy. To maintain this body, I need to give it energy. I just require less than you."

"What do you feel when I touch you?" I asked, my eyes searching him.

He sighed, taking his time answering. "I feel everything inside. Like when someone loses a sense, the others are heightened. I can feel you, I can smell your hair, taste your lips, and they are all very strong sensations…inside of me."

"So you don't…" I swallowed, tracing my fingertips over his arm. "You can't feel that."

"No." Lucas cleared his throat. "Your senses are things your body does. This isn't my body, Care. *My* body is buried in the ground somewhere."

I cringed.

Don't remind me.

"So what am I touching?"

"An illusion. I can't explain it, but it isn't…real, like yours."

I averted my gaze. I didn't know what to make of his answer. So what if he couldn't feel the same way I did? He felt *something*. He felt love for me. He felt turmoil. Emotions. I pondered this as Lucas drove. I stole a few glances his way and, more than once, he grinned back.

"Has this ever happened before? Someone like you falling in love with…someone like me?" I wondered.

He shrugged. "There's so much I don't know, that I don't understand. Most spirits stay away from the human world. It's not important for them to use the power to maintain a body and dwell among the living. We left this world, and the majority doesn't want to go back."

Out my window, the sun reflected off a beautiful lake surrounded by trees. The water glistened, inviting us to join. Brightly painted boats made the lake a colorful sea of recreation. Swimmers cluttered the sandy beaches. Children ran and skipped on the hot sand. Men and boys sat perched with fishing poles on rocks by the shallows.

Lucas made a right turn and followed the winding road to the dock. Campers and boaters unhooked their gear from behind their trucks, ready to take advantage of the summer. Lucas's bright red car didn't stand out among the throng of convertibles. He winked at me before slipping out of the car.

"This way," he said, leading me down the parking lot to a blue and silver motorboat.

"Don't we have to pick up a key or something?"

Lucas dug in his pocket and lifted out a black and silver key on a circular chain. "Done."

I opened my mouth to say something but closed it just as quickly. Lucas had already hopped into the boat and stood on the edge with his hand held out. I shook off my initial thoughts and reached for his hand. He yanked me up and kissed my forehead.

Lucas started the engine and backed the boat out of the shallows.

I raised my face to the sky, drinking in the fresh breeze and sunlight as he sped up. The lake air smelled clean and summery, and I wondered why Snuggle hadn't boxed the scent yet.

I watched Lucas at the wheel, his black sunglasses on, his white t-shirt flapping in the wind. So alive. He seemed so free out in the open. Out here with him, our differences didn't seem so large.

He sped around the lake going nowhere in particular. After a few spins, we came to a stop. We were far enough away from the other boats and anglers, but still in the sun. Lucas grabbed the towels out of the bag, spreading them across the floor. Then he lifted his shirt off, tossing it away.

Oh, good Lord. Wow.

I'd never seen him in so little clothing. His skin was light, somewhat pale, and stunning. Perfect. His body revealed no scars, no moles, and no imperfections of any kind. No signs of death.

He dropped down on one of the towels, his head propped up by one hand. I sat there with my mouth open, admiring the view, not caring if he noticed me staring.

"Carrie," Lucas said, getting my attention.

I blinked, returning to reality. "Yeah?"

"Are you going to continue questioning or would you like me to hula?"

I grinned, suppressing a giggle. "Would you?"

"You wish."

I slipped out of my clothes to my bathing suit underneath. It was a black tankini lined with pink gemstones that Stacy had given me. Unlike Lucas, my body *did* show imperfections. And next to him,

I felt self-conscious. My chicken pox scars, which never bothered me before, suddenly became massive craters covering my flesh. The mole on my back that I'd had removed when I was thirteen left a very noticeable scar. I lay down quickly on my side facing Lucas, my arm draped around my stomach, hoping to hide the flaws.

"How did it happen?" I forced the words out, still unsure if I wanted to know the answer.

"How did I die?" he corrected. "You're going to have to get used to it sometime."

"I know, but…"

"I don't know much. In fact, I can only assume most of it. When I died, I floated out of my body. I didn't know what had happened. It was raining, and I was gaping back on a car that had collided with a tree. I stood in the street and saw my body hunched over the steering wheel, blood covering my face.

"When you die, you don't remember your human life. I tried to remember something, anything, but I couldn't."

My eyes fixed on him. "What did you do?"

Lucas glanced at his hand, which glided over my arm. I shuddered by the coolness of his touch.

"I stood there. Numb. Then, I noticed someone standing next to me. He saw me, or I thought he did. If he couldn't, he at least knew I was there. He called me Lucas. I don't remember everything he said, except that I was dead. I refused to hear more, so I ran."

"Ran?"

I watched his sullen face, his eyes still focused on his own hand. He blinked several times and turned up the corner of his mouth. To me, it looked as if he was reliving the moment.

"Yeah. I just went and kept going. I don't know how much time went by. I didn't want to believe him. I fought myself every second. But I couldn't go back, because I didn't know where I came from."

The green of his irises shone through his lashes.

"I can see other ghosts clearly, no matter what form they're in. One found me. I was in Colorado, in the Rocky Mountains, watching the sunrise and set over and over again like a television rerun. Even though I knew where I was physically, inside I was lost. He sat down and told me I needed help. That things were going to be difficult for a while, and I would eventually get used it—maybe learn to accept it." He stared out to the water before coming back to me.

"Somehow, I ended up in California on a beach studying the waves as they washed over the sand. One day, I saw a person with a silver aura walking toward me. Becca sat next to me on the sand and said nothing for the longest time. She didn't look like the other ghost; she looked human. Real.

"She said, 'I know you're there.' I looked over at her, and she reached out her hand to touch me. I was tired of running. I needed answers."

I ran my fingers over his cheek. He smiled, but his gaze was distant as he relived the scene before his eyes.

"I followed Becca to her little cottage on the beach. She was a sweet woman with silver hair and deep-set blue eyes. She explained that she'd been killed in an accidental shooting almost a hundred years earlier. I was confused, because she looked so *alive*. It took practice, but eventually, she taught me to conjure a body, and I blended in among the living. But still, I longed for what was missing. Something Becca didn't feel, so she couldn't explain. She said there was someone here who could help. So, she gave me some money, and I left. That was almost six months ago."

I sat up, pulling my knees to my chest. "So, you don't remember anything about life?"

"Nothing."

"Your parents? Your age?"

"I have no memory of any of it."

"Have you ever tried to find out?"

He nodded, glancing out at the glittering lake. "That's part of the reason that brought me here, before I found you."

"Me? I'm the reason…"

What have I done?

Lucas cupped my face in his cool hands. "No. You are the reason I'm so happy. You've given me a new reason to exist. And I love this reason so much more."

"But, why me?" My voice shook.

He combed through my hair with his fingers. "I don't know. At first, there was something familiar about you. Something I couldn't wrap my mind around. Still can't. Somehow, you drew me in. I can't explain it, but you make me whole."

"Do you still feel like something's missing?"

He thought for a few moments before nodding. "I do, but it's different. Secondary to my feelings for you." Lucas laughed. "Feelings. It's not a strong enough word for how I…" he chuckled, "feel."

I glided my hand over his bare chest, enjoying his skin, like silk. He caught my hand and held it to where his heart would beat if he had one. "You've replaced my heart with something so much better. *You* make me alive."

I bowed my head and closed my eyes. His words made more sense to me than he knew. Lucas had given me a new definition of what it was to live and to love. Loving meant more than I ever realized it could. For the first time in my life, love actually meant *something*.

"Mike said something once. About ghosts," I said. "He believes you're here because you're lost. That, maybe, you're haunted by your own death, so you can't rest peacefully."

After a moment of silence, Lucas said, "I don't know why I'm still here. In this world, I mean. I don't remember dying, so I can't really be haunted by it."

"You're not out seeking revenge or something?"

Lucas laughed. "Not at all. Didn't I tell you to forget anything you know about ghosts? Movies have it dead wrong!"

I stuck out my tongue at his stupid pun.

He sighed. "I know I don't belong in this world anymore, but I don't know how to leave it. And now that I found you, I don't want to."

"How did you become a ghost? Why didn't you just move on?"

"I've asked myself that a thousand times."

"Mike thinks you had to have had a tragic death

to stay behind on earth. And my superstitious best friend, Jessica, thinks you're out to kill me. Oh, but not anymore," I added, partially as a statement, yet hoping he'd answer my underlying questions.

"Wait," he said. "You told Jessica about me? About what I am?"

I frowned. "Oh, no. Well, I told Jess I was seeing you and that you were...different. She's the one that jumped to conclusions. I haven't told her anything. She thinks you're either an angelic being...or a murderous monster."

Lucas chewed on his lower lip.

"Did I do something wrong?"

He sighed. "No. But, for our safety, I have to be a normal human being, okay?"

"Our safety?"

He nodded. "Yes. There are some in my world that don't look kindly on our involvement with the living, or those not of our world."

"Like other ghosts?"

"Ghosts are not the only *things* in my world," he said. "Demons."

I gulped. "Demons?"

Lucas nodded. "Hauntings. All of the weird stuff you hear about. Everything you believe ghosts do, are done by them."

"Them?"

"Yes. Demons haunt houses. I have one enemy, and they hate humans. They hate all things living and good."

My visions became crystal clear. *They. Them. Demons.* I shivered and stared out onto the busy lake. *Telling me was dangerous and not only for me. I could die. Something worse than death could happen to Lucas.* My heart pounded, and my breath turned shallow. Everything I believed about the world I lived in crashed down around me.

Suddenly, in the warm sun, chills shot through me. While lost in my thoughts, Lucas had wrapped his arms around me and held me close. Though comforted, fear bubbled inside me. What were demons capable of? Where were they? Did they have bodies like Lucas?

He cradled my face between his hands, forcing me to look at him. "I'll do everything in my power to protect you. They don't have to know."

"What can they do to you?" I asked, my voice trembling.

Lucas remained quiet, breathing slowly.

"Lucas?" I asked again.

"They can drag me to Hell...for eternity."

"No." On its own, my hand flew to my mouth.

Lucas smiled then said, "It's not going to happen. Okay? Don't worry about it. Promise?"

I couldn't focus on him. I was too scared for his survival. *Hell.* The word left a hole in my chest. I'd seen Hell. The vision exploded in my mind, taking me back to the attic. My hands trembled, remembering the heat, the fire, and the screaming souls.

"Carrie, promise me?" Lucas said again, this time more urgent.

I nodded, though I didn't know if it was a promise I would be able to keep. The dream of me trapped in Hell, trying to fight my way to Lucas flashed before me. If the demons took him, I'd be the one forced to walk away, unable to do anything.

"It's going to be okay," Lucas said, lacing his fingers through my hair, bringing my attention back to him—sort of.

I nodded again. All I could think about was the new danger. If they took him, would I be able to help? Can the living go to Hell?

"What can they do to me?"

He hesitated. "Anything they want. Mostly, they just feed off the malevolence, greed, anger, and lust of the living, though. Sometimes they'll kill humans or hurt them for fun. They usually make it look like an accident, because they don't want to reveal themselves." He touched my face. "I will never let them hurt you."

"Why would they target me, specifically?" My voice quivered as I returned the intensity of his gaze.

Lucas blinked. His hand dropped from my face. "Because of me."

The sounds of engines and laughter died out, leaving a canopy of silence surrounding us. Sadness burned deep into Lucas's irises.

"I don't understand."

"They will always hunt me. If they were to ever see you with me, they would come after you—for helping me. They thrive on the suffering of others."

"Why do they hate you?"

"They don't exactly hate us," he said, clenching his jaw. "Because we are neither living nor dead, neither a part of earth, Heaven, or Hell—it makes us…We're recruitable."

His fate would be different than mine. I could

die, but Lucas? Lucas would be turned into a monster, thriving in Hell, torturing the trapped souls. Closing my eyes, I took in a deep breath and let it out slowly.

I toyed with the top of my bathing suit, picking at the small rhinestones. "Have they ever tried to recruit you?"

"Yeah, once. I got away, but my friend didn't." Lucas's eyes fell as he said it. "The ghost from the mountain. We're not easy to catch. Night fell, and he and I were talking. We didn't notice the pair of demons creep up behind us. They took him. I disappeared before they had the chance to grab me. Since then, I've done a good job of avoiding them."

I leaned closer to him, kissing him. He didn't return the kiss.

"Hey," I said. "It's not your fault, you know." His gaze swept over the lake. "Yeah. I know."

I didn't believe him.

"Do you swim?" I asked playfully, ready for a less intense time with him.

"Of course," he said, turning to me.

Standing up, I gave him a flirtatious grin and dove into the water. At the surface, Lucas stood on the boat's edge, ready to cannon ball after me. I squealed in delight as he landed next to me, a fountain of water falling on my head. He grabbed a ball from the inside of the boat and tossed it. We stared at each other, childish grins on both of our faces. Knowing exactly what he was thinking, I took off after the ball.

He was a good swimmer. His strokes were graceful and fast. I probably looked like a goldfish without fins in comparison. When I finally caught up, I dunked him under the water. We played together, taking turns throwing the ball and racing after it, until I started to get hungry.

Lucas ducked underwater and then appeared, completely dry, on the deck of the boat. Apparently, my shocked expression humored him as he threw his head back and laughed. He lowered the ladder into the water and helped me up.

"How did you do that?" I asked.

He wrapped a towel around my shoulders and squeezed me against his dry body. "Who do you think you're asking? Your laws of physics don't apply to me."

"So, what did you do?" I asked as Lucas opened the cooler and started digging out some food.

"I can teleport, I guess. That's the best way to describe it. I just have to think of where I want to be, concentrate, and go."

"Anywhere?" I asked, intrigued.

"If I was very good at it," Lucas said, studying my expression. "I'm not. It takes a lot of practice, and I rarely do it. When I do, it's only for small distances."

"Can you take someone with you?"

"I don't know, and I'm not trying with you," he added.

I frowned. "Why not?"

"Did you not hear me say I suck at it? I have no idea what it would do to you. You may end up missing limbs."

"Fine," I pouted.

He reached for the cooler and started to make me

lunch. I took the sandwich from him and grabbed a Pepsi. We sat back down on our towels.

"So," I began again, with my mouth full. "Why do you breathe? You don't need the oxygen."

"I am breath. At least, that's a good way to describe me. Basically, I do it because living people do it. People may start catching on if I never took a breath." Lucas cocked his head to the side. "Imagine what it would be like if the living knew the truth about us?"

"Some people know."

"Do they?" Lucas asked, eyebrows raised high.

"Yeah, I mean you hear ghost stories all the time."

"Ghosts don't haunt, remember?" he said.

I blinked, confused. Then it dawned on me. "Oh. Demons. How did they get here?"

Lucas shrugged. "They've always been here. Guardians balance them out. Thankfully for you, there are more angels than demons."

"Guardian angels, too, huh?"

"Yeah. They have bright golden auras and are the most magnificent creatures you've ever seen. Guardians only protect the living; they don't dwell on the dead."

"Have you ever seen one?"

Lucas grinned, a coy glint in his eye. "They're everywhere."

He moved so that we were cheek-to-cheek and pointed to a sailboat close to us. "There's one leaning against the mast." Then he pointed to a nearby beach. "There's two on the beach, another on the dock, and one perched up on that buoy."

I beamed at him. "Can they have bodies? Like you?"

"They can. As can demons." He continued to run his fingers through my hair. "But I can see them, either way. Invisible to you or not. Demons have red auras—blood red. I can see for miles. I won't let them near you."

"They hate humanity, yet they mimic us?" Fear gripped me at this new revelation.

He nodded. "They exist to wreak turmoil and pain on the living. They're cunning and evil. Demons are fallen souls who know nothing but hatred."

"Are there any here?" I asked, twisting my head around, watching every speck of a person I could see.

"No. They hate light; they live only in darkness."

"How about at home? In Villisca."

Silence again. Deep silence.

"We have to be very careful," Lucas said.

"They're there, aren't they? At the Moore House? Haunting it?"

He nodded again. "Yes, but I've never seen them in town. For some reason, they seem to only stay inside the house."

"I went there," I said so quietly I hoped he hadn't heard me.

"I know," he said just as silently. "I was with you."

His reassuring words made my heart flutter. It made sense. His presence had always soothed me. I'd shivered from the cold the whole time. Lucas stood by my side the whole horrific tour, easing my mind the way only he could.

"I couldn't let you go alone, unprotected, even during the day," he said, playing with a loose strand of my hair. "I hoped you'd decide not to go. What happened in the attic, well..."

"What *did* happen in the attic?" I asked.

"You sensed them, I think because of me. I'm not really sure. I held onto you as tight as I could."

I wanted to tell Lucas what I saw. I wanted to tell him about the screaming and the blood; the nightmares that still haunt me. I could still taste the sulfur. But I didn't want to relive it. Not again.

My mind raced. Demons could do anything. That made them extremely dangerous. And if demons were Lucas's only enemy, did demons fear anything? Did they have enemies?

Thick silence engulfed us. Lucas glanced thoughtfully over the water and then up to the blue sky. I ran my fingers through my hair, wishing I had brought a brush, and stared out into the distance. The lake teemed with real people. For now, I knew, Lucas and I were safe as the sun blared down on us. But when the sun set, and the moon rose bright in the sky, the demons would emerge and begin their hunt.

"We've been out here for a long time. We'd better start heading back," Lucas suggested, breaking my thoughts.

"Do we have to?" I asked. "Can't we stay? I love this, being out here, with you. It's like we're in our own little world."

Lucas grinned, put his arm around me, and kissed my cheek. "I love you," he whispered in my ear. "But we have a meeting. At daybreak."

Taken aback, I stared at him. "A meeting? What do you mean?"

"I chose Villisca for a reason. *She* is here. I found you first and I didn't think I needed her anymore. Now that I've told you, she'll be able to answer all the questions I can't ... for both of us."

The last vision came to mind. *Lucas must take me to Susan.*

"Susan," I whispered.

Lucas stared at me. "How did you know?"

"You know you said you had a vision about me? One that actually happened?"

"Yeah…"

"Well, I've had four about you," I admitted.

He raised his eyebrows. "Really? When?"

"The first was just after you came into the store the first time. You met with someone in an alley."

"Did you see who it was?"

"No. The vision was hazy."

"And the next?"

"She told you to stay away from me—for my own good," I said. "The next one, you decided to tell me what you are. And the last, you met with her and wanted to know if I'd ever come around. She said if I did, you should take me to see Susan. Who's Susan?"

"Susan," Lucas started, "is a necromancer."

"Someone who sees ghosts?"

"We can only be seen if we want to be."

"Is she part of your world? Is she…"

"No, she's completely human," he said. "She's a link between our worlds. Connecting them."

"Why do we have to see her?"

"Let's get back to shore," he suggested.

"You promised to answer…"

As the boat gained speed, I realized he couldn't hear me over the roar of the wind. Then again, maybe he could. I folded my arms across my chest and watched the wake behind us.

Lucas steered the boat into the middle of the lake. We circled once more before returning to the dock. I packed up the towels and cooler as Lucas pulled the boat to shore. He jumped to the ground before holding out his arms to me, catching me effortlessly.

"You're much stronger than you look," I teased.

"I'm just talented."

Lucas slipped the key to the boat into a small wooden box at the edge of the parking lot. We put our things in the back of the car and climbed in.

"Tell me about Susan. Why do we have to see her?" I repeated as soon as he turned onto the highway.

"There are very few necromancers in the world. Susan's one of two in the whole Midwest. They create balance in this world between us and you. They live in places with a lot of demonic activity. Towns with places like the Moore house. Spirits, like me, often seek them for answers. Because there are so few of them, they're visited often by the dead. They know a lot about my world."

"Why do you need to take me?"

"Because you're a part of me now. And to make sure you stay safe. She can tell you more about the danger, and I hope, how to keep you from it." His voice lowered to a deep murmur.

"Who's the girl you met with in the ally?" I asked. She was still a mystery to me, and I *was* dreaming about her.

"She'd rather you not know."

"Is she like you?"

"No. She's like you—sort of."

"But she knows about you?"

"Yes. She's a part of my world. Another link, of sorts." Lucas sighed. "She's a witch. A leader of the supernatural world."

Now I wished I hadn't asked. A whole new world had opened up before my eyes. A world that, until recently, I didn't believe in. I was surrounded by ghosts, demons, witches, and necromancers. Jessica's words kept coming back to me, *'They're out there, Carrie. I know it. I feel it.'*

"Witches and warlocks are born the way they are. They have all types of power at their disposal, and they only use it to protect the living. Like me, they see the auras of supernatural beings. That night, when she wanted to meet me in the alley, was the first time I ever spoke with her. She just wants what's best, and what's best is to keep you safe. She and I agree on that much."

"Are there a lot them?"

"A fair amount. They live among you, unnoticed. They can blend easily because they are like you in every way, except with powers."

"Did you talk to her when you left my house this morning?"

He nodded. "I did."

"Why?"

"To let her know we'd be meeting with Susan tonight."

I was silent. It wasn't that I was out of questions, but I had so much to think about that my head had begun to pound. Lucas took my hand and squeezed. I didn't look at him, lost in thought. The fields and forests flew by the windows. The sun would be setting soon, but for now, it shone bright and beautiful.

Lucas had answered all of my probing questions about his existence without as much as a grimace. I knew he cared for me, but what I didn't know was how long I could have him. It was easy to remember how difficult my life had been without him—a life I didn't want again. He wasn't part of my world, though. His existence was tied to something else, maybe the one thing he so desperately felt compelled to find. And then what? He was lingering on earth for a reason. What would happen when he found that reason? I didn't want him to leave, but I couldn't shake the idea that it was inevitable; he didn't belong here.

I continued to watch trees pass by as Lucas drove. Tears began to fill my eyes that I didn't want Lucas to see. He may have answered all of my questions, but I didn't want to answer his if he saw me crying.

Before long, we entered the Villisca city limits. I had a lifetime worth of new awakening, yet the city hadn't changed. People were out taking walks, holding hands, pushing strollers, and walking dogs. They were the people forever unaware of another world surviving around them, oblivious to the immense amount of power residing in their quiet little town. Everything *looked* the same, but it was different. The people were different.

Lucas squeezed my hand again. I'd been so engrossed in my own thoughts, I forgot he had ahold of it.

"What are you thinking?"

"The people. Are they real? Or do they belong elsewhere?" I said, still peering out my window.

"They're all real. You'll always wonder now, won't you?" he asked, a hint of sadness behind his voice.

I nodded.

"Most of the time, they'll be like you. Even if they're not, they have no reason to bother you."

I said nothing, back in my own head. Lucas turned onto East Second Avenue, pulling up to a white story-and-a-half house. I glanced around the neighborhood—so familiar. My mouth went dry. Down the street loomed the Moore house, completely in view. I shot a stare at Lucas. He smiled at me, leaned over, and kissed my cheek.

"Come on," he urged.

I sighed and opened my door. Dusk had set, and the air was stale. I leaned up against Lucas's car, waiting. He met me and took my hand. I didn't know whether or not to be nervous. I pivoted my head to the house swarming with demons. I shivered; the house frightened me beyond any normal amount of fear.

Lucas knocked on Susan's front door.

"Are you okay?" he asked.

I turned away from the evil house. "Yeah."

No.

We waited at the front step. I stared at my feet, not wanting to look at the Moore house again. Seconds ticked by before I heard footsteps. The knob turned, and I glanced up. A gasp lodged in my throat at the familiar face.

Chapter 14

"Good evening, Lucas, Carrie," Susan Taylor greeted. "Won't you come in?"

Mrs. Taylor stepped to the side allowing Lucas and me to enter. I followed him into the living room, quaint and cheerfully decorated in whites, yellows, and blues. We sat together on the leather sofa. I grabbed one of the square pillows and placed it on my lap. Already uncomfortable, I needed something to toy with, and the conversation hadn't started yet.

"Can I offer you anything to drink?" Mrs. Taylor asked me.

Lucas glanced in my direction.

"Ice...water...please," I stuttered, my hands shaking.

It was different when I didn't know who Susan was, but this woman was friends with my grandmother. What kind of information did they share?

My palms grew clammy as I grasped the tassels on the pillow. Lucas placed his hand against my back. Mrs. Taylor knew that Lucas was ... well, yeah, and I couldn't help but wonder what she thought of me.

Susan sat down on a chair across from us. As with each time I'd seen her, she had a pleasant expression.

"What can I do for you, Lucas?" she asked.

"I need some answers," he said, sitting up a little taller. "I told Carrie everything. Now I need to know how I can protect her."

Susan took a deep breath. "Lucas, I know this has been difficult for you. I've been well informed of your situation, but I must say, I do not agree with the decision you made. I've never dealt with anything like this before. I'm not sure if another exists. But, we cannot take back the past. We must concentrate on Carrie's safety, and yours."

Lucas nodded. "I'm sorry for whatever position I've put you in. I'm thankful for any help you can offer."

"I've been trying to locate other necromancers to find something similar. No one has responded. As of now, my only advice is to stay out of the dark. When the sun begins to set, you must leave her or go somewhere indoors. Carrie's grandparents' home is out of town and secluded; she'll be safe there."

"Spells? Are there any spells that can protect her?"

"Anything that may have even the slightest chance of success has already been cast. Her home is protected as much as it can be. As is Renae's Antiques and both yours and Carrie's vehicles."

Mrs. Taylor glanced my way before turning her

attention back to Lucas.

Spells around my house and car? Cast by the girl in my visions?

"What more can be done?"

Susan shook her head. "Nothing. You are at war against an entity with which you cannot win. You knew that."

Lucas bowed his head and sifted his hand through his dark hair. He looked up at me, his eyes pained. "They won't get you; I won't let them."

I nodded once. Never in my mind had I any idea of how real the danger actually was. I wouldn't go back; I'd still choose Lucas, but now his soul meant more to me than my own.

He faced Susan. "I had no choice; I had to tell her. She needed to make her own decision."

"I understand the integrity of your actions."

"There's some force pulling me to her. When I first saw her, something about her was oddly familiar," he explained.

"I feel it, too," I chimed in, speaking for the first time since the conversation began.

Mrs. Taylor smiled. "Yes. Sometimes, Lucas, something from your human life will be triggered. Carrie must remind you of someone important to you."

"Will I ever remember?"

Her shoulders rose and fell in a heavy sigh. "Only time will tell." Then she turned her attention to me. "How have you been, Carrie?"

"Okay, I guess. I've been having strange dreams, or visions, I guess." I glanced at Lucas for the encouragement to continue. He patted my hand. "I think they're happening as I dream them."

"Lucas?" Susan said tilting her head, her eyes narrowed.

"Yeah, I've had one."

"What events have been dreamt?"

"Major events only," Lucas answered for both of us. "Important decisions regarding our relationship."

Susan sat silent for a few minutes. "You have a strong pull toward each other?"

We nodded, saying nothing. I bit the inside of my cheek, studying Mrs. Taylor.

Susan thought again for a few minutes before she rose from her chair. She walked to the stairs and lifted the wood off the third riser. From inside she drew out a large, ancient book with hard leather binding. "Your dreams have all been real..." she muttered to herself.

She sat back down, book open on her lap. The pages were old and yellowing, some torn. After a few minutes of flipping, a flash of understanding crossed her face. "Yes. Yes, of course," she mused.

Lucas and I exchanged a glance.

"What?" I asked.

"It is a very rare thing, indeed," Susan murmured, thinking out loud. "And absolutely extraordinary for you to find it." She raised her hand to her mouth and caressed her lips as she thought.

"What is it?" Lucas said, watching Mrs. Taylor closely.

"Incenamus," Susan said, raising her eyes to us.

"Incenamus?" I repeated.

"Yes," Susan said. "You two *are* connected. Your souls are matched."

"Our souls?" Lucas's head snapped in my direction.

"Yes. Incenamus happens when two souls, one living and one dead, bind themselves together," Susan said. She stood up and paced the living room. "And you found each other. Truly remarkable, I—"

"Like soul mates?" I asked.

"Many people find their soul mates, dear, if they're looking. This connection fuses two souls together into one. Neither of you have ever felt whole before; it's because you weren't. A small piece was missing. And now, you have found it—in each other."

"How did that happen?" I asked, confused again. Lucas placed his hand over mine.

"The future changes, but there are some things that cannot be changed. You two were meant to be together in life. Lucas dying didn't change that fact. He found you, even in death. Your connection may intensify in ways you can't imagine. It holds powers that I do not know. I'm not sure if many do."

Lucas squeezed my hand. Yes, a confirmation we belonged together.

"But," Susan started, "but you are still here, Lucas."

He cleared his throat.

"Though your souls are connected, yours is lost. Carrie isn't what you were searching for when you came here."

"No," he whispered. "She wasn't."

"And you still don't feel complete, do you?"

"No. Something's missing."

"Your soul, Lucas. It's still a part of you, but it's lost. That's why you didn't cross over."

"My soul?"

"Yes," Susan said. "When you died, you were empty inside. You were in pain—suffering, some great emotional turmoil." She glanced at me. "Do you know the feeling?"

I nodded. "I felt like that when Lucas left. And when I left him. And when..." I let my sentence trail.

And when my parents betrayed me.

Lucas locked my gaze for a few moments before I broke it, staring at the floor.

"The feeling is your soul ripping itself from your spirit. It's unforgiveness. When we don't forgive, it tears us up inside, leaving a void. It's emotionally painful and leaves you hollow. Empty. If you die without forgiving, without your soul reuniting with your spirit, you stay on earth. You become like Lucas," Susan explained.

I shivered. My emptiness with Lucas ended. He returned, and the hole inside healed. But, I couldn't bring myself to forgive my parents. My soul had ripped from my spirit. I was in danger of Lucas's fate.

I didn't know what to say. I harbored what Mrs. Taylor explained—turmoil. Turmoil that I had been trying all summer to ignore. I didn't want to forgive my father. I was angry, and felt like, somehow, I had something to do with it. That I ...

"You're a living being," Susan continued. "That means that you are made up of a spirit, a body, and a soul. If one part dies, you die."

"But if Lucas's soul separated itself from his spirit, doesn't that mean he should have died then?" I asked, putting my own thoughts on hold.

"No. His soul is alive, just separated. Only his body died," she said.

"The pull hasn't been as strong lately," Lucas muttered.

"Of course not," Susan snapped. "You don't feel it in corporeal form. That's the cost of trying to be living when you are not. Ghosts who don't accept their death and want to continue among the living may never find their souls because they no longer sense it. And without it, you'll fade away. You'll cease to exist."

No one spoke. I patted Lucas's hand, but he didn't respond.

Finally, he asked, "Where is it?"

"In something tied to that emotional response that ripped your soul from you in the first place. Something significant—"

"If I can't remember my life, how can I find what is significant to me?" Lucas's voice rose, teetering on angry.

"You must retrace your steps," Susan replied.

"Would the guy who saw Lucas when he died know anything?" I interjected.

Lucas took a few moments to tell Susan about the man at the scene of the accident.

"Maybe," Susan said.

Lucas sighed. "He saw me when I was invisible."

"He could be a very powerful warlock. At least

it's a place to start."

"What will happen if he finds his soul?" I asked.

"He'll be completed and cross over into the next life."

My gaze wandered up to Lucas. His eyes were closed, and he held my hand tighter.

"He must find it, Carrie," Susan encouraged me.

Lucas's eyes shot open. "How much time do I have?"

Susan shrugged. "It varies for everyone. Days for some. Years for others."

Mrs. Taylor glanced in my direction. It was selfish of me, but Lucas belonged with me. She just said as much. How could I live without him?

Danger lurked on our doorstep, and as long as were together, we would fear for our lives. It was a risk I was willing to take just to be with him. What we had, Incenamus was less than a once-in-a-lifetime love. I wasn't about to give that up to save my own life. However, if I died, I'd join Lucas in this limbo-world, neither dead nor living.

I wouldn't try to die, but the thought crossed my mind for like a fraction of a second. What if I didn't forgive? We could be together for eternity.

The idea intrigued me, though I had no doubt Lucas wouldn't be happy about it. The decision belonged to me though, not him.

As I continued to ponder the new idea, my eye caught sight of the Moore House sitting so close. I imagined demons controlling it after sunset. I stared so enthralled out the window that I didn't hear Mrs. Taylor say my name.

"Carrie," she repeated.

Lucas placed his hand on my shoulder. "Carrie," he whispered in my ear.

Startled, I jerked my head to face him. "Yeah. Sorry."

"You're looking at the Moore home," Susan commented.

"We're so close."

A sad look crossed Susan's face.

"Did any of them stay on earth? Like Lucas?" I asked.

Mrs. Taylor nodded. "Sarah did. She came to me seeking help almost thirty years ago. She's since found her soul and passed on. I'm sure she's cradling her children in her arms now."

"What about the demons?"

Susan Taylor sighed. "You must not underestimate them. They're evil and live only to destroy that which is good."

"Can they be killed?"

"No. Powerful witches and warlocks are able to cast a difficult spell that will send them back to Hell, but that's all. You will not escape one." Susan's eyes were serious, her tone soft. She turned to Lucas. "You must be *very* careful."

Lucas's jaw tightened. "We'd better get going," he said.

Mrs. Taylor smiled. "Yes, Carrie probably has much to think about."

She was right. I didn't know if I would ever wrap my mind around everything.

"It's after dark, I suggest you leave separately," Susan said.

"Take my car home." Lucas handed me his keys.

"I'll meet you there. Thank you for your time, Susan."

"You're welcome, Lucas. Let me know if you need anything else. I will help in any way I can," she assured him. "Take care of Carrie."

"I will."

I tucked Lucas's keys into my pocket. He walked with me to the door. I faced Mrs. Taylor.

"Come by anytime," Mrs. Taylor said to me before I had a chance to thank her.

"Thanks".

Mrs. Taylor left the room, giving Lucas and me a moment alone.

"You don't have to hurry. You'll be fine," he said. "I'll be right behind you."

I touched his face. "Be careful."

"Always."

He bent down and brushed his lips over mine, then slid the back of his hand over my cheek. I loved when he did that.

"You better go."

He opened the door, and I stepped out into the starlit night. I didn't want to leave without him, but I understood the necessity. He shot me a reassuring grin before closing the door.

After adjusting the seat, I backed out in the opposite direction of the Moore House. As I glanced into the rearview mirror, the demon-filled house began to fade into the blackness. Behind me, I thought I saw the flash of a blood-red aura. I cut my eyes back to the road ahead of me and slammed on the gas.

Chapter 15

I didn't know if the red light was real or in my head. Either way, it freaked me out. The entire drive I kept looking behind me, paranoid of something following. Inside my grandparents' farmhouse I'd be safe. Mrs. Taylor said protective spells surrounded the house, making my confidence stronger.

I raced up the stairs to my room and turned on the light. Lucas sat in the chair in the corner of my room, his legs extended in front of him and his arms tucked behind his head. Gorgeous.

Quickly forgetting what I'd seen on the drive, a smile spread across my face, and I ran to him. Jumping into his lap, I wrapped my arms around his neck.

"I missed you," I said, kissing him under his ear.

He chuckled. "I missed you more."

"How long have you been here?"

"Since you pulled safely into the driveway."

I shook my head. "You're amazing."

"I know." His dimple took my breath away.

I snuggled up in his chest. I never wanted this moment to end. Right then, everything seemed perfect. Unfortunately, Lucas had other ideas.

"Hey," he said. "Tell me what's on your mind."

"Nothing." Half-lie. "Hold me. That's all I want to think about."

He lifted my chin. "After everything that's happened today, I can't believe you have nothing to say."

His emerald eyes searched mine, and I shook my head.

I don't want to talk.

"I want to know," he said.

At his insistence, all the thoughts I'd had all day made their way from behind the shield I'd created in my brain. Knowing that demons were loose in Villisca and would hunt Lucas and me scared me more by the second. More than that, the knowledge that we could do nothing to prevent it or save ourselves from them ate at me. We were entirely at their mercy.

The nightmares in the Moore House attic still haunted me, too. So many nights I awoke in a cold sweat with a pillow over my face to muffle the screams. Nothing stifled the agonizing cries that continued to echo inside my head. If Lucas got captured, he would be the one screaming, and there was nothing I'd be able to do. He'd be trapped in one of those pits, trying to claw himself out, or he'd be recruited and watching with glee from the sidelines. I couldn't let that happen to him.

Then there was his soul.

As soon as Mrs. Taylor told Lucas he must find

it, I knew *that* would be Lucas's final decision—the one he dreaded making. It would be a choice between himself and me. Either way, we were going to lose each other—we both couldn't win.

Thinking about living the rest of my life if Lucas reunited with his soul was bittersweet. He'd be safe and happy. But how would I ever learn to love again? No one would compare to him.

And what if he never finds it? He'd be trapped on earth until one day when he'd just fade away—as if he'd never existed at all. I couldn't live knowing Lucas didn't exist anywhere.

I sighed, frustrated. I'd just received a slew of new and disturbing information, and I already knew how it would end.

Realizing Lucas probably wouldn't drop it, though, and I couldn't resist, I slid off Lucas's lap and sat cross-legged on the edge of my bed.

"I don't want to be without you," I said, refusing to meet his eyes. Green was the color of greed and selfishness, and I didn't want the reminder.

Lucas said nothing.

"I know it's crazy but, I don't want you to leave. It's selfish, yeah. I'm sorry. I need you."

He rose to his feet and sat beside me. "I've been thinking a lot about what Susan said. I don't want to be without you either."

I fidgeted with my hands. "I sort of have a confession to make. Maybe a solution?" My eyes flitted up to meet his. I pursed my lips, not believing what I was about to say. "You know how she said that your soul ripped itself from your spirit? And that if a person were to die without forgiving, they

230

would become like you?"

His eyes narrowed, and his mouth dropped open.

Stop talking now.

"If I...uh, died right now, I could be like you. We could be together." My whisper sounded so quiet that a normal ear would never have heard. Lucas, however, heard me perfectly clear.

He gaped at me, unblinking.

Oh, crap.

"You can't seriously be thinking about *dying* to be with me?"

I studied him, hoping he'd understand.

"That's absurd, Carrie!" He rose to his feet. "Insane. This is not a life. It's not even death! I couldn't live with myself if something happened to you. I'm doing everything I can to *protect* you!"

"Lucas, don't you see? It's a way for us to be together. Isn't that what you want?" I pleaded.

"I want you to live a long and happy life."

"That's not possible without you."

"Then we'll find a way to make it possible. You dying is *not* an option."

"But Lucas—"

"No. No, Carrie," he interrupted. "It's not going to happen." He dropped to his knee in front of me. His hands covered mine on my lap, his head hung low. Slowly, he lifted his gaze to meet mine. "You have no idea how much it hurts hearing you say you'd die just to be with me. My life, this, means nothing if you're not alive. You, Carrie, you get to live your life for both of us. Our souls are connected, remember. Incenamus. We're one. Live for both of us. Besides, if you become like me, you won't even remember me. Or your parents, your friends, or your grandparents." I hadn't thought about that.

His eyes pleaded with me, more intense than I'd ever seen. His hands clenched onto mine. They felt both cool and warm at the same time.

"I'm sorry, Lucas," I whispered. "I just thought…"

"I know. I'm honored you love me so much, but I love you, too. Death is not the way. It never is."

He let go of my hands and rested his against my face. Then in one motion, he swept me off my bed and into his arms. We were both on our knees on the floor, embraced. My arms wrapped around his neck, my cheek against his. I kissed him, reveling in his touch. He ran his fingers through my hair and pulled me closer.

"I'm really sorry," I whispered in his ear.

Lucas loosened his hold. He kissed me softly.

"I need to find it, Carrie," he said, his forehead pressed against mine.

"I know you do."

"Will you help me?"

The sting of tears burned my eyes. "Of course I will."

"Thank you," he whispered. "I just have to know why."

I let the tears fall—Lucas wiped them away.

"Don't cry," he said. "I don't know how long it will take. And I'm not sure if I'll take it when I find it. I just need to know where it is."

I didn't want to admit it, but I understood. He needed to find his soul, and I would do all I could to help him. He deserved that from me.

"I'd better go," he said.

"Don't." The words were out before I could stop them. "Don't go."

"What would your grandparents think if they see my car in their driveway in the morning?"

"I don't care."

"Yes, you do." He pushed the hair out of my face. "But I'll stay until you fall asleep."

"Is that the best I'm going to get?"

He chuckled. "Yeah."

"I guess I'll take it."

Lucas's lips brushed my lips. "Good guess."

He lay on my bed, his hands behind his head, his ankles crossed. I jumped in beside him and cuddled up next to his cool body.

"Lucas?" I asked, curiosity catching up with me again.

"Yeah."

"Can I ask you something?"

"Sure."

I paused. "What do demons look like?"

Lucas stared at the ceiling as he answered. "Their faces are contorted in all sorts of ways. I've never been close enough to see their eyes, but from a distance they're black with blood-red pupils. Some have horns, some don't." As he spoke, he held me tighter. "Either way, they reek of evil, Carrie. Even humans can smell them. I'd die a thousand deaths before I'd let them get a hold of you."

He grew silent. My heart thudded as I pictured the creatures in my mind. Evil was not a strong enough word for the monsters I saw in my head.

"Lucas?" I said again, nervous.

"Yeah?"

"Can I ask you something else?"

"Yeah."

"You always seem to leave the room whenever you disappear. Why do you do that?"

"Because I don't want you to see."

"Why not?"

He still stared at the ceiling. "I'm scared of what you'd think."

"I won't think anything different. Will you show me if I ask?"

Lucas fell silent for a few moments before he sat up. "Okay," he said. "What do you want to see?"

I sat up, too and crossed my legs. "Can you teleport to the other side of my bed?"

He rolled his eyes. Then he looked at me intently and disappeared. Almost simultaneously, he reappeared on the opposite side of me, beside the closet.

He shrugged. "What else?"

I laughed. "That was really cool!"

"Yeah, if you think so," he muttered.

"You said you could be transparent, right? Like a…ghost." The last word barely made it past my lips.

"I suppose," he grumbled.

This time I saw no concentration behind his eyes. It seemed as if he was letting go; his skin disappeared and in its place formed vapor, filling in his features. He looked the same, only I could see through him. His appearance glowed silvery-white.

Honestly, it was a shocking sight, and I knew after he made the change why he'd insisted I not see him that way. I shuddered.

Lucas closed his eyes for a few moments and returned to "normal."

"Is that enough?" he asked hopefully. "You've seen me invisible an innumerable amount of times."

"Okay. Come back," I said, patting the empty spot next to me.

He lay back down beside me. I wrapped my arm around his chest.

"How was that?"

"I'm glad to know," I said. "I don't think I'd mind seeing you disappear and reappear."

"And the other?"

"Kind of creepy," I admitted.

"And that's why I didn't want to show you."

"Thank you for doing it, though."

Lucas sighed, "You're welcome. Now go to sleep."

I rolled over, turned off my lamp, and cuddled back at Lucas's side. Nestled close to his body, I drifted off to sleep easily.

***

"Goldie's stuff is ready," I said, motioning to the pile I had put out.

"Do you want to ride her today? I'll ride Roxanne."

Though happy to continue our Sunday rides, this sudden jolt of confidence surprised me.

"Really?" I asked. "You think I'm ready?"

"Yeah. Why don't you give it a shot? Just make sure she knows you're the boss."

I nodded. "Yeah. I can do that."

I mounted Goldie with ease and waited patiently for Mike. He led Roxanne through the gate and closed it behind him.

"Let's go," he said as he mounted his large horse.

I kicked Goldie on the side and held the reins. To my surprise, she moved forward on my first command.

"Nice job," Mike commented.

We walked our horses side by side through the pasture, leaving adequate distance between them. Goldie did everything I commanded without fail. My sense of accomplishment soared. Even though horseback riding wasn't exactly an extreme sport, I'd faced my fear. I felt like I could do anything.

I cleared my throat and glanced over at my riding companion. Honestly, I didn't want to tell him. But since I wasn't exactly up front before, *and* hurt him in the process, I figured telling him now was better than him finding out on his own. "Lucas is coming over to meet Rob and Renae this evening. You can meet him then, too, if you'd like."

A few moments ticked by before he answered. "He's back, huh?"

"Yeah."

Mike's shoulders tense as he looked away from me.

We rode in silence for a while. I kept my eyes forward, waiting for his reluctance.

He tottered my way, then back to the field. "Is he

staying for movie night?"

"Uh, yeah. I was hoping so."

He sighed. "I don't know, Carrie."

"Please, Mike? I'd really like for you to be there." I waited for a few seconds. "For me?"

I wished I could see his face; it was hard to read the back of his head. He slowed Roxanne until we were again side-by-side. Without meeting my eye, he half-grinned. "Make sure he knows I have next dibs. And that I'll kill him if he hurts you."

"Oh. Oh, yeah?" I mocked.

If he only knew.

When we returned to the barn, it was past five. I had to hurry if I didn't want to smell like horse when Lucas came over. I yanked off Goldie's saddle and bridle, which was much easier than putting it on, and put each piece in its proper place. Mike said goodbye and promised to return later with a movie for the three of us.

I hurried inside and took a quick shower. There wasn't time to dry my hair, so I ran a brush through it and got dressed. I scurried back downstairs with two minutes to spare.

The day was hot, and as soon as I stepped out, beads of sweat formed on my brow. I sat on the cement step and wrung out my hair onto Grandma's pansies.

It wasn't long before Lucas's red G8 turned into the driveway. I hopped to my feet. He drove as far from the horse barn as he could. So funny! As soon as he parked, he appeared by my side without opening the car door.

"Hey," he said with a smirk.

"What was that? Somebody could have seen." I glanced behind me at the door.

"No one saw. I was trying to avoid your lovely horse."

Lucas leaned down to give me a quick kiss.

"Mike's coming over later to meet you, as well, I hope you don't mind."

"Not at all. It'll be nice to meet him in person."

I took a deep breath and started toward the door, Lucas following. There was every reason to be nervous. Grandma, at least, secretly hoped something would happen between Mike and me, and I worried she'd be disappointed when she met Lucas.

"Calm down," he said, noticing my trembling hands. "It'll be fine."

"If you say so," I muttered.

I opened the door, letting Lucas inside. Usually on a Sunday evening, my grandparents were in their recliners reading, but I peeked into an empty living room. I stood confused until I heard the faint sound of raised voices coming from the downstairs bathroom.

"I said the sink was broken," Grandma insisted.

"Yes. So I checked the kitchen—and it was fine!" Grandpa replied from behind the bathroom sink.

"I didn't say the kitchen, Rob. I said the bathroom sink."

"The bathroom doesn't have a sink. The only sink in the house is in the kitchen. *This* is a basin."

"But I specifically said the bathroom."

"If you wanted the bathroom basin fixed, you

should have said the bathroom *basin*." Grandpa grunted. "I need the wrench."

"Grandma. Grandpa," I said, standing in the doorway trying to hold back my giggles. "I have someone here I'd like you to meet."

"I'm almost done, Care Bear," Grandpa Rob said. "Valve, please, Renae."

I glanced at Lucas, who was fighting a smile. I led him into the living room where we each lost our battles, bursting into laughter.

"They do that," I said. "Grandpa is so technical. I think it drives Grandma crazy, but it's one of the reasons she loves him."

"They're cute." Lucas said. "So, Care Bear, where should I sit?"

I slugged him on the shoulder and tugged him down on the sofa next to me. We didn't wait long.

I jumped to my feet when Grandma walked in. "Grandma. This is Lucas. Lucas, this is my Grandma Renae."

"Nice to meet you, Lucas," she said, shaking his hand. "Rob!"

"Coming," he hollered from the bathroom.

"He'll be right here. Please, sit. Can I get you anything?"

"No, I'm fine. Thank you," Lucas said.

Grandpa Rob appeared at the doorway. Again, Lucas and I stood as I made the introductions. Lucas shook my grandpa's hand and sat back down beside me.

"Where are you from, Lucas?" Grandma asked.

"Red Oak. I have a place there."

"He came into the store earlier this summer," I

explained. "We met then."

"I see," she said, her eyebrows raised. "And you've seen each other ever since?"

"Uh. Not really," I said, feeling squeamish. "Off and on, some." My palms were sweating.

Awkward.

"You still in school?" Grandpa asked, fishing for an age.

"No, Sir. I'm finished."

I was shocked. Lucas handled this uncomfortable situation like a pro. His story wasn't completely untrue, but it wasn't like he could come out and say, "Hey, I'm dead."

"College?"

"I'm undecided. Right now I have a graphic design business I run online. I set up and maintain websites."

Huh?

How did I not know that? It'd never occurred to me that he might have a job or did other things when I wasn't around.

"Who are your parents? I'm in Red Oak quite often," Grandma asked.

"I just recently came to the area, actually."

"Ah. So, what brings you here?" Grandpa asked.

"I have friends here. I came to figure things out for myself."

"Oh. Where did you move here from?" Grandma wondered.

"I was staying with a friend in California before I came here."

Becca, his...friend.

I exhaled, forgetting to breathe for a few

moments. My grandparents asked a swarm of other questions, which Lucas answered without a flinch.

Seriously? Did he rehearse this?

During the second round of Twenty Questions, Mike walked in. I did introductions for the third time. Mike didn't exactly smile when he shook hands with Lucas. I followed Mike with my eyes as he sat down in the wooden rocking chair, leaned back, and crossed his arms over his chest. Whatever had gotten into him, I hoped would be gone by the time the three of us were alone.

Eventually Grandma and Grandpa seemed to run out of questions for Lucas, so the conversation turned to Mike. I was relieved.

"You kids going to watch a movie?" Grandpa asked.

"Yeah, if that's all right with you," Mike said, seeming a little more relaxed.

"No problem. Good night. It was nice to meet you, Lucas."

Grandma nodded at us and followed Grandpa out of the room.

"What did you bring, Mike?" Lucas asked.

"A classic."

I rolled my eyes. "A real classic? *Gone with the Wind?* Or one of *your* classics?"

"This is a real classic," Mike said. "*Star Wars: Return of the Jedi.*"

"Good pick!" Lucas rose his hand to high-five Mike, but Mike ignored him.

I never understood how guys bonded with each other. In 'Guy Land', I wondered if Mike's choice of movie was some sort of test. If Lucas liked it, he was in. If not, Lucas was out.

Lame.

"I feel outnumbered," I mumbled.

"You are. Get over it," Mike teased as he took a spot in Grandpa's chair.

"I'll get some popcorn," I said. I nudged Mike on the shoulder and motioned him to follow.

"You need help with microwave popcorn?" he asked when we stepped into the kitchen.

I grabbed a bag from the cupboard. "What's going on?"

He shrugged. "Nothing."

"Out there? That wasn't nothing."

"I'm being nice."

"Feigning nice is more like it. And the high-five thing doesn't even qualify as 'feigning.'"

"I didn't notice. What more do you want?"

I tossed the popcorn it the microwave. "I want you to be friends."

"Why? You're leaving in two weeks anyway, remember?" His expression was cold.

"Because I want you both in my life. Even if it's only for two more weeks."

Mike ran his fingers through his chestnut hair. "Fine. For you."

Two minutes and thirty seconds later, we returned with two bowls: one for me and one for Mike. Mike engaged Lucas in a "Skywalker" conversation I couldn't care less about. What I did care about was Mike's change in attitude.

The movie lasted forever, as Mike and Lucas felt the need to discuss many of the plot points, pausing the movie to do it.

At least they're getting along.

The best part of the movie was when the credits started rolling, except that Mike and Lucas had started a new conversation over the newer *Star Wars* films. I laid my head on the pillow at the far end of the sofa, drowning out the boring conversation between them.

The next thing I knew, Lucas was carrying me to my room. He laid me on my bed and pulled the blankets over me. Warm under my covers, I felt the coolness of Lucas beside me. He kissed me softly on the forehead and then on my lips.

"Sweet dreams," he whispered as he brushed his hand over my hair. "I'll see you tomorrow. I love you."

I moaned something that I intended to be "I love you, too." I didn't hear my bedroom door open or close, because it probably didn't.

Chapter 16

Monday began overcast, and gray clouds lingered throughout the day. It was cold, a mere sixty-eight degrees at noon. The rain hadn't started yet, but The National Weather Service had issued severe thunderstorm and tornado watches all over the state. Drizzle coated my jacket as I walked up to Renae's Antiques for my afternoon shift.

I stepped through the glass door, ringing the golden bell. The store seemed darker than usual, probably just the sunless day.

I greeted Megan at the counter. "How's the day been?"

"Deathly boring," she answered. "I've had one customer since eight-thirty. I hope you brought a book."

"Yeah, but I'm getting close to being done with it."

She shrugged. "Maybe this afternoon will pick up."

"Yeah. Maybe," I said. "What are you doing today?"

"Helping my mom out. And Mrs. Taylor wants her garden tilled again before it rains."

"Didn't you say Mrs. Taylor was your neighbor?" I asked, trying not to sound awkward.

"Yeah. Why?"

I swallowed, hoping she didn't notice the break in my voice. "Oh, I was driving around and saw her outside the other day. I didn't even think about you living so close to her."

Poor Megan!

She lived so close to a place with ghosts coming and going at all hours of the day. I wondered if she ever noticed anything strange at Susan's. Though, ghosts seldom went to see her in the flesh. Yeah, Megan was better off not knowing that she lived between a necromancer and a house filled with demons.

"Ours is the blue house on the left. I need to get that garden done before it rains, and it looks like that's going to happen real soon," she mused, grabbing her bag and an umbrella. "See you later."

As soon as the bell rang behind her, I moseyed behind the counter and plopped on the stool. I only had four hours to be here, but I had the feeling the day would drag on for an eternity. My only solace was wondering when I'd see Lucas.

Other than Mike, the night before had gone smoother than I'd anticipated. My grandparents seemed to approve, although Grandma had yet to say anything to me—it would be coming soon. Grandpa said something about his "good, strong handshake," whatever that meant.

I tapped my fingers on the counter and circled

the store with my eyes. It looked like Megan had cleaned the showroom in her boredom. I sighed.

I opened a can of Pepsi and took my book out of my bag. Bilbo and the rest of the dwarves were trapped in the mountain, deciding on a way to escape. I flipped my book open and began to read.

I loved fantasy novels. They were a wonderful escape from reality. However, my view of reality had changed dramatically in the last forty-eight hours. It was almost as if I was now a part of my own fantasy novel filled with demons, ghosts, and witches. I massaged my brow, losing myself in the story.

An hour passed without me looking anywhere but the words on the page. A door opened and closed behind me, and Grandma's footsteps echoed in the stillness.

"Hey, there," she said as she reached the counter. "Have a good morning to yourself?"

I glanced up at her. "Hi, Grandma." I purposely ignored her question since I didn't want to admit that I'd slept until eleven.

"Slow day, huh?"

"Very," I replied. "Megan said she only had one person come in all morning."

"It is a good day to get a lot done in the back, though." Grandma smiled. "By the way, I wanted to talk to you."

Right. Here we go.

"Oh. About what?" I tucked the bookmark between the pages and set the book on the counter, pretending I didn't know what she wanted.

"Your friend, Lucas."

I squirmed a little on the stool. "What about him?"

"It's just that you'll be going back to Texas in two weeks. And, well, he lives here. Is this a wise idea?"

I sighed, thankful it wasn't the "he's-too-old-for-you" speech I half-expected. "Grandma, it's okay. He knows I'm not staying. We've just hung out a few times this summer," I lied.

"You two looked awfully snug last night."

"I like him," I said. This was the other conversation I'd expected, but it was still uncomfortable. "He knows I live in Texas. Long distance relationships sometimes work out."

"All right, I guess you're old enough to make some decisions on your own."

I caught the undertone in her voice. She meant I was old enough to make my own mistakes and hopefully learn from them.

"Thanks," I said.

"I'm going to run some errands. Are you okay by yourself?" Grandma asked, picking up a stack of stamped envelopes from under the counter.

"Yeah. Go ahead."

"I'll be back soon."

I'd been thinking about what would happen in two weeks. School in Texas would be starting soon. There were a few scenarios roaming in and out of my mind, but none seemed plausible. It wasn't fair to ask Lucas to come with me. He'd come to Villisca because Susan lived here. His search started in Villisca, not Texas.

I wiped the thoughts from my mind and returned

to my book. As predicted, the next person to ring the bell was Grandma returning from her errands. So little time had passed, I thought I was about to lose my mind. Four-thirty couldn't come soon enough.

To my surprise, at four twenty-nine, the golden bell above the door rang and in walked the most handsome guy I'd ever seen.

"Lucas!" I cried, running to him and throwing my arms around his neck.

He hugged me back and kissed the top of my head. "Someone's happy to see me."

"I've been crazy-bored today!" I whined. "Other than Grandma and me, you're the only person to walk through that door."

He chuckled. "Well, it sounds like you need a nice walk and dinner before it gets too dark."

Before it gets dark. Right.

"I'd say I have to agree with that," I answered. "I'm almost done here."

"Take your time. But not too much."

I gathered my things behind the counter. My finished book was back in my bag and the empty can of soda tucked away in a box. I hurried to the back of the store and knocked on the door.

"Grandma?" I peeked my head inside. "Grandma, I'm ready to go."

"Oh, is it that time already?" Grandma glanced up from underneath an end table. "Is everything done?"

"Except flipping the sign."

"Okay. Flip it, and I'll see you at home."

"Um, actually, I was wondering if it was okay to

go out with Lucas? He's here."

"Oh, sure. When will you be home?"

"Um, ten? Maybe before."

"I'll keep the light on for you. Don't be out too late."

If I do, demons can drag us to Hell. No worries.

"Thanks," I exclaimed and danced out the door into Lucas's arms. "You feel so good."

"I'm sure you do, too."

I frowned, hating that he couldn't feel me in the same ways I felt him.

"Hey," he said, taking my hand. "Just because I can't feel you on the outside, doesn't mean I don't feel you in here." He patted the place where his heart should be.

"Still," I said quietly.

"It doesn't make me love you any less." He drew me into him. "We'd better go before it gets too late."

I flipped the sign to "closed" as we walked out the door. The misting cold stung my cheeks, but I didn't care. I was with Lucas, and that meant the boredom from the afternoon wouldn't linger. I put my cinch-sac in my car and followed Lucas to his.

"I thought we were going for a walk?"

"We are, but I thought you'd get cold," he said, grabbing a black fleece jacket from the backseat. He wrapped the coat around me; it smelled like him.

"What did you and Mike talk about last night?"

"I like Mike," Lucas said nodding. "He's a good guy. He likes you. I guess I can overlook that—for now. It just means he has good taste." Lucas grinned. "We talked about Star Wars, other films, football—guy stuff."

"I didn't know you liked Star Wars and football."

"Just because I'm dead doesn't mean I'm not male! What do you think I did wandering around for so long?"

I shrugged.

"I went to movies and games. I did what any normal guy would do. Whatever I *could* to keep myself from going crazy."

"That reminds me. Graphic design? I didn't know that."

Lucas laughed. "Becca taught me. Besides, how else am I supposed to buy a car and pay rent?"

"I guess I never thought about that."

"It's perfect. I only do business online."

A thought crossed my mind, wondering how many dead people were actually online.

Weird.

We walked around the square a few times, talking about nothing. Neither of us brought up the impossibilities of our relationship. The nonchalance felt like a huge weight lifted off my shoulders, even if it was just for a few hours.

Tonight, we were normal. Two living people in love, taking a stroll in the mist. This was the life we were meant to have.

The thought of having to go back to Texas unwillingly entered into my thoughts. Now that I had Lucas, I didn't want to go home. My life was taking a different direction—a direction I didn't ask for, but one I gladly embraced.

Lucas led us to a bench at the center of the

square, overlooking the park. It was empty, of course; the cold and the threat of rain kept everyone indoors.

Lucas wrapped an arm around my waist and tugged me close to his side. I laid my head on his shoulder, taking in the moment. I felt at home.

I sighed and buried my head into him, wishing I could just enjoy this time without my stupid thoughts getting in the way. Lucas rested his chin on my head, and I heaved another sigh, triggering an immediate response from him.

"You're upset about something," he observed. He knew me so well.

"Just thinking," I answered, trying not to.

"What about?"

"The future. I'm going back to Texas in a couple of weeks," I said as I faced him. "And I don't want to go."

"Yeah." His chin left my head, and he tilted my face up to him.

"I don't want to leave you," I murmured.

"You don't have to," he said. "I'm coming with you."

"That sounds amazing Lucas, but … I just don't see how that's possible. I mean, Susan's here, and you have a soul to find. I'm not going to be the one to stand in the way."

"I'll start my search from Texas. We'll figure it out. Together."

"What if something happens to you?"

"Nothing will. And if it does, I have no regrets. I spent the time I had with you. And that's enough."

Lucas's words sounded too good to be true. But I

couldn't live knowing I'd cheated him out of eternity. Years on earth were nothing but milliseconds in forever.

"Let's get you some dinner," he said, rising to his feet.

We walked to Dan's Bar and Grill, where we shared our first date. The mist slowed, but it was getting colder. I shivered under Lucas's warm coat.

Inside, it looked as if everyone had the same idea as us. The small restaurant was full. With every table taken, a group of people meandered around the waiting area. Lucas glanced over at me, and I shrugged. More than likely the other restaurants in town had a similar situation. And given the gloomy evening, darkness would come sooner than usual— driving to the next town wasn't an option.

"Even though it's day, the sun's hidden," I whispered to him.

He pulled me closer. "They won't risk it. One crack in the clouds, and they're dust."

I giggled, thinking of Jessica's blond-man-out-to-kill-me theory. "Like a vampire."

Lucas's body tightened. "Uh, yeah. Something like that."

I shot him a quick glare, but he didn't elaborate. The pending nightfall had put him on edge.

We leaned against the wall, watching as people left and those standing around took over their tables. Lucas kept his eyes fixed outside.

When the next table emptied, a server came and directed us to our seats. We both ordered soda and a meal to share.

"Have I told you that you look beautiful today?"

Lucas asked, cutting the tension.

"No," I shook my head. "No, I don't believe you have."

"Well, remind me, and I'll tell you later!"

I laughed.

"You look beautiful today, as always."

The minutes ticked by with our server bringing only our drinks. I tapped my fingers on the table and noticed Lucas glancing out the window in regular intervals. His glowing eyes concentrated on the outdoors, making the tension between us thick.

"It's getting dark," he mused.

"I think we'll be fine."

"I do, too. It's just that after what Susan said last night..." He paused, chewing on his lip. "Never mind, you're probably right. I've never seen any red glows in town. It's unlikely I'll see one tonight." He turned his attention back to me. I wondered if he really believed what he just said.

"Are we always going to have to be this careful?" I asked, already knowing the answer.

"It's a necessary precaution."

The server arrived and set a full plate of food in the middle of the table with an extra plate. Lucas thanked him.

"Help yourself," he said. "I don't need much."

I, on the other hand, was famished. Lucas ate a few fries and the tomato from the hamburger—I finished the rest in record time.

The restaurant had cleared substantially since we'd first walked in. Lucas placed some money in the black folder on the table and reached for his jacket to put around me.

We walked out into the dark, cold evening. The mist picked up again, this time with a sprinkle of rain. The starless sky hung above us like a blackout curtain. Night had fallen, and my heart raced. Lucas held me close as we started back toward Renae's Antiques.

"Are you coming over later?" I asked, trying to calm myself with words.

"I planned on it, if that's okay?"

"I don't have to work tomorrow, so we can stay up late...or all night, if you want," I said, hoping he'd catch my meaning.

The corner of his lips rose, his dimple sinking deep into his cheek. Then, suddenly, he jerked me hard to the side. Clutching my hand, he stooped and whisked past the stores, dragging me along. He ducked between two closely set buildings, yanking me down with him. Lucas crouched low to the ground.

"What are you doing?"

"Shhhh," he hissed.

He peered around the corner and snapped back.

"What?" I whispered. "What's going on?"

Slowly, he faced me. His intense stare settled directly on me, but he seemed like he saw something else. The hint of terror in his stare didn't escape me.

"Lucas?"

"We need to get to the car," he said as softly as he could.

"Why?" I urged. "Lucas, tell me what's happening."

He shook his head, his eyes squeezed together.

"We don't have much time."

"What's wrong?" I pleaded.

"Demon."

"What?"

"I don't think he saw us."

"What does that mean?"

"I don't know. We must get to Susan's. And fast."

"Can *I* see him?"

Lucas nodded. He peered again, and this time he didn't turn back as fast.

"He's around the corner, on the next street," he murmured. "Listen. We have to get to my car. It's only a half a block away. You can make it."

He dug in his pocket.

"Take these," he said, folding the keys in my hand. "You have to drive. The spell on the car should hold. You'll be able to drive unnoticed—he can't feel you in there. I don't think he'll pay much attention to a random car driving by … I hope."

"Are you coming with me?" I breathed, my mouth going dry.

Lucas cradled my face in his hands. "I'm not leaving without you. Okay? Just get to the car and start driving to Susan's. Do you remember how to get there?"

I nodded too fast.

"Good. I'll tell you when to go. As soon as you get to the car and start it, I'll be there. It'll be okay."

Lucas's hand gripped my shoulders. He pulled me forward and kissed me hard. He peeked around the corner and tugged me closer.

He whispered in my ear. "Walk casually and

whatever you do, don't look behind you. Do *not* make him suspicious. Go. Now!"

On Lucas's command, I crept from the space between the brick buildings. I did as he told me and walked as calmly as possible, fighting the urge to glance over my shoulder.

I hurried to Lucas's car, fiddling with the keys in my hand. The cold metal jingled as I shuffled the keys in the dark, searching for the one to unlock the door. It was quiet, too quiet. The second key slid into the lock and clicked, ringing out into the empty street. I closed my eyes and gulped, my body trembling. My breath cast a white cloud in front of me.

I opened the door, trying not to make noise. I edged it open only far enough to slide behind the wheel. As I did, I saw the outline of a muscular man round the corner a block away. I shifted my eyes to where Lucas was hiding. It was dark, but I didn't think he was there. I fumbled with the keys again as I closed the car door.

I took a deep breath and jabbed the key in the ignition; the car purred to life. I flipped the switch, and the headlights cast a glow on the sidewalk and buildings. The man, dressed in a dark long-sleeve shirt and jeans, was almost to the small breeze-way where we'd been hiding.

Lucas wasn't in the car.

My hands clammed up. Sweat beads formed on my hairline as I watched out the windshield. It wasn't too late. It couldn't be.

"Carrie...Move!...Now!" a voice growled from behind me.

I jerked my head around.

Nothing.

"Go!" Lucas pressed again.

I shifted to reverse and backed onto the street. My eyes blazed forward as the man passed the car on the sidewalk. I held my breath and stepped on the gas hard enough to feel the lurch.

"Damn it."

The man turned his head and looked directly at the car. I felt his stare settling on me.

"Don't worry about it. Just go," Lucas commanded.

I sped the car forward, focused on the road in front of me. Small drops of rain began to plop onto the windshield. Red taillights appeared, and I slammed on the brakes. I rocked forward, almost hitting the car in front of me.

I stole a glance in my rearview mirror. The man was still standing on the sidewalk, watching.

"Hurry. Hurry." I tapped my fingers on the steering wheel.

"Calm down," Lucas rasped out. "Pull out slow."

I moved my foot off the brake and placed my toes on the gas. The car crept forward.

"Lucas?" I said. "Where are you?"

"Trunk."

"Why?"

"No windows."

"Are you okay?"

"I'm fine. You all right?"

"Yes." I didn't recognize my own voice. "We're almost there."

"Look around. Do you see anyone?"

I shifted my eyes, too scared to pivot my head, and scanned the surroundings. All the sidewalks looked empty. The streets were bare. Not a soul in sight.

"I don't see anyone," I responded.

"Good. Park in Susan's driveway, as far back as you can."

I could barely see Mrs. Taylor's house in the distance, two blocks away. I pushed down on the gas a little harder. There was no one in view, but I didn't feel safe—in fact, I was terrified.

Mrs. Taylor had her porch light on as if she were expecting us. I inched into the drive and parked as closely to the garage as I could.

I turned off the engine and the lights and left the keys in the ignition.

"We're here."

"Go to the back door," Lucas instructed. "I'll meet you inside."

I opened the car door and vomited on the pavement. I heaved in a last breath before stumbling out. The back door opened before I had the chance to knock. Lucas stood there with a damp towel.

"You okay?"

"I'm fine," I said, taking the towel.

"You'd better lay down," he said, leading me into the living room. "You're pale."

"I'll get a glass of water," I heard Mrs. Taylor say.

I lay down on the white leather sofa, and Lucas placed a pillow under my head. He placed a blanket over me then bent low, kissing me.

Mrs. Taylor appeared with a tall glass of ice

water and set it on the coffee table in front of me. She took a seat in the same chair she sat in the night before and crossed her legs.

My head spun in circles and the cheery living room with it. The blurs of blues and yellows blended together in a dizzy cloud. I closed my eyes, fighting off the need to throw up again. Lucas positioned himself on the floor, holding my hand.

"Demons are roaming the town," Susan speculated. She paused for a long while. When I opened my eyes, she had a book on her lap. She scanned the words on the page and every so often she'd say, "Hmm."

Lucas broke the silence. "Do they know about Carrie? Are they here for me?"

"I don't know how they *could* know about the two of you," Mrs. Taylor responded, a hint of frustration in her tone. "Demons don't target and hunt down specific spirits. It's more of a 'grab and bag' thing."

"This one was searching for something." His words were rough and serious; I was too scared to look at his face. "Have they ever left the grounds of the house before?"

"The house," Susan mused, shaking her head. "No. It can't be. The house has strong containment spells surrounding it that have held for over a hundred years. They *cannot* leave the house."

"Containment spells? What containment spells?" he asked, letting go of my hand and straightening up. His shoulders tensed.

A spell? Around the Moore House? My mouth went dry. I reached for the glass of water and finished it off.

Susan shifted in her chair. "When the murders happened, a powerful witch who lived in the area put containment spells around the house. The demons were stuck inside."

"So, this demon is from the Moore House?" Lucas asked, running his hands through his dark hair.

Her eyes flitted to the window and back to Lucas. "I don't know. There's always at least a pair. You saw only one?"

"Yeah." Lucas's shoulders fell. We were no closer to figuring out why they were here. The frustration in Lucas's gaze was difficult to miss.

Susan's voice lowered. "There must be another."

"What's the connection with the house and the demons?" I asked, my voice shaking.

Susan shifted her attention from Lucas to me. Her fingers toyed with the corner of the book sitting in her lap. She focused at me for a few seconds, shifted her gaze to the closed window again, then back to me. "Demons, as is their nature, thrive on evil. They prosper, feeding off the malevolence done by humans, gaining strength through our fears and doubts. Murder, in the face of malice, is the ultimate transgression. The place of such a horrendous crime opens up a rift to Hell, allowing demons access to the earth. The more murders committed in one place, the larger the rift. One murder doesn't create a large enough hole for a demon to pass through; there must be at least three. Inside the Moore house, there were eight and six of them children—this is one of the largest rifts in

America." Mrs. Taylor paused as I lifted my head from my pillow. "A containment spell was of absolute necessity. Without it, demons would be running more rampant than they already are, and the majority coming from here."

A rift to Hell. A passageway from the fires to earth was only a hundred yards away from where I sat. From Lucas.

I covered my mouth with my hand and stared blankly at the coffee table. The vision from the attic re-played back in my mind. Screams rung in my ears. I closed my eyes as moisture began to form behind the lids. I was reminded of the souls on fire, trying to claw their way out. How the smell of sulfur burned my insides. Fire crept toward me, ready to consume me.

My eyes shot open. "But you said the spell has held for a century."

"It has." Susan didn't look up from her book. She turned the page and continued to scan. "What if it's been broken?" she mumbled to herself, biting the nail on her index finger. Her eyes moved up and down the next two pages of the book.

"Can't someone cast another?" Lucas asked. "You know, just to make sure."

"Yes, but only by a witch powerful enough to do it. They're difficult to come by. The soonest it can be done is daybreak." Susan still didn't glance up. She stopped flipping through the pages and stared on the words in front of her.

"That's hours away!" I cried.

Susan sighed. "By then it may be too late if they're after you."

"How could the spell have been broken?" I asked, scared to know the answer, but wondering if I already did. The flash of blood and fire returned in vividness to my memory.

"There are a few ways: A reverse spell, but I can't imagine anyone doing that. If there was another murder done in the house after the spell was cast, which hasn't happened. The only other way,"—she paused and shifted her gaze between us several times-"is that the house has been disturbed by another, stronger, supernatural force."

I watched the expression on Lucas's face. His irises shrunk and the muscles in his cheeks relaxed.

"Like what?" I whispered.

Susan bit her lip. A realization slowly emerged in her thoughts. She went back to her book and turned the page. Her index finger moved down each page until she finally looked up.

"Lucas," she started. "Have you and Carrie been in the Moore House at the same time?"

"Sort of."

"When?"

Lucas glanced at me; I stared at the floor. "Um, Carrie decided to go on a tour of the house just over a month ago. She didn't know I followed. I stayed by her the whole time, even in the attic. It was only after she darted from the house that I backed off," he explained.

Susan's shoulders dropped, and her lids closed. "What happened in the attic, Carrie?"

"I saw it." My voice was hoarse and shaky in my ears. "A vision of Hell. I saw flames and blood. I heard screaming." I swallowed. "I saw them: souls, spirits, trapped in fire. Unable to escape. Unable to die."

The room went silent. Only the sound of the clock ticking gave any hint of life. My eyes locked on Lucas's. I wished now I had told him earlier, but I was too scared. Scared that if I said something, he'd somehow become one of those trapped souls.

"The spell broke," Susan said under her breath. She closed her book, placing it on the table beside her. She moved her gaze to the closed curtains, behind which hid the demon-infested house.

"How exactly? By Carrie's vision?"

Susan shook her head. "The vision was just the proof. The spell broke as soon as the two of you set foot inside. Together, you entered a place shining the one thing demons hate above all else. Love. Not just any love. Soul-binding love. Love shared between two people who have connected souls."

Lucas clenched his jaw. "Incenamus."

"By nature, demons do not like being trapped. They're constantly trying to get out."

"Wait." I leaned forward. "How can our love let evil loose? Isn't love stronger than evil?"

"Of course it is, Carrie. But this has nothing to do with good and evil. You see, the power of Incenamus is stronger than that of the containment spell, causing a disturbance in the energy field, and—"

Susan stopped, seeing the confused look on my face. "It's like when you have a cell phone by a microwave. There's a disturbance because one field is stronger than the other. You can hear that disturbance when you're next to the microwave while talking on your phone. Incenamus weakened the field enough for the demons to break through." Susan picked back up her book and handed it to Lucas. "Tonight is the first night you've seen them?"

"Yeah. I guess I haven't been paying much attention lately," Lucas said, taking it from Susan and opening it to where she had marked, reading it.

"They've felt the power between the two of you," Susan said to me. "And now they're hunting you."

"Why? We let them out! Shouldn't they owe us?"

Lucas rubbed my back and chuckled. I turned my head to face him. Even in the insanity of the moment, hearing his laugh brought back a sense of what had become normalcy. "I don't think they think like that. Love is good, so they hate it. They want it destroyed."

"They know it was us?" My throat tightened and goose bumps appeared on my arms.

"They only know what they felt that day. That's what they're searching for—the power between you," Mrs. Taylor said.

Lucas's rough voice sent chills up my spine. "What do we do?"

"You must leave town. Tonight."

Chapter 17

"Tonight?" I cried, heat returning to my body. A rush of adrenaline coupled with a surge of anxiety burst through me at the sound of my own voice.

"Where can we go?" Lucas asked, his tone steady and matter-of-fact.

"It's especially not safe here," Susan said, drawing the rest of the drapes as quickly as she could. "The protective spells can only do so much. They can still find you here. Then we'll all be at risk."

"I'll go," Lucas said to me. "*You'll* be safe here with Susan."

Susan stopped and faced us. "No, she won't, Lucas. Not now." For the first time in the last several minutes, she was calm and collected. "They can feel her now, separate from you. You have to take Carrie out of here, as far away as you can, as fast as you can."

Lucas sighed, his eyes darting around the room, trying to figure out a different solution. He ran his fingers through his disheveled hair and clenched his jaw, tapping his fingers nervously on his thigh.

Finally, he shook his head in dismay. "Okay. Fine. We'll drive to Omaha. It's a large enough city. They won't try anything with an audience."

"You need to go now," Susan warned. "You *must* be careful. The drive won't be safe."

Lucas helped me off the sofa. "Thank you, Susan, for all of your help," he said. We followed her through the kitchen to the back door.

"Be safe. I'll find someone to re-cast the spell as soon as possible. There is a coven of powerful witches in Omaha. I'll try to make contact. Godspeed, Lucas," she said.

Lucas took my hand and pulled me closer. Giving Susan a slight nod before turning to me, he squeezed my hand so tightly it hurt.

"Run to the car. Now!" he commanded.

I shot out the back door with Lucas at my heels. I swung open the driver's door and crawled over the seat to the other side. He was behind the wheel with the door closed and the car started before I was in my seat.

"Buckle up."

I fumbled with the seatbelt. Lucas peeled out of the driveway when the buckle finally clicked. He sped down the road in the opposite direction of the Moore House. My eyes grew wide. I stared out the window, concentrating on nothing but breathing. It was difficult; my whole body trembled. Lucas looked calm—a façade.

"Is he following us?" I asked.

"I don't know. I haven't seen anything," Lucas said, his eyes shifting in every direction.

"Susan said there has to be more than one."

"I've only seen one," he said. "Hang on."

Lucas threw the steering wheel hard to the left and skidded onto Highway 71. The car fishtailed, and the tires squealed. The force slammed me into the passenger door, making me bite the inside of my cheek, then against Lucas as he corrected. I grunted, breathless.

Darkness covered the skies and ground below. The only lights were the ones shining from the car. I stared at Lucas's face—hard and expressionless. Swallowing the blood in my mouth, I reached out to him. He jumped as my fingers made contact.

"I'm sorry," I stammered, jerking back.

"No. I'm sorry," he said, taking my hand in his. He raised it to his mouth and kissed the back of it before letting go.

Voices, even frightened ones, had a less deafening effect. The only sounds, though, were the slow drone of the tires on the pavement. Anxiety coursed through my veins, my leg bouncing on its own.

Lucas kept his eyes forward. "I just need to get you to safety as soon as I can. I hope the coven finds us quickly. I can leave you with them; you'll be safe."

"Where would you go? They can feel you now," I said, more nervous than before. I couldn't bear the thought of not knowing where Lucas would be and if he was safe.

"To lead them away from you."

"No! You can't leave me," I pleaded. "You can't."

"I swore I'd protect you, Carrie. And if that means sacrificing myself for your safety, I *will* do it." His voice was stiff, almost angry.

"You're not the only one who can make decisions, you know," I said, louder than I intended, matching Lucas's tone. "This is my life, too. I have a say. If they get you, they get me, too."

Lucas swiveled his face to me, something that resembled a mixture of fear and anger in his eyes. "Don't. Say. That. I won't let you die because of me. Do you understand? I am *not* going to lose you that way. Not to them!"

I was taken aback by the force of his words. I fell silent and stared out my window. The cornfields passed at unthinkable speeds, but in the dark it was all a blur. I didn't care, though, his senses were unparalleled, and so were his reflexes. I felt safe, even though I knew that if anyone else was driving like a suicidal maniac, I would be freaking out.

"Lucas, there's no guarantee they won't come after me if you…" I let my sentence trail off. I couldn't let them take him. I saw the fire and the souls burning in Hell. He couldn't sacrifice himself for me. There could be no worse fate. For either of us.

I ran my fingers through my hair and held my lower lip between my teeth, fighting back the tears I didn't mean to create. Holding my breath the best I could, I thought about the days before. I thought about our first date, our night under the stars. It hadn't really been that long ago, and it was the night that changed everything for both of us.

Lucas's eyes flitted out each window several

times a minute. His apprehension made mine worse. As I watched him, I noticed his jaw clenching and the muscles in his hands contracting. He was more alive than he realized.

My heart ached for him. He suffered now because he feared for my life. I didn't want him to feel responsible for what was happening, even though I had a striking sensation that was exactly what he thought. Our next play was just as much my choice as his. If death was my fate, I'd take it without regret. It *was* better "to have lived and loved than to have never loved at all." And now, on the brink of death, I loved Lucas more than ever.

"Lucas," I murmured.

He glanced quickly in my direction and then turned his attention back to the road before answering.

"Yeah?"

"I just want to let you know I wouldn't change anything. Being with you has been amazing and something I'll never forget. Thank you for choosing me." My eyes shifted to his hands, gripping the steering wheel.

"Carrie," he said, curving up the corner of his mouth into something resembling a grin. "Don't say goodbye. This isn't the end. I *will* be with you tomorrow."

"I know," I lied. "But I wanted you to know I'd still make the same choices."

"I know you would have," he said, shooting me a half-smile. "And that's one of the many reasons I love you so much. I don't want us to be in this situation any more than I want you to be in danger.

269

But, I also know what you have given me. I wouldn't trade that for anything."

He cradled my hand in his.

"No matter what happens to me tonight, I know you'll be safe. Because you're a part of me, I'll always be with you," he said. "Love never fails, Carrie. You have to believe in us."

He seemed so sure. What if he was wrong? Maybe our love wasn't that strong, like my parents'. Theirs wasn't.

I didn't have the fortitude to dwell on my thoughts, however. Just then, the thunder boomed from behind us. A flash of lightning lit up the sky, and I could see everything around me.

On all sides of the car were endless fields of corn. The sky was black with monstrous clouds hovering over our small vehicle. We seemed so insignificant under the vastness of the storming sky. Small drops of rain hit the windshield, splattering in every direction.

Lucas broke his gaze and sped the car forward.

"He's coming," Lucas said, his voice deep.

"What?" I squeaked. "You can see him?"

"Not yet, but you just saw and heard his fury."

"They can control the weather?" My eyes narrowed, and I threw my head to look out the back.

"If it benefits their goals. He'll use this storm to his advantage."

"How far away is he?" I asked swallowing.

"Not far enough." Lucas slammed his hands on the steering wheel. "Damn it! It's not enough time."

The thunder roared again. Fear gripped at my inner core; he was coming. We were out of time and there was nowhere to hide. In the rainy darkness surrounded by cornfields, Lucas and I would meet our final fate. At least we'd be together. I'd rather die with Lucas by my side than alone.

I felt the car beginning to slow. My heart skipped a beat as I peered at Lucas. His head bowed, and he sat perfectly still.

"Carrie," he said. "You're going to drive now."

"No." I shook my head. "I can't. I can't go that fast."

Lucas pulled over to the gravel shoulder and came to a stop.

"Slide over."

"I can't," I insisted. "Please."

"You have to, Carrie," he replied, something unfamiliar behind his words. "Hurry."

"I can't." I barely heard myself whimper as I slid behind the wheel in the empty seat beside me. He materialized next to me as soon as I was over. I yanked the seat belt across my lap and put the car in gear. We moved forward slowly at first, and as soon as I hit the pavement, I stomped on the gas.

I didn't know what Lucas was thinking, but I had a suspicion I wouldn't like it. Driving in the dark, and in the pouring rain, wasn't my forte. Speeding away from a demon didn't add any less stress.

"Listen," he started. "Drive to Omaha as fast as you can. Drive safely and be careful. As soon as you get there, go downtown. Stay in the lights and around large groups of people."

"Where are *you* going?" I said, understanding I would be doing all of this by myself.

"I'm going to save you."

271

"Please. Please don't leave me," I pleaded.

"I'll always be with you. Always." Lucas stared at me for a few moments before caressing my face.

Tears started falling down my cheeks. "Don't say goodbye."

"I'm not." He paused as if memorizing my face.

"Don't go," I whispered. I wiped the drops from my eyes and turned to face him again; he was gone.

"Lucas?"

No answer.

"Lucas?" I said again, louder.

No answer.

"Lucas! Lucas!" I screamed in terror, my hands shaking at the wheel.

"Lucas!" My voice cracked as I shrieked his name over and over again.

Nothing. I was alone.

Fear paralyzed my body. Besides being chased by an angry demon, I couldn't fathom never seeing Lucas again. He was out there risking his eternity for me. I didn't know if he'd be captured or if, somehow, it was possible he could return to me. The odds were not in our favor.

My body started shaking. The road in front of me disappeared as tears continued to swell and fall from my eyes. With each blink, more escaped. My lips trembled. Everything was dark—the road in front of me and the road behind. There wasn't a star in the sky. I clenched the steering wheel until my fingers hurt. The only sounds were coming from my mouth—my gasps, my sobs, my uneven breaths.

I had no idea if the demon was still after me, but my foot pressed on the gas pedal harder. No matter what, I knew tonight I was going to die. I couldn't outrun the demon. I took comfort in knowing my death would be quick. He had others to hunt. He wouldn't waste his time on me. And if, by some miracle, I *did* survive, Lucas wouldn't. He'd be gone. I'd never hear his sweet voice again. I'd never gaze into his adoring eyes. I'd never touch his soft skin. Lucas would be lost forever. It was *that* death I feared the most, the slow agonizing death I'd be forced to endure if I never saw Lucas again.

Rain fell harder in a steady rhythm. The sound of the drops hitting the car reminded me of how alone I was in the middle of nowhere—just the darkness, the demon, and me. I wondered if I should just get it over with. Pull over to the side of the road, stand in the rain, and wait for the demon to kill me. It would make my inevitable fate much quicker.

Unconsciously, I lifted my foot from the pedal. My hand let go of the wheel to wipe away tears.

What if Lucas could somehow escape, though? I realized the chances were slim, but he was still alive then...

No, I couldn't accept my fate. Not if there was even the tiniest sliver of hope. Lucas had spoken so confidently about us before he disappeared. I couldn't damn him to any eternity where he knew I wasn't alive. He was risking his fate for me, and I wouldn't let him down. And if possible, I would save him. I didn't know how, but maybe this coven of witches would. Determination surged in my mind as I slammed my foot on the gas.

Thunder and lightning crashed above me. It was hard to see through the downpour, but I managed.

The windshield wipers moved rapidly, trying to keep up. I kept my eyes on the road, no use looking behind. If the demon was still there, I couldn't see him anyway.

I thought about what Lucas said about love and about us. I had doubts; love faded all the time. I didn't know what he was talking about—love never fails. But it does fail, doesn't it?

If I believed in us, would love save us? Lucas seemed to believe it. If love could bear this, if it could endure through this, I knew *we'd* make it, even if the bounds of life and death separated us. I took a deep breath, contemplating Lucas's words. '*You have to believe in us, Carrie,*' he'd said.

"Lucas," I said aloud for my own benefit while trying to hold back the sobs. "I have faith in us—in you."

After I said it, I began to believe it. A surge of resolve filled my limbs and spread to the rest of my body. My eyes dried, and I once again concentrated on driving.

Behind me, the thunder rumbled again. A flash of lightning struck the cornfield next to me. I jumped, my head jerking to the right. It was close. *He* was close. I watched in horror as a large tree fell onto the highway just feet behind me. My mouth went dry, and I fought to keep my composure.

Just a few more miles and I'd be in the next town. Even a few minutes of comfort would help my nerves. I pushed on, keeping my eyes on my surroundings.

My mind wandered to Jessica and Stacy, safe in Texas. To my grandparents, who had expected me home at ten. To my parents, clueless about where I was and what I was doing.

I didn't slow when I reached the small town, but I took a couple of minutes to reassure myself and loosen my muscles. It was a long journey; more than half still lay before me.

Back in the darkness, my eyes flashed around, surveying every little detail. There were no lights, not even from the town I just passed through. Nothing lay ahead of me, only trees and cornstalks leaning in the wind.

Small clicks filled my ears as tiny pieces of ice mixed with the rain began to pelt into the windshield. The hail started falling, slowly at first, then picked up as more and more fell from the sky.

I squeezed the steering wheel tighter, and I squinted. I could barely see two feet in front of me. My foot let up on the accelerator. Fear rushed through me, and a chill ran down my spine.

Oh, yeah. *Demons use the weather to their advantage*. Great.

Rain and ice poured down hurricane-style, blinding me.

Suddenly, I slammed on the brakes as a large tree branch swept past the windshield, barely missing the front of the car. Cold stunned my body, and perspiration fell from my brow.

My head jerked to the passenger-side window as small sticks and twigs hit the glass. Hail fell harder, thudding on the roof. Golf-ball sized hail flew toward me.

Another bright flash of lightning lit up the sky.

This time, ahead of me.

I swallowed hard.

Another roll of thunder.

Louder.

Then another.

He was pissed. And he'd found me.

The hail increased in size and banged harder against the windshield until, with one large blow, it cracked. Spider-web lines spread across the windshield, making it virtually impossible to see.

The blurry outline of a tree lying across the road made me squint. It was too late, though. I threw my foot on the brake. The car wrenched and slid; then it started to roll. I'd lost control. There was no denying it now; the demon had won.

I covered my head with my arms, ducking as low as I could. Bracing myself with my legs against the floor, I pushed myself backward against the seat. Windows shattered, and glass flew through the vehicle. My arm scraped against the cement as the car flipped over and over again toward the tree.

Images of Lucas's face flashed through my mind. I smiled. His was the only face I wanted to see as I took my final breaths.

I sucked in a breath as the car collided with the tree. The impact jolted me from side to side, my shoulder smacking against the door. In as tight of a ball as I could pull myself into, I felt my elbow hit something hard twice, and my head bounce before it came to rest on the steering wheel.

I wasn't sure how long the pain would last or how many breaths I had left. My eyes fluttered open and closed again. Blood dripped from my face and my arm. My head was numb, but my elbow hurt like crazy. I couldn't move it.

I took breaths slowly, in and out.

Blinking, I waited for everything to end. In and out.

"I'm sorry, Lucas. So sorry."

In and out.

Rain dripped onto my face, and I shivered, closing my eyes.

In and…

I tried to open my lids again: blurred darkness.

In…

I moaned as I took one final breath in the cold.

And…

Then everything went black.

Chapter 18

The demon saw Lucas above the highway, a bright silver glow in the sky. He growled, his face contorted with hate. Lurching for the ghost, he missed as Lucas moved quickly out of reach.

"Come and get me," Lucas offered, taking off through the air toward Villisca.

From the right, another demon appeared out of nowhere. Both stared at each other for a moment before they howled and shrieked. Their black eyes blazed in vehemence, foreheads creased in a constant scowl. Small and pointed, their nostrils flared with indignation. Their skin resembled stone, and in the blackness, it glowed a deep red.

Lucas glanced over his shoulder. The first demon nodded at the second and took off after Lucas. The second went in the opposite direction.

Damn it!

Anger seized him. This had *to work.*

He took a deep breath and waited for the first demon to get closer. Determined, Lucas led him back to Villisca. The demon stayed close on his heels. They both floated through the night sky flying faster than any vehicle could travel. Lucas looked back frequently, making sure the demon was still following him.

The demon smirked; he was easily gaining on the ghost.

Lucas's face was hard as he pushed with all of his strength through the air. He had to get to there and then go after the second demon. There wasn't much time. Lucas closed his eyes.

He believed in her. If anyone could survive this, she could. He had no intention of going to Hell tonight, or ever for that matter. But he would go under for her, if that's what it took to keep her alive.

Lucas's eyes shot open, drawing closer to his destination. Just a few more miles. He had to stay ahead of the demon, but close enough for the demon to continue pursuing him instead of giving up and turning back. This had *to work. Then he'd go back for Carrie.*

The Moore House loomed in front of him. He could see it clearly now. Susan did her job, he knew. She'd be waiting for him with someone who could fight. Someone who could easily handle the demon who was only feet behind him now.

Lucas urged himself forward.

Closer. Closer.

Every inch made him closer to saving Carrie— his final goal. He could see two green auras shining in the darkness. They glowed behind a group of trees in the back of the house, staying out of sight.

The demon's concentration would only be on

him. It wouldn't be looking for anyone else.

Closer. Closer.

Lucas crossed the property line just as the demon reached for him. Stunned with a blast of yellow light, the demon writhed inside the bubble.

He was contained.

Lucas nodded in the direction of the green glow. The demon shrieked as more flashes of light hit him time after time. Slowly, the demon faded.

With a smile, Lucas closed his eyes and disappeared into the darkness.

***

I didn't know how long I laid in the car, shivering in the cold. It could have been minutes, or hours, or even days for all I knew.

My eyes flickered open. In the dark, with rain splattering against the windshield, I groaned.

What happened?

I stared out what used to be the driver's side window of Lucas's car. The road lay out below me, the sky above, the tree hugging the passenger's door. At least I landed upright.

The air bag had deployed, and my cheek was lying against what was left of it. Both of my arms draped above my head holding each other loosely.

I didn't want to move; it hurt to breathe. I blinked several times as I stared out the window, afraid to lift my head. Flashbacks of the tree lying across the highway enveloped my mind. The sound of the car rolling and smashing into the massive trunk echoed in my ears, making me wince. When I hit it, I blacked out, and Incenamus had taken over my consciousness, transporting me into Lucas's mind.

I didn't know what the vision meant, but I knew I was still in danger. If the other demon still wanted me, he'd come back. He'd set this trap hoping it would kill me. Lucas said they made deaths look like accidents. I had to move. Now.

Joke's on you, demon. I'm still alive.

My hand went directly to the pain on my forehead, just above my eye. It felt wet and sticky—blood. I groaned; my whole body ached. After wiping my brow with my forearm, I noticed that it, too, was covered in blood.

I shifted around in the seat, cringing with every movement. Most of my body parts were surprisingly free, except for a leg crushed under the dashboard. Pounding up the plastic, I managed to shift myself enough to be mobile. Without the extra weight on my thigh cutting off the circulation to my lower extremities, the shock of tiny razors shooting through my veins immobilized me for a moment. I maneuvered around the limp air bag and steering wheel, fumbling for the door handle. It wasn't easy; I was disoriented. When I found it, I tugged and tried to push the door open; it didn't move.

I took a painful, heaving breath and slammed at it again using whatever body weight I could. It wasn't much, and my shoulder hurt like hell, but the door finally swung open. I held still for a few moments waiting for the sting to subside. It lessened only slightly. I didn't have time to wait it out.

I stepped on one leg and pulled the other with my hands, unsure of its steadiness. Clutching a hold of the door jamb, I scooted forward and lifted myself up. As my weight pushed into the pavement, daggers shot through both legs. I gasped and held my breath, falling back into my seat.

The rain let up, but the brisk wind made my muscles tighten. I wrapped my hands around my neck, massaging the muscles. My eyesight blurred, and I had to grab onto the steering wheel to keep my balance from the dizziness that swept over me.

Everything around me looked hazy all blurred together. From what I could make out, I was still alone...for now. I had to make a run for it, and the cover of darkness wouldn't be enough. The cornfields were full of stalks reaching higher than my head. I made for them, the one shot I had.

Panic struck, and my body shook in fear. This was it. Making it to Omaha wasn't going to happen. The only thing I could do now was try to survive until daylight. I didn't know how long I had.

I put my hands on the seat, on either side of my body, and pushed with all of my strength. Pain rushed through me like a crushing wave. I held back the screams as I made it to my feet, clinging to the mangled car door for balance. My head spun, and my eyes blurred again. I felt exposed out in the open. Knowing I didn't have time to stop at every excruciating movement I made, I took a step forward. At this pace I'd die for sure. I had to suck it up and fight through the torture.

I used the car for support as I walked around it, holding my left arm against my body. The thunder and lightning had both stopped. Looking around, the eerie silence of absolutely nothing invaded my senses, increasing the dread.

As I let go of the car, I wobbled and fell to the ground. My hand hit the pavement hard, and I heard my wrist pop.

"Damn!"

I snapped it up and twirled it in a circle. Ignoring the pain, I took a deep breath and picked myself back up.

The field wasn't too far, but under the light of the moon, I noticed a fence running the perimeter between the embankment and the corn. I staggered across the street.

I lurched forward to the gravel shoulder. My body reminded me with each step that death would be easier, less painful. I couldn't give in. As I stepped onto the wet grass, I slipped and landed on my side, rolling down the bank to the ditch below. Reeds broke my fall and scratched up my arms.

I cried out, tasting the blood in my mouth.

A dull pang flowed in my left ankle. I sat up, rubbing it. Hopefully, it was just sprained. No matter. I crawled on my hands and knees over the puddles of water in the ditch, making my way to the fence.

Rust caked the metal lines giving them a burnt orange color. I grabbed a hold of one of the barbed wires, trying to separate them enough to crawl between; they didn't budge. Lowering myself slowly, I groaned; they were also too low to slip under.

I guess I'll have to climb over it.

The fence came up to my chest. I gasped as I used one of the rotted-out wooden posts to help me to my feet. I stepped my less-injured foot onto the lowest wire and used the post to heave myself upward. Leftover from the crash, my disoriented sense of balance teetered. Grabbing for anything I could, I steadied myself on each line as I climbed. Luckily the wires held my weight. At the top, I swung my leg over the last strand of metal, securing it on the rung beneath. I turned my body and walked my other leg over. Then, on the wet wire, my foot slipped and I fell backward, landing with a hard thud on my back.

Heaving for air, I clutched my chest. I rolled onto my stomach and lay on the ground, clenching the dirt between my fingers. The world began to spin around me. I wanted to scream, but my body lacked the necessary oxygen.

I can't be defeated like this. Get up! Get up!

I pushed my knees under me and put all of my weight on my hands. My left forearm and ankle screamed out in painful protest. I fell back onto my stomach and laid there with my face in the mud. Air returned to my lungs in small gasps. Shaking, I forced myself to my knees, trying to use my hands as little as possible. I climbed to my feet, grabbing onto a corn stalk. It shifted at my weight, and I tumbled back to the ground. I laid there for a few moments, shaking in the cold. I was getting nowhere.

I lifted my head to the sky and closed my eyes.

Water. I need water.

My mouth opened as tiny drops of rain—not

nearly enough—fell inside. I swallowed what I could before trying again to stand. This time, I only depended on myself for support. Tensing my whole body, I used my wobbling arms to tilt myself back onto my heels. Then I sunk my fingers into the mud and walked my hands back to my feet.

"Ahh," I groaned as my back cracked.

I took a few limps forward into the stalks. With each step, I used the corn to steady myself. It wasn't a lot of help, but it was the only thing I had. The uneven ground made it difficult to walk, though walking wasn't nearly fast enough. I pivoted to look behind me. I could still make out the outline of the car; I wasn't far enough into the field.

I limped faster, hobbling over the mud and puddles. Once again, my eyes blurred and my head started to spin. Dead quiet and shadows squeezed in from all sides.

"Lucas," I whispered into the darkness. "I need you."

He wasn't there, but I had hope. Hope that he was on his way.

I concentrated on moving forward, watching my feet as I walked. With each step, the pain in my ankle increased. I wondered when it would give out.

One foot in front of the other. One step at a time.

Behind me, the frame of the car began to fade. I moved deeper into the field, hidden from the road behind me.

The rain began to pick up, getting heavier. I wished it would let up again, but I wished in vain. The farther I hobbled into the field the faster it fell. Surrounded by corn, I pushed myself to walk quicker.

Then I heard it: Thunder. Loud thunder.

Terror returned, and goose bumps spread across my body. It sounded far away, though getting closer.

I had to move—like, now! I wiped the water out of my face. My being alive would be easily proven when the demon reached an empty car in the middle of the highway. After that, he'd just have to concentrate before he'd feel me and follow me into the fields. I was no longer alone.

"Lucas," I cried. "Hurry."

I picked up the pace. My thighs protested as I lurched myself further into the field. Air filled my lungs, burning them behind my ribs.

Rain poured in heavy sheets now, stinging my skin. Lightning flashed in the sky, illuminating the endless rows of corn. All of a sudden, claustrophobia set in. Stalks began to push in on me; I couldn't see an end to them.

I gasped for air and my walk turned into a jog. The adrenaline that had been filling my veins cleared my vision, setting a clear path through the corn. I had to move faster.

Survival mode took over. With more effort than my body had, I began to run, no longer aware of any pain. The ground sloshed beneath my feet. I tripped several times, but remained standing, grabbing corn stalks to maintain balance. The wind blew harder. I didn't know what lay beyond the corn, or even if I'd make it that far.

Another flash of lightning.

Yes, he was getting closer.

BOOM!

Deafening thunder pounded in my ears. The demon was livid. I pushed myself harder, cornstalks cutting my arms as I ran.

More lightning.

I could still see only corn in front of me. I sprinted, throwing the cornstalks off to the side as I thrust myself onward.

Slash of lightning.

Ear-splitting thunder.

He was right behind me now. It would be soon. He could easily overtake me. And then what? What would he do? How would he finish me out here?

The wind howled, and the swish of the cornstalks rushed past me as I dashed through them. The cold burned my muscles.

With the next flash of lightning, I flew forward, landing face-first into the cold wet mud. I bit my lip as I toppled to the ground. Blood began to trickle down my chin. I was out of breath and out of energy. Everything went fuzzy again.

I stopped moving, lying on the ground. Energy drained from my body. It was over. I just wanted it to end. I took a few deep breaths, sucking in water and mud.

No! No! Lucas is coming.

Grunting, I forced myself up. Back on my feet, I staggered again through the field. My head throbbed under the cut. More blood trickled down my face. As it slipped over my lips, the bitter taste made me wince.

I coughed out dirt and started running again. Somehow, if I could only stay far enough ahead of the demon, maybe it would give Lucas enough time to reach me. I didn't know how he could save me, but having him near as we both died would be enough.

I pushed past the stalks, heaving my body forward in the sheets of falling rain and hail. At last, I made out the edge of the field in front of me. Beyond the field was a massive blur of shapes I couldn't make out.

I squinted as lightning filled the sky.

Trees.

A forest ballooned up less than a hundred feet in front of me. The cluster looked thick, but I didn't know if it would be enough cover. My choices lacked: either make for the woods or run in circles in the cornfield.

I sidestepped through the last few stalks of corn as the woods loomed before me. The rain hurt my skin less under the canopy of trees. In here, though, I'd have to watch my step more closely. I didn't know how many more tumbles I could afford before I stayed down.

The cackle of corn underfoot interrupted my thoughts. I froze, gulping.

Crunch. Crunch.

He's here!

Darting for the cover of trees, I stepped over logs, branches, and roots, my eyes searching for which direction would be the most concealing.

No. NO!

Everywhere looked the same. I shook violently, the cold already consuming me.

I stopped and glanced around a dark forest in the

dead of night—alone.

Only, I wasn't alone. The demon was closing in.

My breathing slowed, and I stared at the ground then up to the tops of the trees. Everything would end here. I still clung to the tiny sliver of hope it would end in my favor.

White clouds billowed from my mouth with each exhale. I took a few deep breaths before trudging deeper between the trees. My legs struggled to move, the icy air making my muscles rigid. As my eyes rolled back, a hand grabbed a hold of my shoulder from behind.

I let out a blood-curdling scream and flung myself forward. He'd caught me. Game over. The demon was here.

The cool hand clasped over my mouth, stifling my screams. Unable to run any more, I closed my eyes and fell to my knees.

The voice followed me to the ground. "I'm here, Carrie. I'm here."

Arms enveloped me and lifted me off the ground. I couldn't bear opening my eyes to the demonic face I knew I'd see. My mind flashed images of Lucas, and that was all I wanted to remember as death folded over me.

The arms held me tighter. In the cold air and coolness of the skin holding me, somehow it felt warmer. Safer. Lips pressed hard against my bleeding mouth, and my eyes shot open.

I gasped and threw my arms around Lucas's neck.

He's here. Lucas is safe.

He smiled.

"Lucas," I breathed.

His eyes wandered over me, catching sight of the blood flowing down the side of my face. Lines in his brow deepening, he wiped the crimson away, swearing. "He's almost here," Lucas said, setting me on my feet. "Can you stand?"

"I think so." A renewed sense of energy filled me.

"We need to go deeper into the forest," he instructed. "We need to find a clearing. We'll be easier to find."

"What?"

Is this a demonic trick to get me to follow him?

"Come on. There's only one now." Lucas took my hand and pulled me along.

I swallowed, debating whether or not to follow, but he already had a hold on me.

We trekked over the forest floor, Lucas never releasing my hand.

A strip of silver flashed through the sky.

We both looked up to see it strike a large maple directly in front of us. Lucas yanked me to his side and jumped out of the way just as it fell to the ground, barely missing us.

"He's *really* pissed off now," Lucas said, helping me up. "We're together now, and *he's* the one alone."

"What happened to the other one?"

"Sent back to Hell where he belongs," Lucas said. "You okay?"

I nodded.

"We need to keep moving. Come on." He grabbed my hand again, and we continued through the trees.

The thunder growled above us. The demon was right on top of us, and I didn't know why Lucas was leading us somewhere we'd be easier to find.

"Look out!" Lucas screamed, pushing me to the ground. He flung himself over me, covering me with his body as large branches fell from the trees above us. Thumping onto Lucas's back, they vibrated through him. I held my breath, feeling the beats against my back.

Buried beneath the pile, Lucas groaned. Losing some concentration, he evaporated into transparency for a second before regaining control.

"Sorry," he muttered.

He lifted one of his hands and shoved the branches away. One by one, he moved enough to create a hole for me to crawl through.

"Go," he instructed.

He lifted himself up, and I crawled on my elbows. I clenched my teeth together as my elbow dug into the ground. The cut opened, and fresh blood eased out. Cleared from the pile, I staggered to my feet. Lucas materialized next to me.

"Keep moving," he said, taking my hand and tugging me forward. "We need to keep him chasing us."

I stumbled forward, trying to stay on my feet. None of what Lucas said made any sense. My vision started to fail again and dizziness took over. I didn't have the energy to be paranoid.

I lost my balance and fell to the ground, scraping my skin. Without a word, Lucas picked me up and continued the journey with me in his arms.

Everything spun in a blur of blackness. I dug my face into Lucas's shoulder.

"We're gonna make it, Carrie. We're gonna make it."

He ran—or floated—carrying me, until suddenly, he thrust me through the air. I landed hard on the ground, feet away from where Lucas laid facedown. I turned my head to see him scrambling to his feet. As though he slipped on a sheet of ice, he plummeted back down on his stomach. One of his legs outstretched behind him, it rose up in the air on its own. He tried to fight free, kicking behind him.

"Run, Carrie!" he screamed. "Run! Go!"

Frozen, I watched the demon solidify into the brute man we'd seen on the town square. An evil grin on his face, he pulled Lucas by the ankle toward him. The shrill laughter rising from the demon burned my ears.

Lucas's hands dug into the ground, his body wiggling in agony. He fluttered in and out of transparency as his concentration began to fade. He glared up at me, his eyes glowing a deep, dark green.

"Run!" he screamed again.

I stood up and started backwards, my eyes glued on Lucas and the way he struggled against the demon. Tears swelled in my eyes. I was losing him, and there was nothing I could do.

"RUN!"

Lucas's voice invigorated me. When the demon finished with Lucas, he would come for me, and Lucas's destruction would be for nothing. I swung around and began to run through darkness.

Without warning, I stumbled forward. As I fell, I glanced back to Lucas, needing to see him one last time.

Nothing.

He must've disappeared down to the fires of Hell. My head hit something cold and hard; blackness engulfed me.

***

I moaned when I heard footsteps approaching. My eyes fluttered but refused to open. I swallowed the blood pooling in my mouth, waiting for the demon to take me just as he took Lucas. I wouldn't fight him; I had no fight left.

The footsteps stopped abruptly above my head.

Yes, my struggles were over. My life would end quickly. I sucked in my last breath of fresh air. Even happy endings end, and this was mine. I held my breath as I awaited the demon's grip.

Instead, two people began speaking words that I didn't understand.

Daemon Tenebrae
Audi vocationis vestrae
Vade revertere ad umbras
Ubi tu pertinent
Expectat Infernus Te,
Semel pro semper
Daemon Tenebrae
Cadetis...

I forced my eyes open. Yellow light sprayed over

my head. Beyond me, it encircled a shadow. Terrible screams filled the night. The demon shrieked inside the ball of light, fighting for his life. Minutes passed and the brightness began to fade away. I tried desperately to keep my eyes open.

Lucas, are you there?

I struggled, but my lids gave in. I saw nothing more.

Chapter 19

"She doesn't look good," I heard a familiar female voice say.

"She's been through a lot tonight," Lucas's voice answered.

Lucas! Lucas!

I screamed his name in my head, but I couldn't get the words past my lips.

"We can take her back to my house. Mom may be able to heal her," the first voice replied.

"Good idea. Fewer explanations," Lucas agreed.

"We need to make for the clearing. She'll be waiting for us there when she's finished cleaning the mess on the highway."

I groaned and tried to move. Pain shot down my torso and into my legs. My neck stiffened. Somehow, I managed to turn it a little in the direction of the voices.

"Lucas," I managed. "Lucas."

I wasn't sure if the words were recognizable or just mumbling sounds. I coughed, and my lungs tightened. The taste of blood in my throat made me gag.

His hand squeezed mine. "I'm here," he said. "Try not to move."

I forced a giggle, clenching my hand over my stomach. "Easy for you to say."

Lucas puffed a laugh, his adorable dimple flashing me in my mind.

He stroked my hair, combing through the wet mess with his fingers. I struggled to raise my hand to his face. My lids fluttered when I tried to force them open. His face was blurry, but I could make out some of his features, especially his eyes.

Yes, he was *real*.

I touched his cheek, trying to focus on it. Choking, I grimaced from the stitch in my ribs. My vision stabilized on him.

A deep sense of relief filled me. I knew what I had seen; the demon dragging Lucas into the abyss. But *somehow* he was here. I wanted to jump with excitement into his arms, but my body refused.

He'd been right—love had endured.

I caressed his face like I was touching him for the first time. Lucas's soft, smooth skin against my hand was all the comfort I needed. I shifted on the ground and contorted my face as I held back a groan. The pain soared, and my body drowned in it.

"We need to go, Lucas," the girl said.

I'd forgotten we weren't alone. I squinted as I tried to see through the darkness to the figure standing behind him. I thought there were two women, but now I only saw one. And I *barely* saw her. Although there was something about her I recognized, I just couldn't figure it out. She wore a dark hooded cape with her hood covering her face. Auburn hair flowed past her shoulders.

"I'm going to carry you," Lucas said.

I nodded, turning my attention back to him. I took a deep breath as I waited for him to lift me.

He bent low to the ground and slipped one hand behind my knees and the other around my back. I squeezed my eyelids shut, anticipating the lift.

"Ahh!" The wail came out involuntarily.

"I'm sorry," he whispered.

I wrapped my arms around his neck, burrowing my face in his shoulder.

"This way," the female voice instructed. "We must hurry."

Lucas followed the girl to the outskirts of the woods. I clung to him, my eyes never leaving his face. He grinned down at me, his loving smile reassuring me.

The trees around me faded out of focus, and my skin became numb to the drizzle of rain. Yes, I was in Lucas's arms where I belonged. We were safe; the demons were gone.

When Lucas stopped, I looked around. A circular clearing surrounded us. The sky opened up above us and the mist fell unobstructed to the surface below. I wiped my face with the back of my hand.

"She's awake," a new female voice noted.

"Yes," said the girl. "She's in a lot of pain."

"At least she's conscious. That's a good sign," the first voice replied. "I can take care of the cuts later. Lucas, I'm sending you and Carrie back to our house. Put Carrie on the sofa, and give her plenty of fluids. She's probably dehydrated, and I don't want her going into shock. We'll be there after the sun rises. The containment spell shouldn't take long to replace."

My eyelids began to fall against my will as I heard a soft chant wafting in the breeze. I saw Lucas nod at the woman and say something I couldn't hear. The voices chanting slowly dissolved, and I saw a bright flash of light. Instantly, warmth and dryness engulfed me.

I had difficulty making anything out through the haze. Lucas laid me on a blanket of spongy cushions, then he disappeared. He returned seconds later, handing me a glass of water. I took it and sipped.

"You need to drink all of it, Carrie," he instructed. "I'll be right here." He paused. "I'm not leaving."

I took another sip. "Lucas, what happened?"

"Later. Right now, you need to rest."

"Where am I?"

"You're safe, just as I promised. Drink," he urged.

I took a longer drink this time. The mud in my mouth started to dissolve, replaced by the refreshing coolness of the water. I sighed and took another drink. I handed the empty glass back to Lucas.

"I'll get you more," he said, and took off for the kitchen.

The sofa felt comfortable under me, unlike the hard ground in the woods. The warmth of the room made me drowsy, and my lids began to fall again.

Exhaustion overtook me; I didn't try to fight it this time.

Lucas is safe.
I fell asleep before he returned.

***

When I awoke, sunlight poured in through the large windows in the unfamiliar living room. I tried to sit up, but it hurt so much to move. My hand flew instinctively to my forehead.

The cut was gone.

I frantically felt my face and then my elbow. No blood, no gashes. Had everything just been a terrible nightmare?

The empty room contained two ivory armchairs on opposite ends of a light green rug. The coffee table in front of the sofa was home to a beautiful arrangement of roses, half a dozen magazines, and a full glass of ice water—probably for me. A fireplace stood at the far end of the room with a white mantel holding various pictures. Over the mantel hung a large painting of black roses.

I reached for the glass and gulped down the water in one swig. Voices wafted in from another room, but I couldn't make out what was being said. They didn't sound angry, just talking. Laughing?

I shifted on the sofa and let out a small moan of pain. My body stiffened and wanted nothing more than to be still.

Footsteps sounded from the adjacent room. Glancing up, I saw Lucas walking toward me, perfect and whole. I smiled until my cheeks hurt.

"Good morning." As he came closer, I could smell his clean fresh scent, so much nicer than the muddy stench I smelled on myself. "How are you feeling?"

"Better, I think," I said, trying again to sit up.

He hurried to my side, placing two pillows behind my back to prop me up. Then he sat at my feet, lifting my legs onto his lap.

"What time is it?" I asked.

"Almost two," he replied. "You've been out since four-thirty this morning."

"Where am I?" I whispered scanning the room again.

"You are at Vanessa Miller's house."

Miller?

I shook my head, unable to place the name. "Who?"

"Megan's mother."

My eyes widened. "Megan? From the store?"

"One and the same."

"Why? Do they know about us? About what happened?" I said quietly just in case anyone else happened to be within earshot.

"Yes, they know. They saved our lives last night," he explained.

My head swam in confusion. I searched my memory, trying to pull up all the events from the night before. There was one demon at first. Lucas and I were on our way to Omaha, to a coven of witches. But then Lucas left, and I was alone. Then what?

The memories came flooding back, almost engulfing me like waves. None of them were good, but I didn't fight it.

"You left me. I kept driving...I knew nothing. I

didn't know if he was still after me or whether you were all right." Tears swelled in my eyes. "You didn't even say goodbye. I didn't know what to do. I couldn't breathe. I couldn't…"

"I'm so sorry, Carrie. There wasn't enough time to explain. It was the only way to save you," Lucas said, pushing a lock of my hair to the side.

"I was so scared. A tree fell into the road behind me, and I knew he was there to kill me. I thought he'd already gotten you." I swallowed. "I thought I was going to die. When I opened my eyes, my head and my arm were bleeding."

I looked over at Lucas for an explanation as I touched my head. He caressed my face with his hand, his fingertips tracing the areas where the cuts used to be.

"Vanessa healed it," he said.

"Healed it? How?"

"I'll let her explain. It's not my story to tell."

I dropped my hand and continued with my thoughts, shifting my gaze back to the floor. I told him about the car accident and how I made my way through the field and into the forest where he found me.

"I told you I'd see you today. I didn't break my promise, did I?" Lucas said, stroking my hair.

"No. You didn't. But…"

Lucas moved to cradle me in his arms, holding me close. It still hurt—the memory of losing him. I didn't want to ever feel like that again. As Lucas held me in his arms, I wanted him to keep me there forever.

We stayed in our embrace, thankful for each

other. I held him as tightly as I was able. It wasn't long enough, though. He pulled back and ran his fingers through my hair.

"I'm sorry it took me so long to get to you," he murmured. "You don't know how relieved I was when I found you after I saw the car. It was important for us to find a clearing. That made it easier for Megan and Vanessa to find us. We didn't make it, so it took longer. Vanessa found us just in time."

"I heard them in the forest," I recalled. "Megan and Vanessa."

"Yes," he said. "They sent the demon back to the shadows. The rift is contained. We can never go back into the house."

I half-smiled. "Like I ever want to."

Lucas grinned. "Yeah, me neither."

I laid my head back on the pillow and closed my eyes. Lucas pulled the blanket back over me. I could feel his cool hands on my cheek and in my hair. His lips delicately brushed mine. I smiled, opening my eyes to drink him in one more time. He sat on the floor at my side, his face soft, his eyes narrowed slightly. He leaned over me and kissed me. The kiss was light but lasted. Maybe Lucas didn't want to let me go just as much as I didn't want him to.

"Rest," he whispered.

I nodded and closed my eyes again, still feeling his presence next to me for the next few minutes. Then I felt him stand up.

"I've got some stuff to take care of. I'll be back soon."

"Can't it wait?" I mumbled, drowsy.

Lucas hesitated. "Unfortunately, no."

He brushed the back of his hand over my cheek, and suddenly, it was gone. When I peeked, the room was empty. Sleep threatening to engulf me, I closed my eyes again.

I relived the whole thing in my dreams, like a 4D movie. Pain bit into me over and over again.

Then, like a bullet, it hit me. Together, we'd always be running. Always be fighting for our lives. Next time, we may not be this lucky.

The look on Lucas's face as the demon held him flashed through my mind. So did the souls in the fiery pits in Hell. Lucas had come so close, trapped in the demon's grip. His screams would forever haunt me.

I was only human after all—weak and vulnerable. If it had been just him last night, he could have gotten away from the demons easily. He'd have disappeared and reappeared somewhere far away; he wouldn't have had to come back for me.

This was too dangerous. I rolled over to face the back of the sofa and covered my face with the blanket. Lucas couldn't be held down by me. Now it was my turn to make the difficult decision. In two weeks, I'd go back home to Texas. Back to life without Lucas. That was the way it was supposed to be. The way it *had* to be.

My heart already hurt. I had to make him see that this was the best way. I would be safer, too, and I knew he wanted that for me. He'd continue his journey and find his soul, and cross over to the next life where he belonged. It was the right thing to do.

Tonight was the night Lucas and I would say goodbye forever.

Chapter 20

My lashes fluttered open. Lucas sat perched on the arm of the sofa at my feet. Megan relaxed in one of the ivory-colored armchairs with her legs tucked under her. A woman with coal-black hair, cut chin-length with wisps of bangs hanging over her forehead—Vanessa, I assumed—sat cross-legged in the other. She had large dark eyes, practically black. Absolutely stunning.

They were discussing the weather—of all things.

"It's been a while since we've had a storm that rough," Vanessa said.

"The basement flooded again," Megan said. "I tried another concealment charm on the cracks, but as usual, it made it worse. I think I may have created a waterfall down there."

"I'll bet it's very pretty," her mother joked.

Lucas snickered.

"Don't worry, you'll get it eventually." Vanessa patted her daughter's arm.

"I still don't see why you can't do it," Megan said, glaring at her mother.

"You know I gave up practicing magic."

"What about last night?"

"That was different. It was an emergency," Vanessa said. "Besides, what would your father think if the basement was suddenly fixed?"

"That you hired someone to come and fix it."

"For free?"

"Oh, come on, Mom!" Megan said. "Haven't you kept this a secret from Dad long enough?"

"Megan, your father would have a heart attack if he knew. Besides, there's nothing to tell. I don't do magic anymore," Vanessa reasoned. "So, the next time it rains, you get to practice on the basement again."

"What are you going to do when I'm at college?"

"I'm sure I can conjure up some buckets for your father and me." Vanessa giggled. "Or we can leave it for you when you get back. We'll just have a nice swimming pool in the basement."

Megan rolled her eyes. "I hate rain."

Lucas laughed. I loved his laugh.

I chuckled slightly and watched as three heads popped in my direction. I blushed.

"Hey, Carrie," Megan said.

Lucas stood and helped me up, replacing the fluffed pillows behind my back. "Hey there, beautiful," he whispered in my ear before taking the cushion next to me.

So close to me, our thighs touching, warmth instead of coolness engulfed me. I sucked in a breath, feeling sorry for him. I was going to break his heart, and he had no idea.

"How do you feel?" Vanessa asked.

"Still sore," I said. "But better."

"Good," Vanessa replied. "The soreness will linger for a few days. You had a few broken bones and three fairly deep cuts, which all healed beautifully."

I nodded. "Uh, thanks for that."

"I'm sure we'd all have to answer to Rob and Renae if we took you back looking like you'd been in a boxing match."

Rob and Renae—Grandma and Grandpa! I had completely forgotten about them. What did they think? Did they know I didn't come home last night?

I shot a stare at Lucas, my mouth gaping.

"Don't worry, Carrie," Megan said. "They don't know anything. I made sure this morning. I told them you were staying here for dinner tonight, and we were going to go see a movie. They're not expecting you until late, after they've gone to bed."

"What about my car?"

"Already taken care of," Megan replied. "It's in our driveway. Besides, I think you owe Lucas a new one."

Lucas shook his head and smirked. "That reminds me, Megan, I'm going to need a new car. Can you conjure me up a '67 Corvette? Red, preferably."

"Sure thing," Megan said, her voice dripping in sarcasm. "I'll get right on that. *After* I fix the basement."

"You're..." I paused, finally putting it all together. "You're a witch, aren't you?"

How did I miss that one?

Megan chuckled. "Yes. I'm sorry for being so secretive. As you can see, it's necessary."

"Our family has lived in Villisca for generations," Vanessa said. "We were here in 1912 when the Moore family was murdered. My grandmother cast the original containment spell around the house. After her death, my mother watched over the house. She placed more protective charms on it over the years. Overseeing the house, protecting others from it, is the job that has fallen to me. When I am gone, the duty will go to Megan."

"I'm not very powerful," Megan stated. "Our powers grow as we use them. When Mom married my dad, she vowed never to use her powers again. We were cut off from the family—or most of them. So my powers are not well developed."

"I wasn't even sure if she had any as I married someone without magical powers. But, when Megan turned thirteen, she started showing signs of magic. Most witches and warlocks begin training their children from birth; Megan didn't start until she was a teenager," Vanessa explained.

"Is marrying an ordinary human forbidden or something?" I asked.

"No. But giving up your powers is frowned upon. Most who marry non-magics let them in, not keep them out. I kept Kevin out because I wanted an ordinary life. I said I'd watch the house to try and make amends with the family," Vanessa said.

"I want to be trained, though," Megan cut in. "Mom did all she's willing to do. I'm going to Iowa City for college and training there with my aunt."

"Why would anyone care if you give up your

powers?" I wondered.

"Because our family, the Pouvoirs, is among the oldest and most powerful magical families alive today. There are very few of us left," Vanessa explained. "Megan and I are Fey witches, meaning we're clairvoyant. There are others with different powers. Telepaths can read the thoughts or feelings of others, Precogs can see the future, Recogs can see the past, and Healers can heal with the touch of their hands—much more than what I did."

"I never realized. I mean, I always knew psychics existed, but I never knew they were this advanced," I said.

Megan rolled her eyes in disgust. "The psychics you know are one of two things. They are either complete frauds or witches who don't know they are. Their abilities are untrained."

"I thought you said most are trained from the day they're born?"

"There are some whose knowledge has left the family line. They don't know they have powers," Vanessa said.

"My dreams," I muttered, piecing things together little by little.

It was Megan I saw in my dreams—Megan, who tried to convince Lucas to leave. *She* was the one who didn't want us together. Megan didn't want me to know about her, afraid of being exposed. Yet it was Megan who saved our lives.

"How long have the two of you known each other?" I asked, glancing at Lucas.

"The day I first appeared to you at your grandma's store, I saw her green aura and knew.

That's why she left the room. She saw me for who I was and thought I was there to ask a favor of her. Many ghosts do that of witches. When I went to you, she sensed something else was going on. She didn't want to be involved," he said.

"Why?"

Megan opened her mouth to answer, but Lucas cut in. "For you." He laced his fingers through mine. "She wanted to protect you. She thinks I am being selfish for wanting to be with you, and she's right. She kept an eye on you, especially while I was away." He paused as he stroked my hand.

"I'm sorry for all the secrets," Megan murmured. "I thought keeping you two apart was the best thing for both of you." She paused. "I was wrong."

"It's over now," Lucas said.

"Yeah...over," Megan mumbled to herself.

I frowned. "What about the other dreams? The ones with only you at the Moore House?"

Megan pressed her lips together, her eyelids squeezing shut.

"You inserted yourself in her dreams?" Vanessa glared at her daughter.

Shifting uncomfortably in her chair, Megan met her mother's eye.

"More like nightmares," I grumbled under my breath.

Vanessa rose to her feet. "Megan Elizabeth Miller!"

"Well...I...it was to..." Megan stammered.

Her mother placed her hands on her hips. "You know what happens to witches who meddle with fate."

"I was trying to warn her. It was subtle," Megan turned to me. "Wasn't it?"

"Um, yeah. I never did figure it out," I answered, wishing I could disappear and materialize somewhere else like Lucas.

A buzzing noise sounded in the kitchen.

"We will talk about this later, young lady," Vanessa said before heading off to the kitchen to turn off the timer.

Megan slumped into the chair.

"Sorry," I said.

"That's all right. She'd have figured it out anyway. I'm shocked it took her so long."

"So, you can invade people's dreams but you can't fix a crack in the basement wall?" I asked partly teasing.

"Oh, well, dream magic is easy. Burn some DNA with a cluster of poppies and there you go. Concealing a leak, however, that's something else entirely!"

"Wait," I said, sitting up a little, the pain still throbbing in my ribs. "How did you get my DNA?"

Megan crinkled her nose. "I may have taken some of your hair from the hairbrush I found in your bag."

"Seriously?"

The cautious grin on Megan's face almost made me laugh.

"Even?" she asked hopefully with the same goofy expression.

I sighed, glancing up at Lucas. Trying unsuccessfully to keep a straight face, he shrugged.

"Deal," I agreed. "I don't want you to turn me

into a toad or something."

Megan nodded. "You seem to have a lot of faith in my abilities. I'm not Merlin you know."

Vanessa called us in for dinner, and Lucas helped me to my feet. I wobbled slightly.

"Whoa, there!" Lucas steadied me. "Here, I'll carry you."

"No," I said too quickly.

His brows narrowed a little.

"I mean, I can manage. Just … just hold my hand." I refused to meet his gaze.

After dinner, Megan, Lucas, and I went back to the living room. Lucas tucked me back on the sofa, my head resting on his lap. Megan popped in a movie and sat in one of the ivory armchairs. I relaxed, wishing to freeze the moment.

With no such luck, time continued to tick forward. As soon as the sun had set and the stars shone brightly in the clear night sky, a lump formed in my throat. It was time to go home, and I only had a couple hours left with Lucas.

Vanessa met us at the door to say good night.

"Thank you again for all that you've done," I said, standing by Lucas's side.

"It was my pleasure, Carrie. Lucas, you take good care of her, you hear?" She nodded toward Lucas.

"Don't worry, I will," he assured her.

He held my hand and led me outside. Megan followed us to my car waiting in the driveway.

"I'll see you at work tomorrow, Carrie," Megan said.

"Sure. And thanks for all you did."

"Yeah." Megan smiled. "Welcome to our world."

The ride home was quiet.

I'm not sure what was on Lucas's mind, but mine focused on the one thing I dreaded doing: we had to talk.

As Lucas turned onto my street, he swiveled his head to me. "Are you okay?"

I gave a fake smile, hoping he wouldn't notice. "Yeah. I'm fine."

My grandparents had left the light on for me, as expected. I let out a sigh as Lucas rounded the front of the car to help me out. He opened the door and offered his hand. I debated for a moment whether or not to take it. Touching him again, feeling his skin on mine, just made what I was about to do even harder.

But I needed the extra help. I took his hand, and he gently pulled me out of the car and closed the door behind me.

"I'll meet you upstairs," he said. "Do you think you can make it by yourself?"

"Yeah. I'll be fine."

The house was dark, and I stared at the stairs for a few moments before attempting the climb. Each step felt like lifting fifty extra pounds. I looked up and saw Lucas standing at the top, waiting. I didn't want his help, so I gritted my teeth and finished the climb by myself.

He wrapped his arm around my shoulders as soon as I reached the top. There was a note taped to my door.

Your mom called today. She wants you to call her back as soon as possible.

She probably wanted to talk about my trip back home.

Home.

Lucas.

I squeezed my eyes shut. Maybe if I tried, I'd melt into my bed and disappear.

"Do you want to clean up?" Lucas asked, sitting on the bed next to me.

I hadn't thought about it, but taking a hot shower and brushing my teeth would prolong the upcoming conversation.

"Yeah. That'd be good."

Lucas cleared his throat and looked at the floor. "If you need help...I can...you know...close my eyes."

My breath caught in my lungs. Of course I wanted his help.

Don't go there, Carrie.

"I'll be fine," I croaked, longing to have him follow me anyway.

He nodded, balling his hands into fists.

The expression on Lucas's face was heartbreaking, and I hated knowing that I was about to make it worse. I grabbed my pajamas and limped awkwardly to the bathroom.

I took as long as I dared in the bathroom, stalling. The water flowed over me like rain on a warm summer day. I tried not to think about what I was going to say to Lucas. Instead, I imagined what our lives would have been like if we had met sooner. Before he'd died. It was only a dream, though. A wonderful dream—one that I knew I'd relive in my mind time and time again for the rest of my life.

Reality check: Dreams end.

Taking a moment in the hallway, peering through the crack in the door, I saw Lucas. He was sitting casually on my bed, staring out the window. Even though it was dark outside, I wondered how far out he could see and what he was watching.

As I entered the room, his head turned. I forced a smile, not wanting this to be more painful than I already feared it would be.

Damn, he was breathtaking. His striking features, amazing eyes, and tender touch made me shiver. I already missed it.

I sat on the opposite side of the bed, away from the man I was about to hurt. Lucas kept his eyes on me.

"Lucas," I started. "We need to talk."

He let out a breath and smirked. "What do you need to say?"

Why can't he take this seriously? It's hard enough as it is.

I waited for a few moments, deciding where to start. "I think," I sighed. "I think it would be best if I went back home to Texas."

Lucas's eyebrows shifted upward, waiting for more.

"Alone."

He said nothing, just looked in my direction with an oddly pleasant look on his face.

"I can't let you risk everything for me. You'll

always have to run from them, and you'll always come back for me. I slow you down." I paused. "Tonight, if it weren't for me, you could have gotten away so much easier."

Lucas remained silent, pursing his lips.

I bit into the insides of my cheeks and continued. "I've loved being with you more than you know. I hate doing this, but I think it's best. The safest way."

I waited for Lucas to say something. To contradict me in some way. To reach out and hold me. To kiss me and make me shut up. Anything!

He didn't.

"You mean too much to me. Being without you is going to be hard, but not as hard as it will be if something happens to you." I sniffled, swallowing my sobs. "I'd have to live with the fact that it was me who threw you into Hell, and I just can't bear that."

I wiped the moisture from my cheeks. Lucas stared at me, a grin spread across his face. He stretched out across my bed so that his face was next to me, his hand under his head, leaning on his elbow.

"I'll always love you," I whispered.

Lucas took my hand in his and pressed his lips to each of my fingers. He pulled my arm closer to him, kissing as he went. Tears fell from my eyes until we were face to face. He continued up my shoulder to my neck. His touch felt so amazing, it was hard to let go of him.

"Are you done talking now?" he asked softly into my ear.

I nodded. I couldn't think with him stirring up hungry feelings inside me.

"Good," he said against my mouth before pushing his lips against mine, kissing me with more intensity than he had since under the weeping willows. His hands folded around the back of my head, pulling me closer. I fell limp and sank into him. My arms wrapped themselves around his neck.

"This isn't about me," he said.

"No?"

He shook his head. "No."

"What do you mean?"

"You've bottled up so much anger this summer that you've been waiting for opportunities to torture yourself," he said. "You don't believe that you deserve to be loved, because those who love you betrayed you."

I shook my head. "I really think it's the best thing, Lucas."

"No, you don't," he said. "You want to stay in pain. You can't allow yourself to be happy, because if you do, God forbid, that means you don't care about the pain your parents caused you. And you want to care. You care deeply."

"How do you know about that?" I asked, dropping my gaze to the bed.

"I've known most of the summer. Your grandma told Megan why you were here. Megan told me."

A surge of anger rushed through my body. How dare he not tell me!

"Before you get mad," he continued, sensing my mood change, "I've been waiting for you to open up and talk about it with me. You can leave, that's up to you. But know this, I *am* coming with you."

What?

I was speechless. The anger vanished just as quickly as it appeared. My eyes darted around the room and finally came to rest on Lucas. I felt naked, and exposed now that he knew what I'd been hiding from him.

Well, from myself.

"Stop blaming yourself. It was never about you. Loving someone's not simple. Anything easy isn't worth having. Love takes work," he said. "I'm not saying they didn't work at it. What I am saying is that it's not your fault."

I peered into his eyes. "It was my life, too."

"Yes, it *was*. Now, you have your own life to live." He shrugged. "And you have me, if you still want me."

I smiled and scooted toward him, cuddling up at his side. He wrapped his cool arms around me. All of my anger, fear, and pain remained bottled up inside me, just as I had intended. Lying to myself all summer that if I just ignored what was happening, it would disappear was not working out as well as I'd hoped. Lucas saw through me. I wondered if Mike and Megan had, too.

Safe in Lucas's safe arms, I wanted to spill it all. There was no more hiding behind the false assumption that I was brave and strong and that none of it really bothered me.

"I didn't even get a choice," I said.

"It isn't fair, I know. How you choose to deal with it *is* up to you. That *is* your choice," he said, holding me closer. "Ignoring it will only prolong the pain. Trust me. You have to find a way to let it go. You need to forgive them. Both of them."

I wiped my eyes. He knew all along of the war that ensued inside me. Betrayal didn't go away overnight, though. Pain didn't evaporate as quickly as water. And the fire of anger wasn't put out with a blow of air. Reconnecting with my mother would be much easier than anything with my father, whom I didn't know if I'd ever forgive. He destroyed everything.

"What about you?" I asked.

"What about me?"

"I put you in more danger than I'm worth."

"The only thing I fear, the only thing that would be unbearably torturous, is being without you."

"But…"

Lucas cut me off. "But nothing. I love you. I'm not going on without you."

I lifted my head to face him, and he kissed me gently on the forehead. "I'm not saying goodbye."

Yes, I loved him no matter the danger. I loved him so deeply, so genuinely, so intensely, that all obstacles were irrelevant. We beat the odds twice and given a third time, we'd beat them again.

"I'm not saying goodbye either."

Chapter 21

I walked into Renae's Antiques just after eight-thirty in the morning. Megan was already there, rearranging the displays.

"Good morning, Carrie," she greeted, turning to me after placing the wooden wheel against the table.

"Good morning!" I couldn't wipe the permanent smile off my face. Lucas had stayed all night, me wrapped in his arms. We were together. It was a fantastic day!

"You look better," she said quietly.

"I'm a little tender, but, yeah, better."

"That's good." Megan's grin faded as she moved closer to my side. Her voice lowered. "We need to talk. Can you and Lucas meet me at my place later tonight?"

My stomach dropped.

"Sure," I replied. "What about?" The demons were trapped again, the spell recast, everyone was safe. Now what?

"I have some thoughts, among other things," she

began. "And if…"

Both of us straightened up and took a step away from each other as we heard the back door open and Grandma's footsteps crossing the room.

"Megan, did you hear about Susan Taylor?" Grandma asked her face ashen.

Oh, God!

I shot Megan a questioning look. She didn't return it, though she seemed to notice. "I did. The police came over and spoke with us this morning."

My eyes grew wide and swung back and forth between Megan and Grandma.

"What do they know?" Grandma asked.

"Not much. They think it was an accident," Megan explained, shooting me a quick glance that I couldn't read. "Mr. Taylor was in bed and says he didn't hear anything. He found her at the bottom of the stairs early this morning with one of his lanterns in her hand."

"Such a shock." Grandma shook her head. "Is he a suspect?"

"I'm sure the police reports will show it was just an accident."

"We'll close the store for the funeral," Grandma said, patting Megan on the shoulder. "Keep me informed if you find out anything else."

The room began to spin around me, swirling into a blur of colors. I grabbed a hold of the stool behind me to keep my balance.

Megan nodded. "I will."

"I'm so sorry. I know the two of you were close." Grandma gave her a sympathetic grin. "How are you this morning, Carrie?" she asked, turning her attention to me.

"Fine," I replied too quickly, hoping my voice didn't sound shaken.

"I haven't seen much of you the last couple of days."

"I know. I'll be home for dinner tonight, though. Would you mind if Lucas joins us?"

"The more the merrier," Grandma grinned. "Mike will be there, too. Megan, would you care to join us, as well?"

"Thanks for the offer, Mrs. Reese, but I think I should stay home tonight."

"I suppose so." Grandma started back to her workshop then spun around.

"Oh, Carrie. Did you call your mother?"

I shook my head. "Not yet."

"Make sure you call her today. It was kind of important."

As soon as I heard the workshop door close, I faced Megan. "Mrs. Taylor's *dead*?"

How? Why? Is it my fault?

I knew all of the answers I asked myself already.

"Last night."

"How?"

"That was one of the things we need to talk about," Megan answered. "But not here."

My mind reeled. How could she be dead? We had just spoken to her the night before. Was I one of the last people to see her alive? A knife jabbed into my stomach at the thought. Did I have a hand in orchestrating her death? Because she helped me— us? She was so alive last night. So...

I started to heave.

No. NO!

Demons. They made it look like an accident. Of course. My shoulders dropped, and my lids closed.

My fault.

Mrs. Taylor's blood was on my hands. Hyperventilation took over as the realization hit.

A hand slapped my back, and my eyes flew open. I twirled to face my attacker.

"It wasn't your fault," Megan growled. "Stop worrying about it."

My eyes narrowed. "Can you read my mind or something?"

Megan shook her head. "You didn't kill Susan. Put the blame where it belongs, Carrie."

I rolled my eyes.

"Later," Megan repeated, her voice stern. "Now let's run the store."

I had no other option than to shake it off; I didn't need Megan hitting me all day.

When noon rolled around, I walked to The Coffee Shop for a turkey sandwich. Lucas met me there—this time in person.

"Did you hear about Mrs. Taylor?" I whispered as we sat down at one of the circular tables.

Lucas straightened up in his seat, his eyes scanning the room. "Yeah."

"What hap—"

"We'll talk in private, later."

"That's a common response today," I grumbled.

"It has to be. Our lives must remain a secret."

I took a bite of my sandwich. Around me, people were staring at Lucas. It was still amusing. Of course, he acted as if he didn't notice.

"Would you like to join us for dinner tonight?" I asked.

"I'd be honored."

I ate my lunch quickly, wanting to call my mom during break. When I went to stand, Lucas grabbed my hand and walked me out into the warm summer day. Even in the humidity with the sun beating down on us, the air still smelled sweet like lilacs.

"Did you get your car replaced?" I asked, glancing down the street at the parked cars.

"This morning."

"Where is it?" I skimmed the line of parked cars trying to guess what he chose.

"You can't figure it out?"

As he said it, my eye caught the large vehicle at the far corner of the street. A black Jeep Compass glistened in the sunlight. I glared at him.

"I thought I needed something bigger. You know, you'd be safer if you decided to drive this one into a tree," he teased. "State-of-the-art air bag system."

"Thanks."

"I thought you'd like it."

I punched him playfully on the shoulder. "You're a goon."

He kissed me. "I'll see you later. Around six? I love you."

"Sounds good. I love you." I tucked my lip between my teeth, watching him walk away.

So hot.

I slipped my phone out of my pocket and dialed my mom's number. The summer passed quickly, and I had barely spoken to her.

"Carrie!" I heard her exclaim on the other end.

"Hi, Mom."

"How have you been?" she said very mom-like.

"Just fine," I assured her. "Grandma said you called."

"I'm not sure how you'll feel about this. I know how upset you were when we didn't ask you about going to Iowa for the summer, so I'm asking now. You get a choice on this, okay?"

She paused for a few moments. "I know you probably want to come back to Sherman and finish your senior year with Stacy and Jessica, but I was wondering if you wanted to stay in Iowa for school this year instead?"

Her words shocked me, taking the breath out of my lungs. I didn't know why she was asking. I wasn't upset; in fact, I was somewhat relieved.

I searched for words—I had none. "Uh," I uttered, trying to think of something to say. "Um, what about Grandma and Grandpa?"

"I've already spoken with Renae. She said that it would be fine if you wanted to stay. She said you've made some friends there."

I exhaled loudly and ran my fingers through my hair. "Uh. Why do you want me to stay here?"

"Carrie, this is a really hard time for me right now. I'm in therapy, and honestly, I can barely take care of myself. I think you may be happier there, at least for now." The reluctant sadness in her voice made me feel sorry for her.

I knew she wanted me home to help ease the pain. But, I figured she didn't want to depress me or lean on me for support, either.

"You need to live your own life and not be bothered by my regrets."

"Oh, Mom, I just want you to be happy." She was taking this harder than I imagined. Apparently, sending me to Iowa hadn't only been a coping mechanism for me. "I'll stay. I actually like it up here."

I could sense my mom smiling. "Your grandma said she thought you'd say that. She tells me you have a boyfriend?"

I laughed. "Yeah. He's great."

"And very attractive, I hear."

I blushed. "Oh, Grandma."

Silence.

"Well, thank you, Carrie, for understanding. It shows maturity above your years. I never imagined how much you'd grow up in one summer."

"Thank you, Mom. Just concentrate on yourself right now. You'll get there. And you know where to find me if you need me." I said, and I meant it.

"I love you, Carrie."

"I love you, too, Mom. I need to go. My break's almost over."

"Call me, all right?"

"I will," I promised.

We're going to make it, Mom and me.

I smiled to myself.

Tucking my phone back in my pocket, I went inside the store.

"You can go to lunch now," I told Megan.

"Thanks," she replied grabbing her things. "I'll be back in half an hour."

I sat down on the stool. A sense of relief washed

over me, thinking about the phone call with my mother. Now I wouldn't have to make a decision. It had been, in a way, made for me. I was given an out. The anticipation of telling Lucas bubbled in my veins.

As quickly as the happiness came, it vanished. What about Jess? And Stacy? We wouldn't be spending our final year of high school strutting through halls, finally on the top of the food chain. How was I going to tell them? What would they say?

I leaned back in my chair stressing over the best way to tell my best friends that I wouldn't be back for senior year. This also meant that I would have to start at a new, unfamiliar—not to mention tiny—high school in a few weeks. At least I'd know one person there: Mike.

I tapped my fingernails nervously on the counter. The bell over the door rang, and I looked up. Grandma walked in with a stack of mail in one hand and a sack in the other.

"Hi, Grandma. I talked to Mom."

She nodded. "What was your decision?"

"I'm staying," I said grinning, unable to think of anything but being with Lucas.

"I figured you would. Boys will do that to you."

I blushed again.

"We'll have to get you registered for school. I don't imagine it will be too different than what you're used to." Grandma tossed the stack of mail on the counter. "We'll talk later; I need to get this hutch finished. Someone is picking it up this afternoon."

After work, I sat in my room with my phone in one hand and my computer open to my email sitting on my bed. Calling would be more personal, but an e-mail would be easier.

What to do?

Finally deciding not to think about it, I dialed Jessica's number. It only rang once before I heard Jess's voice on the other end.

"Carrie! I'm so glad you called! When are you coming home? I want to go to Dallas again before school starts."

"Hey, Jess," I answered, much less excited. "How's it going?"

"Good. My last day at the paper is Friday. Will you be home by then? We need to check our class schedules. I'm going to need you in Lit again this year. Stacy suggested trying to get at least one class all together. We haven't done that since junior high."

I bit my lower lip. Jessica already made plans.

Crap.

"Jess," I said. "I have something to tell you."

"What happened, Care?" Her tone did a complete one-eighty. "You're scaring me."

"I'm not dead or anything. I talked to my mom earlier today. It seems that she is taking this divorce worse than I am and asked if I wanted to stay in Iowa for the school year."

The words made it out of my mouth very slowly, and when they were finally out, silence filled the other end.

"Jess?" I asked, hoping she hadn't hung up on me. "Jess? Are you there?"

I heard a long exhale. "Yeah, I'm still here. Is this about Lucas or Mike?"

I sighed. "Neither, but honestly, I'm happy to stay here with Lucas."

A few moments passed before Jessica said, "I think I already knew that you'd stay. I dreamt it last week. We were having this exact conversation. It's like déjà vu, but more exact."

"You dreamt that I'd stay in Villisca?"

"Yeah. I've been having all sorts of strange dreams, and all of them are coming true. I think … I think there may be something wrong with me." Jessica's voice shook on the other end.

"Nothing's wrong with you," I assured her. "What stuff is coming true?"

"Well, this. And I saw Stacy dump Ben before it happened. I saw you get into a car accident, although it wasn't your car, it was red." She paused for a moment. "Oh, no! You haven't been in a car accident, have you?"

My mouth went dry. What did this mean? Was it the same as my visions? Was my soul connected to hers as well? How could I tell her? The simple answer was that I couldn't. I couldn't out Lucas or Megan.

"Um. Yeah, I did," I breathed. "Lucas's car is red. I was driving and rolled it." I paused as I listened to Jessica gasp on the other end. "Oh. I'm fine, though."

"Carrie, what's happening to me?"

"I don't know. You're usually the one with those answers, Jess."

"There are people with ESP that can see the

future, but…" She stopped. "Carrie, I'm scared."

I dropped my head and closed my eyes. I didn't know how to console Jessica or even if I could.

"Like you said, it's probably is just déjà vu. I mean, you also dreamt that I'd die at the mercy of a blond man. I'm still very much alive with no blond men in sight."

"That's true." Silence. "Yeah. Yeah, you're probably right."

I hope so.

"Let me know if you see anything else, okay?"

"I will. Anyway, are you sure you want to stay in Villisca?"

I smiled to myself. "Yeah. I think it would be best for Mom right now, too."

"It's not going to be the same without you."

"I know. Maybe you and Stacy can come up during Christmas break. It might be fun. They have snow up here!"

"Yeah, that'd be fun."

"I'd better go. I still need to call Stacy."

"Oh, sure. Call more often, okay?"

"Sure thing. Have a good year. Take lots of pictures for me," I added.

"Okay. Bye."

I frowned. "Bye, Jess."

I missed her already.

For a split second, I considered telling Lucas and Megan about Jess's odd dreams. They did seem strange, even for her. More than likely, though, they were probably nothing. Besides, it wasn't my place to tell people Jess didn't even know.

I fell back onto my pillows. Now, I had to call

Stacy. Spectacular.

I made the call while lying on my bed. Stacy cried and tried to convince me to come back home. I spent most of our conversation soothing her. Each time I thought she'd calmed down, she or I would say something that started the sobs all over again. After mentioning that she and Jess could visit over Christmas, the cries ceased momentarily. Letting her go took some work on my part. When we finally hung up, I thought I heard a smile in her voice.

I glanced at the clock, then rushed down the stairs to wait for Lucas. I stood at the door and peered out the window until I saw his black Jeep pull onto the gravel. He stepped gracefully out of the vehicle and walked to the door, glancing behind him toward Goldie. I laughed to myself; his hesitation was adorable.

A new wave of electricity shocked my body as I opened the door, and Lucas swept me into his arms. I wrapped my hands around his neck and kissed his neck. The excitement swelled in my mouth.

I giggled. Lucas's arms loosened around my back as my feet touched the floor. I lifted myself onto my toes and kissed him hard on his lips. A few seconds passed before he returned it. I could tell he was uncomfortable kissing me where my grandparents could see. His body tensed, and he pulled back slowly.

"What was that all about?"

"Guess what?"

He threw up his arms and shrugged. "I don't know. You just remembered how much you love me?"

"No. I always remember that. I'm staying in Villisca for the school year."

Lucas stared at me skeptically for a moment before a grin spread across his face. Suddenly he swept me off my feet again and swung me in a circle. I could feel his subtle enthusiasm as he squeezed me into himself.

Happiness stayed plastered on my face as I led Lucas into the kitchen. Grandma was tearing lettuce at the counter when we walked in. Noticing my overwhelming zeal, she couldn't help but smile back at us.

"You told him," she said, handing us a bowl. "Well, make yourselves useful. I need the carrots and celery cut, please."

Lucas and I sat at the table where Grandma had set a cutting board and the bags of vegetables. She handed me a second knife.

"I assume we'll be seeing more of you now, Lucas?"

"If that's all right with you, ma'am."

"Please," Grandma said facing us. "Call me Renae. You are very much welcome. Although, Carrie will have a curfew on school nights." She paused. "And probably all nights. I'll have to speak with your mother."

"I figured as much." I groaned.

We finished making the tossed salad, waiting for Grandpa and Mike. The door opened, and we heard them walk in and begin washing up. It wasn't long before we were all circled around the table.

"So, Mike," I started after the milk-pouring ceremony was over. "I'm staying here for senior year. Any tips?"

Mike choked on his milk and set the glass down with half of the contents remaining. He wiped his mouth with his hand. "Really?"

"Yeah. Just found out today."

His eyes cut to Lucas and back to me. He tried to suppress a smile. "Cool. I can show you around. It will be nice to see a new face in the halls. We don't get new students often."

"Any teacher recommendations?"

"Uh, you don't really get a choice. Small school. Only one teacher per subject," Mike said, wrinkling his nose.

"Oh," I grumbled.

Weird.

"Please tell me you're good at Math, because my tutor graduated last year," he said, his grin growing wider.

"No, sorry," I said, glancing toward Lucas, whose eyes were narrowed at Mike.

"How about Literature? Or Science? History is rough, too."

I laughed. "Do you need help with every subject?"

Mike cocked his head to the side and looked playfully at the ceiling. "Hmm, no. I passed PE without any help whatsoever."

I shook my head. "I can help you with Lit."

He shot a quick glance in Lucas's direction. "Good. It's my worst subject."

Lucas shifted in his seat and cleared his throat a little louder than necessary.

"How about you, Lucas," Mike said. "Any good

at school stuff?"

Lucas smirked, "I don't think you want me tutoring you."

Grandma caught my eye. Her eyebrows rose as she nodded to each of the guys, but kept her eyes locked on me. She chuckled.

"That bad, huh?" Mike jabbed. "Hey, you coming to the game next Friday night?"

"*Carrie and I* will be cheering you on from the top of the bleachers," Lucas said.

Mike nodded slightly. "Not from the track, Carrie?" He winked at me.

Lucas pursed his lips together.

"HA! I'm no cheerleader. I think I'll stick to the bleachers."

Mike shrugged. "Too bad."

Lucas picked at his food throughout dinner. He ate more than I'd ever seen, though no one seemed to notice his lack of appetite. Sometime during the meal, Lucas slid his left hand onto my thigh. His touch sent small shock waves down my spine. I held my breath until the feeling passed.

"Well, Mike," Grandpa said. "We need to finish up outside."

Mike grabbed his glass and finished it with one swig before standing. "All right. Good to see you again, Lucas. I'll talk to you later, Carrie."

Grandpa leaned over and kissed Grandma on the cheek. "Thanks for dinner, darling."

I looked up at Mike who returned the shocked expression, both of us with raised eyebrows and playful grins on our faces. The just-witnessed-scene had never taken place in front of my eyes before, and from the look on Mike's face, it was his first time, too.

"Love is catching," Lucas whispered to me.

Mike followed Grandpa out of the kitchen. I smiled at Grandma, who offered nothing in return.

"Oh, Grandma? Can Lucas and I go over to Megan's for a little while?" I asked as I gathered mine and Lucas's dishes to take to the sink.

"I really think you need to stay here for once. You've barely been home."

Home.

Yeah. I feel at home.

"We won't be long. I'll be back by eight. Eight-thirty at the latest."

Grandma sighed. "Eight-thirty." Then she added, "Teenagers," under her breath.

"Thanks," I said, grabbing Lucas's hand and leading him out of the kitchen.

Lucas drove us to Megan's. I held on to his hand the entire drive, feeling his cool skin; it was a touch I never wanted to forget. The way his hand felt holding mine, his soft skin always made my heart lurch. I wished he could feel it, too.

I moved my thumb over the top of his hand, hoping that our visit would be short. The sooner it was over, the sooner I would be cuddled up on Lucas's chest.

He pulled up the drive, neither of us stealing a glance at Susan's house but well aware of its presence. I gave Lucas's hand a small squeeze before letting go.

"Good evening, Lucas, Carrie. How are you?" Vanessa greeted, opening the door for us.

"Good," I said, knowing she was addressing me. "Much better. The soreness is pretty much gone."

"Glad to hear it," Vanessa said, motioning us inside.

Lucas continued to hold my hand as we followed her to the den. Megan was sitting on the floor, legs crossed, reading a magazine. She looked up when we entered the room.

"Come on in. I wanted to discuss something Susan told me."

"I want to know the truth about Susan—Mrs. Taylor," I cut in.

Megan deferred the answers to Lucas. "The demons knew she was helping us. I believe that's where the second demon was. When that deed was done, he came after us."

"What? Did they push her down the stairs?" I asked confused.

"That's what it looks like."

"How? I mean, didn't she have protective spells around her house? How did they get in?"

Megan took a few moments before she answered. "The containment spell was broken when you saw the vision, but it wasn't until last night that the demons actually left the house. They've been planning this whole thing, watching Susan's house—figuring out exactly how to break through the spell. The spell isn't foolproof, but it's not easy to get past, either. Susan was their first target, you two were their second.

"Another necromancer will rise up and take her place. Villisca will always have one," Megan said.

"We killed her," I said silently. "It's my fault."

Megan and Lucas shook their heads simultaneously. "No. It's a risk of living her life, doing what she did. She had a choice, you know. She didn't have to answer her calling. They murdered her for helping all ghosts, not just Lucas," Megan said. "Don't blame yourself. She helped you fully knowing the possible outcome. In fact, she expected it."

"She knew she was going to die?"

"She knew it was a possibility. After you left, she came to us and told us everything. She also asked that we keep an eye on her husband, make sure he didn't take the fall." Megan's eyes drifted to the window facing the Taylors' home.

"The police think Mr. Taylor murdered her?"

"There was one of those antique lanterns of his, broken, at the bottom of the stairs. It's not good evidence. Mom's taking care of it; he'll be fine."

I shook my head in disbelief. Mr. Taylor was just as much a victim as Susan.

"We need to discuss some things Susan told us," Megan continued. "Lucas, you spoke of a man seeing you after your death?"

"Yeah. I don't know any more than what I told Susan."

"I *think* we may be looking for a vampire. Or some other cambion."

I caught two words that sent chills up my spine. The first one, "we", implied that Megan would be helping us. I didn't want Megan's life to be endangered by me, too. Enough people have died on my account.

The second word made my palms sweat.

Vampire. They were real? How have I lived in this world for seventeen—almost eighteen—years and never knew about any of this?

"That thought crossed my mind, too," Lucas admitted. "I didn't want it to be true because it's so unlikely. Cambions are not known for being helpful."

"I don't know what else to think, but it's a good place to start. I checked into your warlock theory, and I came up empty."

"I don't remember much about him. We don't have a whole lot to go on."

"I know. We'll find him," Megan said, and then groaned. "Ugh. I think I'd rather deal with werewolves."

What? Have I entered some alternate universe?...Again?

I shot Lucas a shocked glare before turning to face Megan. "Werewolves? Vampires? And what's a cambion?"

Megan laughed. "Cambions are half-demons. Vampires are a breed of cambion. Werewolves, though not demonic, are a lot like vamps but without the ego."

"You know, Carrie," Lucas said, putting his arm around my shoulders and pulling me close. "You really shouldn't be surprised about anything anymore. You're in love with a ghost, you're sitting in a house of witches, and you had a near-death experience involving demons."

There was nothing to say. I just leaned against Lucas, sinking into him. He and Megan laughed. This, I realized, was only the beginning of my new life with Lucas.

Chapter 22

The stars glittered like fairy dust in the sky. I inhaled the freshness of the August air. None of it compared to Lucas's mouthwatering scent lying beside me.

I curled up next to him on the blanket, my head on his chest. The absence of a heartbeat went almost unnoticed.

I kissed Lucas on the neck and smiled at the soft hum in his throat.

"Mmmmm," he purred.

I nestled my face into the nape of his neck. "I love you."

He squeezed me close, pressing his lips to my forehead. "You've made my life worthwhile, and my death bearable."

I trembled.

"You've got to accept it."

I said nothing, biting the inside of my check instead. *Do I?*

"Death is a permanent condition, Care. There's no coming back." The regret in his tone left my mouth dry.

"You're here now, though."

Lucas's chest rose and fell. "Sort of."

I glanced up to see the distant look in his eyes. Dead or alive, eyes were indeed the windows to the soul. And Lucas's cut through me like a knife.

My fingers caressed the side of his face and swept through his hair. "Can you feel that?"

He didn't say anything.

I brushed my lips over his. "Or that?"

Silence fell around us.

"Please," I urged. "Feel me."

Lucas stroked my hair. His fingers glided over my jaw and down my neck. I closed my eyes, concentrating on the wake left by his touch. I felt his wintery breath against my lips before he kissed me. My arms folded around him, pressing him closer.

Waves of urgency crashed through me. If I could only hold him tighter, kiss him harder, then maybe he'd be able to feel what I felt. I knew he loved me, but I couldn't help wonder if …

I ran my hands under his shirt, enjoying how the muscles hardened under my fingers. When I pressed my palms into his chest, Lucas shuddered. My lids shot open, and I stared at him.

"Did you feel that?"

Lucas sank back into the blanket, defeated. "Not like you. Just inside as always."

"Maybe there's a magical—"

"No. There's no potion, no spell that can give me a body. Trust me, I've looked."

I nodded, dropping my gaze.

"Hey." Lucas lifted my chin. "We'll figure it out, though. Together, right?"

The moon illuminated Lucas's face, making it glow in a ghostly haze. So beautiful.

"Forever."

The dimple on Lucas's cheek deepened. He hugged me against him, kissing my temple.

"Look," he said, pointing up at the sky.

Directly above us, a shooting star flew through the heavens.

"Make a wish," Lucas whispered.

I closed my eyes. My mouth turned up in a smile as I realized that my wish already had come true.

Life was mine for the taking and after seventeen years, I was finally grasping it. I'd found love! A love that was so wonderful I still didn't fully understand it. I'd do anything for him.

And death? Death was inevitable. You can only hope that it waits until you've lived your life.

Through death, Lucas's death, I found my life. Whatever awaited us, whatever choices were left, Lucas and I would always share something deeper, stronger than life. We'd been given a second chance to find each other, and neither of us was going to let it go.

"What did you wish for?"

"Hmm-mmm." I shook my head. "If I tell you, it won't come true."

"I'll find out soon enough."

"What?" I squinted at him. "How?"

His low chuckle hit my ear in a cool tickle. "In your dreams."

The End

Acknowledgements

Behind every great writer is an amazing team of support: family, friends, beta readers, CP's, editors, marketing people, cover designers, formatters, submissions teams, and everyone else at the publishing house. This is my chance to say 'thanks,' and I sincerely hope I don't leave anyone out!

First and foremost, I thank God, for without Him, none of this would be possible.

Secondly, my family. To my husband, David, for his encouragement to chase my dream, his analytical thoughts when I had problems figuring something out, his willing ear, and the fire he lit under me to start sending out query letters. I couldn't have done this without you!

To my children, David Michael, Brennan, Natalie Anne, and Abigaylle, for making me smile when the story wasn't moving like I wanted, and for finding things to do while Mommy worked. You four are the best!

To my parents, siblings, and in-laws for being among the first readers and for being there when I had good and bad news to share. Thanks for letting me count on you!

Thank you to my friends and various beta readers who read through my stories with a keen eye. Your thoughts have been very helpful, as well as your encouragement and kind words. Holly Hendrian, Tonille Burrows, Karen Robison, Pam Negley, Kristen King, Sarah Hart, Kimberly Pollard, Bekah Hart, Suzy Hart, Heather Jelsma,

Paula Reece, Kim Jackson, Landon King, and I hope I'm not missing anyone, I appreciate you all very much. Your insights have been invaluable.

A special thanks to Heather Jelsma and Angela Rothfus for helping me put together my website! Seriously, I wouldn't have one if it weren't for you!

I've been blessed with some amazing critique partners (CP's), and I can't even begin to express my thanks for the hard work they put in making my stories shine their brightest. Sunniva Dee: You were the first non-family/non-friend to read my work, and not only did you fall in love with it, it spawned a great friendship. Your honesty and thorough eye has made me a better writer, editor, and has made my manuscripts look more polished than I could ever have done on my own. Temperance Elisabeth: Your logic questions in THE SPIRIT blew me away. I'd never thought of those things before! You know how to ask the right questions in the right places to make my stories come alive even more. I'm so grateful for our newfound friendship! Ashland R.: Wow, you really fished out the guy stuff in THE SPIRIT that I never would have figured out on my own! Thanks for your insight with Mike Carson and your car knowledge. Marie Caseri: Thank you for your personal touches in THE SPIRIT. Your input really brought out each character and made them more relatable. Laura Carlson: The first chapter of THE SPIRIT would not rock like it does without you! You know how essential you were to the publishing of this book, and 'thank you' doesn't seem like strong enough words. Thank you, friend!

Thank you to my editors, Kristin Scearce and Becky Johnson. I'd also like to thank the beta readers, Teri, Amy, Sue, and Sonja from Hot Tree Editing. I appreciate all of your hard work on this novel! It's been a pleasure working with you!

Thank you to *Limitless Publishing* for taking a chance on me! Jennifer O'Neill, Jessica Gunhammer, Dixie Matthews, Olivia Oswald, Jen Snowden and everyone else who had a hand in getting my book out there, you're all amazing!

And of course to the readers! Without you, there'd be no books! So a huge, sincere, round of applause for each and every one of you! You're the best!

Sweet Dreams,
d.

About the Author

Born and raised in Iowa, d. Nichole King writes her stories close to home. There's nothing like small-town Midwest scenery to create the perfect backdrop for an amazing tale.

She wrote her first book in junior high and loved every second of it. However, she couldn't bring herself to share her passion with anyone. She packed it away until one day, with the encouragement of her husband, she sat down at the computer and began to type. Now, she can't stop.

When not writing, d. is usually curled up with a book, scrapbooking, or doing yet another load of laundry.

Along with her incredible husband, she lives in small-town Iowa with her four adorable children and their dog, Peaches.

Facebook:
www.facebook.com/dnichole.king

Twitter:
https://twitter.com/dNicholeKing

Goodreads:
www.goodreads.com/author/show/7762889.D_Nich
ole_King

Website:
www.dnicholeking.com/